DARK PRISON

Gray Tower Series Book One

J. M. Brister

Cover designed by The Cover Collection

This book is a work of fiction. Names, characters, places, and incidents either are products of the author's imagination or are used fictitiously. Any resemblance to actual persons, living or dead, events, or locales is entirely coincidental.

J. M. Brister
Visit my website at http://jmbrister.blogspot.com

Printed in the United States of America

First Printing: December 2018
Kindle Direct Publishing

ISBN: 9781790194919

Dedication
To Michael, for not giving up on me when I was ready to give up on myself.

CONTENTS

PROLOGUE

Congratulations, Keira," everyone at the party said in unison as they lifted their glasses for a toast. A group of twenty or so people were gathered around a large, ornate dining room table. Everyone had finished eating, so a toast seemed appropriate.

Keira Amherst smiled and thanked the guests, taking a sip of her wine. She hadn't wanted her father to throw her such an elaborate bash for finally graduating with her MBA, but he had insisted that he wanted to do something special. She would have preferred to not have the celebration at Amherst Manor, a large estate in Virginia that was only an hour drive away from D.C. However, her father, Damien Amherst, had gotten his way as always.

Everything seemed a little over the top in the formal dining room with the dark, paneled wood walls and the one hundred-thousand-dollar chandelier that loomed overhead. She would have rather had a small intimate bash with her friends. Instead, she was staring out into a sea of faces that she barely recognized. They were a lot of her father's business associates. Keira had been told all throughout her life that she was being groomed for a top spot in her father's business. The get-together felt more like a coronation than a graduation party.

One of her father's colleagues turned toward her and asked, "When do you think you'll start at Amherst Global? Do you know what you want to do there, yet?"

"I don't..." Keira trailed off.

She had been concentrating so hard on school for so long that she hadn't quite thought that far ahead. It had all been about graduating with her masters. Now, everything suddenly felt so real.

"I'm sure there will be time to discuss that later," her father interrupted, sensing her apprehension.

Keira smiled at him. He was always so overprotective of her since her mother had died years ago in a fatal car crash. It had just been the two of them since that time.

Well, it was more like the two of them, a slew of staff that kept the mansion running, her dad's personal bodyguards and security associates, and his work colleagues who visited quite often. Somehow, though, she always felt lonely when she was home from college. It felt empty without her mother.

"I've interned at several companies every summer that I've had off," she said, suddenly snapping back into business mode.

If this was what she wanted to do with the rest of her life, she was going to have to learn to schmooze.

"I'm sure I'll find an appropriate spot," she continued and smiled as best as she could.

Then Keira realized: Was this even what she wanted to do? It was a sinking feeling that wouldn't quite go away, even though she had largely ignored it while dutifully working through school. It had always been expected that she would take over her father's business eventually. She had never been given the option otherwise. She was an Amherst. Taking some part in Amherst Global was inevitable.

"Since we're all finished with dinner, why don't we all move to the drawing room for some cognac and cigars?" Her father said with one of his dazzling smiles.

Her father was a handsome man and was also extremely charismatic. Damien Amherst stood a little over six feet tall with a great head of pepper and salt hair, but he always felt like the biggest guy in the room. Keira knew that was how he had amassed his wealth from almost nothing to owning one of the largest privately-owned companies in the world.

Her graduation party guests were mostly made of men from Amherst Global, so it that was appropriate to do the "good old boys thing." Keira didn't like cognac, and she really hated cigar smoke. However, her father had always told her to suck it up. This was apparently the way things had to be if you wanted to connect with the higher-ups. In a way, Keira felt like this was more about her father than her. His progeny now had an MBA from an Ivy league school. It was really all about him.

Keira sighed as she got up from the table and followed the chatty group down the long corridors of Amherst Manor to the drawing room, a favorite place to entertain for her father. More of the same dark-paneled wood followed the hallways until they reached a large room with a fireplace, a bar with bartender ready to serve, and a grouping of soft brown leather seats. Yes, this was the good old boys club. She felt out of place among the sea of expensive suits in her little black cocktail dress and strappy heels.

"Keira, you are the spitting image of your mother," one of the guests told her as they gathered into the room. "We all miss her very much."

She didn't really want to be reminded constantly that her mother, Lily Amherst, wasn't here to share in this celebration, but she did have to agree that the resemblance was uncanny. They both had straight mousy brown hair, a tall frame, doe-like hazel eyes, and a slender build. Keira liked to wear her hair a little bit shorter than her mother's at about shoulder length, and she had surpassed her mother in height by an inch at five foot eight. Yet, they looked so much alike that their pictures had an eerie resemblance.

"Yes, I miss her a lot," Keira said, smiling as politely as she could, though she wanted to do nothing but shrink back into the crowd and disappear.

She dodged most of her father's associates and went straight for the back of the room. Cigars were passed out, and the high-end booze was flowing. Keira declined. She had had enough. Wanting desperately to get away, she ducked outside to the hallway. Happy for a bit of peace and quiet, she shut her eyes for just a moment and began to take a few deep breaths.

"Are you all right, Keira?" Asked a familiar male voice from behind her.

Opening her eyes and turning around, she saw John Stratton, one of her father's closest friends. Damien Amherst may have been the head of Amherst Global, but Stratton was the one working behind the scenes, making sure everything ran smoothly. Because of the nature of his job, Keira saw him constantly at the house and used to call him "Uncle John" when she was younger, even though there was no relation.

John was a tall man, like her father, with dark brown hair and eyes. They were both around the same age from what Keira understood. While her father was more of a commanding man, John seemed softer somehow. He wasn't the flashy type, and he rarely went to any of her father's events. He liked to stay on the business side of things and wasn't much for socializing or small talk. However, she knew that he could get whatever he wanted done just like her father. They were like opposite sides of the same coin.

"I'm fine," she told him, though she wasn't quite sure if that was the truth.

John cocked his head slightly.

"You don't look fine. What's bothering you?"

Did she really want to open this can of worms in front of her father's right-hand man? She's always thought that John had been more approachable than her own father, but she didn't want it to get back to her dad that she was having second thoughts about joining the business.

She sighed.

"It just feels like my whole life has been planned out for me. It's a bit overwhelming."

John frowned, and asked, "Have you ever told your father about this?"

Of course, she hadn't. Trying to talk to her father about anything important was always intimidating to her. He was hard to approach and had extremely high expectations of her. She didn't want to let him down.

"I don't want to disappoint him," Keira replied, beginning to get flustered.

"I try not to get involved between you and your father, but have you ever thought about talking to him? It might not be a bad idea, especially before you start to really get involved in the company," he told her.

"I suppose," Keira said with a sigh. "I'll try and talk with him later."

One of John's eyebrows raised slightly. He wasn't going to let this one go.

"I'm sure he has time right now," he told her. "This is your party, remember?"

Keira shifted uneasily in her heels.

"Yeah, sure," she agreed, though she wasn't sure if she meant it.

John pulled a small headset from his pocket, put it in his ear, and turned it on.

"Stratton to security. Where is Mr. Amherst? Over."

There was a slight pause before he continued.

"Okay, tell him I'm bringing Keira by. Over."

He turned toward Keira.

"Your father stepped out of the party and is in his office. Care to come with me?"

That was the way things worked in Amherst Manor. Keira usually needed an appointment to see her own father, even during her own graduation party.

"Okay," she agreed, though she really wasn't all that keen on talking to her father about the whole thing.

As they walked the long hallways of the Manor, she had butterflies in her stomach. Why did she agree to this? She didn't want to upset her father, especially during her graduation party. Yet, she knew (and probably John as well), that if she didn't say something now, she would stay on her current path forever.

When they arrived at her father's office doors, she had to do a couple of quick breaths. Her father was a workaholic, and it wasn't uncommon for him to slip off to work during any of his parties. She was a little peeved that it was *her* party that he chose to leave, but that was typical of him.

John opened the door and showed Keira into her father's office. It was a little over the top in design (at least for her taste). There were expensive pictures on the wall of people hunting foxes on horseback. Lush couches lined the perimeter, while her father's massive mahogany desk sat in the middle. The whole room was lined with bookshelves, displaying leather titles that had probably never been read. It was all for show, just like most of the décor in Amherst Manor.

Her father was sitting in his huge leather-backed chair, still on a phone call. When he noticed them, he held up a finger for them to wait.

"Just get it done," he said in a stern voice into the receiver and slammed down the phone.

Then, he looked up at Keira and smiled thinly.

"Sorry about that, sweetheart. Business as usual. What did you need?"

"I just wanted to..." Keira trailed off for a moment.

There was a short pause.

"Hey, can we talk?"

Her father's face remained emotionless as he said, "Certainly."

Keira turned around to see where John was, but he had slipped out without saying a word. She was now alone to face her father.

"What do you need?" Her father asked, the tone of his voice gave no emotion. It was all-business with him.

She walked forward hesitantly. Her black heels clicking on the hardwood floor a little too loudly for her liking. She attempted to speak, but her father interrupted her.

"Before you say anything, I really have something that I must show you. I believe it's appropriate for today, since you are getting ready to be an important member of the company. Eventually, you will run everything. You understand that, right?"

Keira couldn't really respond. She had lost control of the conversation before it had even started. Her father was getting too sentimental about his legacy. Perhaps her objections were a lost cause at this point? He would probably break if she told him she didn't want to work for Amherst Global.

"Yes," she said, trying to keep herself calm.

"It's important that I have an offspring who will continue this company to its fullest. It's always been my greatest dream."

Why did he have to say it in such an impersonal manner? She suddenly felt small, like her father couldn't care less about her feelings in the matter. To him, she was still a child who needed to be guided.

"Come here. I want to show you something," her father continued.

Keira stepped forward to his desk, her stomach in complete knots. The opportunity had passed. Her courage was suddenly gone.

"I know you just graduated, but I want to make sure we are on the same page," her father said. "Amherst Global is a great organization. Its reach crosses the globe, and it is one of the most influential companies in the world. But I want you to realize that it does much more than what you think."

He pushed a manila folder toward her. Keira reached out and took it in her hands, trying not to tremble. She pulled it open and began to study its contents. It was an Amherst Global file.

As she began to read, she furrowed her brow. What was this? It didn't make any sense to her. Although finance was not her specialty, there was a set of earnings reports that seemed off to her.

After a few moments of studying, she began to feel sick.

"What is all of this?" She asked, a knot in her stomach had formed, and she suddenly wished that she hadn't had any wine.

Her father stared at her intently and said, "There's more to Amherst Global than you think. I want you to be completely on board before you take a leadership position in the company."

Keira continued to study the files intently for a few more moments. Then she suddenly jerked up her head. What was her father trying to pull?

"These are business transactions that I don't recognize. What is all of this?"

Her father gave her a wide smile, and it was a bit disturbing to Keira. Something felt wrong.

"I don't understand," she told him.

"I know you don't," her father said. "But I want you to truly comprehend what you are getting into with this company."

Keira's hands began to tremble, so she tried to steady them as best as she could. What was he talking about?

"My company has expanded to many different avenues," her father said. "Some are off the books. That hadn't initially been the plan when I started my business. But as with anything, time and pressure can change a man."

Keira's throat was so tight that she couldn't even speak. She wasn't sure what her father was about to reveal to her, but she just knew it would be bad.

When she hadn't responded, her father continued, "There are a few dubious transactions that I wish you to know about."

Something didn't feel right, and she wanted to flee. But it was her father, what exactly was she supposed to do?

"The company does more than just shipping regular goods, Keira."

Oh, no. No. No! She thought.

What was he saying? She almost stumbled backwards, but she caught herself on one of her father's plush leather sofas. The huge office suddenly felt small.

"No," he said with more intensity. "I want you to understand exactly what I've had to do to make my company what is has become."

Her father reached out to her and grasped her arm, hard. Keira gasped. Her arm throbbed with the pressure. Was he drunk? She couldn't tell. She had never seen her father this way. He appeared to be dead serious.

"We don't just ship electronics. Or cars. Or materials. Since the very beginning, the company has done some very *special* deliveries.

"I found that as I was struggling to keep the company afloat with local delivery that I could gain more influence and power by adding illegal items to the shipments: drugs, guns, and sometimes even people. Within a short amount of time, my struggling business took off because I could make things happen for some very influential people. I got a lot of investors from my back-room deals and the small Amherst Freight company transformed into Amherst Global. That was almost thirty years ago."

Keira felt sick, and she couldn't seem to say anything. What was she supposed to say? The man who she had loved, respected, and looked up to was just a crook? How could she have been so wrong about him?

"Don't look so surprised, Keira," he continued. "This family would have never gotten as far as it has without some of my decisions. Besides, you've certainly benefited from it."

Keira wanted to fling back some kind of retort, but her mouth had gone completely dry.

"You need to understand all of this before you take on responsibility for the company. I've done this for you and for your mother..."

He trailed off for a moment staring away from her, seemingly looking at nothing. His expression was emotionless.

Then he continued.

"You've always had a good head on your shoulders, but you've always been naïve to the way the world really works. It's time that you open up your eyes."

At least the last part of what her father said was true. It *was* time to open her eyes and realize how much of a creep her father was. How could she have been so blind not to see it before?

Or, maybe she had known all along and had never been able to admit it to herself? The warning signs had been there the whole time.

"I don't want to be a part of your company," she told him firmly. It had been the first time that she had ever stood up to him, and it felt damned good. "And I don't want anything to do with you."

Her father crossed the space between him and her so quickly that Keira didn't have time to react. It was only an instant later that he slapped her hard across the face. Pain and shock stung across her face. The force of his blow made her jerk back so suddenly that she fell to the floor.

"Keep your mouth shut!" Her father growled harshly. "It would have been a lot easier if you had just gone along with my plans."

He stood over her and glowered. The man had to be insane, Keira realized.

"You'll learn to go along with whatever I say, eventually."

Looming over her, he pulled one of his legs back and kicked her forcefully in the gut. Keira cried out in pain and tried to shield herself before another blow connected with her. The wind seemed to get knocked out of her as she tried to crawl away; she was in too much pain to try and stand up. It seemed to radiate up and down her entire body.

"This is for your own good," her father bit out and kicked her again.

It was another blow to her chest and gut that left her breathless and in agonizing pain. She gasped and tried to scream, but she could barely catch her breath, let alone call out for help.

Her father sneered down at her, a creepy smile forming on his face. He kicked her again and again. She instinctively clutched her abdomen to try and protect herself.

Pain radiated throughout her body. Meanwhile, she was still in disbelief that this was happening. How could her own father do this to her?

For a moment, the kicks stopped, and Keira thought that it was over. She struggled for breath while she tried to crawl away.

Then, there was a forceful knock to her head. Her vision shook for a moment; reality seemed like a blur. A wave of nausea overcame her, and everything went cloudy.

Then, there was darkness.

CHAPTER 1

Two Years Later

Keira pulled the comforter over her head. She had no idea how long she had been in bed, but the heavy floral curtains in her room had light shining through the cracks along the edges.

Of course, she didn't care what time it was. What exactly did she have to live for? She had been a prisoner of her father for too long. He would never let her go. She knew too much about what kind of company Amherst Global really was. She knew what kind of person he really was. He was a monster.

She would have shed a tear at the thought of her situation, but she had already cried enough over the past two years. Her father, not wanting to just kill her and get it over with, had decided to keep her hostage in her room at Amherst Manor. Keira had literally spent years of her life living in one room, shut off from the outside world. No Internet. No phone calls. No social contact. Nothing.

Well, nothing but loneliness and despair.

It was her father's wrath that was responsible for her situation. She had defied him; therefore, she would be punished. And he would continue punishing her until she would submit. Still, she didn't want anything to do with the company, and she certainly didn't want anything to do with him. Her father was obsessed with the idea of her eventually taking over everything at Amherst Global.

That wasn't going to happen.

Keira wasn't going to sell her soul to get out of this prison. Damien Amherst was evil. If the way he ran his company hadn't cemented that realization, then the physical abuse that he had dealt to her during her graduation party had been the death knell.

Her father's true nature should have been more obvious beforehand, but she had been too blind to see it. Perhaps he had been right about one thing: she had been naïve.

As much as she didn't want to dwell on the way her life had gone, it was the only thing that she could do. Keira lived in a prison of her father's making: trapped in her childhood bedroom for the last two years, under lock and key by her father's security. She was depressed and had pretty much given up hope of anything good happening in her life. Her father controlled everything that she did, but that wasn't surprising. In a way, he had always been controlling her life. Now, it was just more obvious.

Unfortunately, there was nothing for her to do now but sit around and allow life to pass her by. When her father had initially locked Keira in her room, she had just been grateful that he wasn't hurting her anymore. Her father had broken a few of her ribs during their confrontation at her graduation party and had given her a concussion. However, after the days and weeks and months had passed, her life had become less about being content with being left alone and more about the soul shattering loneliness and isolation that she had to deal with every day.

Keira had been deprived of any electronics, even just a plain television. She was at least lucky that she had several built-in bookshelves that kept her sane. Even that was starting to get old as she had read and re-read every book that she owned.

Other than that, it was either sleep or being lost in her own thoughts. Sometimes there was the occasional fantasy that she would be rescued, but she had lost hope on that a long time ago.

Keira hated what her life had become, but there was nothing she could do about it. She was trapped.

There was a sudden knock at her door, interrupting Keira's train of thought. She jerked her head out from the blankets.

What now? She thought.

It was odd for her to be disturbed, unless it was for her meals. Those were delivered by her father's security guards. She almost never left her room.

"Yes?" She said meekly as she peeked her head out from underneath the covers.

"Miss Amherst, your father is requesting a luncheon with you today," said one of her father's men.

He was dressed in the typical security uniform for the manor. His expression seemed cold and unfeeling. This was just business for him.

Keira groaned.

Once a week, her father insisted on dining with her. She hadn't spoken a word to him in over two years since he had her confined to her room. Yet, once a week without fail, they ate lunch together on the weekends. It was a silent and horrendous task for Keira. She hated seeing her father. He was the keeper to her cage.

"Okay," she said meekly.

There was no use in trying to get out of it. She had tried to defy him earlier on in her captivity, but her father had ways of coercing her into compliance. He hadn't physically touched her since her graduation party, but there were other ways to inflict pain. Withholding food was one of his favorites. Keira had lost a considerable amount of weight since being imprisoned on her already thin frame. She felt like a shell of a person at this point.

"Can you give me a few minutes?" She told the guard, eyeing him warily.

Keira was expected to look presentable during their weekly meal together. If she didn't, there was a good chance that she wouldn't eat for the next few days. She despised how her father could manipulate her so easily, but Keira was stuck in survival mode. All she could do was concentrate on getting through each day.

There was a pause before the guard said, "Yes, but hurry it up. Mr. Amherst was very clear that he wants you immediately."

Of course, he does, she thought.

Her father had his schedule. She just fit into it when it was convenient. He didn't care about her. She was more of an object than a human being to him.

Keira spent the next few minutes dragging herself out of bed, finding a suitable outfit, and trying to fix her hair up a bit. She had chosen a bright blue, long-sleeved 1950s-style A-line dress with a pair of silver pumps. Once upon a time, she would have thought the look cute, but her heart wasn't into it. She just wanted this over as soon as possible with the least bit of hassle.

As she brushed her hair, she couldn't help but wince at the reflection that stared back at her in the bathroom mirror. Her face was pale, and her eyes looked haunted. Sometimes, she didn't recognize herself.

When she was ready, she called outside for the guard. There was always one posted by her door. Always. There was no chance of escape.

Another nondescript guard (the same old tall, foreboding male guard) walked her to the informal dining room. The steps that she took seemed like a somber funeral procession.

She hated all of this. She hated her life. There were points in time that she thought about ending it if she could. What was the purpose of life as a prisoner? There was no contact to the outside world. Just isolation and utter loneliness.

When they reached the informal dining room, a wave of anxiety came over Keira. The room was decorated much lighter than the rest of the house in more yellows and whites, but the place felt like doom to her. Outside, she could see a dusting of snow on the ground, reminding her that it was a bit after Christmas and New Year's. Time seemed to blur together when there wasn't much to differentiate the days and weeks.

Damien Amherst sat there in his expensive suit and tie (she rarely ever saw him wearing anything else). The look on his face was stern as always. However, there was another person in the room. That was a first. The only people who she had contact with was her father and his security team.

Keira's eyes darted over to a handsome blonde man in a charcoal gray suit with sharp blue eyes. His haircut and clothing spoke of wealth. The expression on his face said cocky. She studied him for a moment and immediately realized she didn't like him. He reminded her of her father too much.

"Ah, Keira," her father said in a sickeningly smooth voice and stood up from the table. "Just in time. I want you to meet someone."

Keira just stared at her father. She would not speak to him, and he knew that. However, he didn't seem to miss a beat despite her silence.

"This is Jason Savage. He will be the new COO of Amherst Global. He'll be joining us today for lunch."

Keira glanced in his direction, but still said nothing. Jason Savage was a young pick for the position; however, she was more concerned about why he was even here. Wasn't her father concerned that she might say something about her treatment? Then again, if Savage was that high up in the company, he was one of her father's cronies and would most likely follow Damien Amherst without question.

"It's a pleasure to meet you, Keira," Savage told her, his voice low and honeyed.

She still said nothing. He was an incredibly handsome man, but his whole demeanor seemed off. Keira immediately knew that she didn't like him.

Jason stood up and walked over to her. He pulled out a chair for her, and she wearily sat down, suddenly feeling her hands start to shake. What was her father up to now? This whole situation was out of the ordinary.

Keira watched as Jason strolled back to his seat and turned to look at her father saying, "I like her. She's quiet. Knows her place. I think it's a good match already."

Her head started to spin, and she let out a short gasp.

Oh, no! No, no, no, no! She thought.

She knew exactly what was going on: her father was setting her up with one of his company men.

"No!" She exclaimed, her voice choked with emotion.

"Quiet," her father said sternly. "This is your own damned doing. If you had been more obedient and gone along with the plan, you wouldn't be in this situation."

He stared at her intently, a vicious smile spreading across his face.

"I need a legacy willing to take over the company when I die. I feel like a marriage to Jason is the perfect arrangement. We have the same views on how Amherst Global should be run, and I want grandchildren to keep the legacy going. Jason has graciously agreed with this endeavor. He is the type of person I want raising my grandchildren."

Marriage? Grandchildren? Keira couldn't quite believe what she was hearing. She knew that her father was an evil bastard, but he was apparently also insane. Could he really marry off his own daughter?

"You can't do this," she said quietly, trying to hold back tears.

Don't cry. Don't cry. Don't let him see you cry, she thought.

"You can't force someone to get married."

"I can do whatever the hell I want to, Keira," her father snapped. "At this point, I own this town, this county, this state. I have a mega-empire. You are going to marry Jason, and that's the end of the discussion."

Keep it together, she told herself, though she was starting to come unraveled.

Her father was nuts. He was hell-bent on establishing a legacy, no matter what the cost. Before she had learned of her father's secret, she wouldn't have believed that he would sell her off to another man. But after two years of confinement, she'd believe anything. He had previously beat the hell out of her. She now understood that he was capable of anything.

"Keira, I didn't mean to come off too strongly," Jason told her. "I think this is for the best. You are a gorgeous woman, and you'll make a good wife, eventually. You just need to learn to submit."

Keira was sick to her stomach, and if she had eaten anything that day, she was sure she would have thrown it up. Was her father going to force her to marry this man? Was he going to force her to bear his grandchildren? She shuddered. No, that couldn't be possible.

Then, an even darker thought came to her: In order to have children, she'd have to be intimate with a man she didn't know, one who appeared to be a harsh and cruel person. Keira could already see that he was just as controlling as her father. Who in their right might would agree to such a farce? He may have been handsome, but the thought of sex with that man made her sick to her stomach.

No, she reminded herself firmly. *It wouldn't be consensual sex. It would just be plain rape.*

Keira was suddenly dizzy and got up from the table without thinking. She felt like she was suffocating, and the room seemed to lose focus for a moment.

"I need to go..." She mumbled, stumbling around her chair.

Her life was spinning out of control way too fast, and it had already been a mess for the last two years.

She began to stagger away when her father commanded, "Sit down!"

"No!" She exclaimed and suddenly had the urge to run.

Keira, unfortunately, didn't make it that far. A pair of strong hands grabbed her arms and pushed her against the wall. Where exactly she thought she was going, she didn't really know. Of course, one of her father's security associates would have been standing by. She was always being watched.

"Sit her down here now!" Her father yelled, his voice snarling.

Keira felt herself literally being picked up like a rag doll and moved back to her chair where she was forced to sit by a mean-looking security associate dressed in black.

She felt utterly defeated.

"You have been nothing but a disappointment to me," her father said.

He was calmer now, but his voice was like ice.

"You are lucky that I've been so forgiving of your behavior, but my patience will not last forever."

Keira felt shaky, like her blood sugar had suddenly dropped. The room around her didn't feel real, as if all of this was just a dream. But she knew it wasn't. Her father was a monster who was going to force her to marry another monster.

"Now, where were we?" Her father asked as if nothing had happened. "Oh, yes! I think we were discussing your engagement. After talking to Jason, I feel like we don't want to waste too much time for such a perfect couple. You two will look wonderful together."

"I agree with your father, Keira," Jason added.

There was some sort of glint in his eye.

"It's why I got you this."

From out of his suit pocket, he pulled out a box that obviously had a ring in it and slid it forward to her.

"I think you'll like this."

Knowing that there was a security guy hanging right over her head, she complied.

Hands trembling, she opened the box to see a huge, practically flawless diamond surrounded by a ring of smaller diamonds. It was a beautiful piece of jewelry, but everything about it seemed wrong. It was too big—almost tacky in a way. She couldn't even imagine its worth. The glittering stone in front of her felt more like a bribe than anything else.

Was Jason Savage trying to persuade her into liking him? Into loving him? It was a disgusting thought. She didn't need money to win her love. She had never been into grandiose living.

"No," she said firmly after a moment in a moment of courage. "No. No! No!"

Without another thought in her head, she snapped the jewelry box closed and flung it at Jason. He easily dodged it, and it bounced softly to the floor. When she saw the expression on his face, she immediately regretted throwing the box at him.

"You are going to learn how to be obedient," Jason said darkly.

His piercing blue eyes glared menacingly at her.

"Eventually, you will be mine. And you will obey."

"I think Jason and I are on the same page here," her father interjected. "You have been out of control for too long. I think a man in your life will change that. I'm thinking a short engagement. I'll have something set up within the next week for the ceremony."

Keira couldn't help but start to cry. It was hopeless. Her father would force her to marry Jason Savage. Then Savage would force himself on her, probably repeatedly, and she would have to follow along with his will for the rest of her life. Life felt bleaker than it had ever been. She had thought for a while now that her father would just keep her locked up forever, but her new fate appeared to be even worse.

"I know you probably wanted a larger ceremony, Keira," her father continued. "But I'm thinking we could do something for next weekend. Everything will be taken care of: dress, make-up, hair. Don't worry. I'll do the best that I can."

Keira wasn't sure if her father sincerely meant what he had just said or if he was trying to toy with her emotions some more. At this point, all she could do was cry. She had held it in for so long that it just didn't matter to her anymore what her appearance was. She wanted to be strong—to show that her father couldn't get to her—but everything was falling apart so quickly.

"We'll have you try on a few dresses in the next day or so," her father continued. "I have a seamstress on hold who will come at a moment's notice. I'm sorry that there will be no reception, as I think your behavior will be in question, but I'm sure that you understand."

Keira could barely hear him. Her head was pounding, and all she wanted to do was escape, even if it was just back up to her room.

"Just let me go," she heard herself saying. "I'll leave. Disappear. You won't ever hear from me again."

Her father sighed and shook his head.

"I can't take that chance. I'm sorry. This is the best for you, anyhow. I wanted more for you, but that just doesn't seem to be in the cards."

Completely changing the subject, he said, "I think the soup course is ready. Shall we eat?"

Keira debated between trying to choke down some food for sustenance or try and forgo it because of her nauseated stomach. A staff member brought out a tray of some sort of creamy soup. Her father and Jason dug in. Meanwhile, Keira tried to gulp down a few bites but couldn't quite stomach it.

"What's wrong, Keira? Not hungry?" Jason asked with a sly smile.

Keira studied him for a moment. Then, she suddenly realized that he was *toying* with her. Jason Savage was an absolute creep. The thought of being married to him disgusted her.

"You're a little too skinny at this point," Jason continued. "Let's work on that a bit before our wedding. I know it's short notice, but I think a few good meals would do you good."

Keira had had enough. In a spurt of confidence, she pushed her bowl across the table.

"Go to hell," she said firmly.

Instead of any anger that she thought Jason would have, his smirk seemed to widen.

"You are very feisty," Jason told her. "A lot more than I thought. That's good. But your father and I agreed that I will have to break you eventually."

Break me? Keira thought.

Her head was spinning. She let out a scream, something primal from within her. She stumbled out of her seat again just to be grabbed by a security associate.

"Take her back up to her room," her father said forcefully. "She'll learn soon enough."

Keira wondered as she was being escorted off if her father and Jason would wear her down to the point where she didn't care anymore. It was a scary thought, one that made her sob even more as she was hauled off back to her prison.

CHAPTER 2

Keira sat wide-awake in her bed. It was night-time, and the room was in complete darkness. She couldn't sleep, though she wished that she could sink into the comforting oblivion for a bit. It had been two days since the fateful lunch with her father and Jason Savage. Since that time, her life had been a whirlwind. She had already been fitted for a dress. Her father had procured a marriage license and had apparently paid off someone to officiate, even though it would be against Keira's will. There really was no way of stopping this now. It was hopeless for her.

She began to cry again, which surprised Keira because she really felt like she had no more tears to shed over her problems. For the last few hours, she had tried to think positively about the situation. It had even crossed her mind that if she were to marry Jason, it would at least get her out of her room and out of her father's house. Then she realized that she would have to be intimate with him, and that's where the tears started back up again.

Keira couldn't imagine what sex would be like with a man like Jason. He was just as cruel as her father, if not more so. Her only experience with intimacy was with a college boyfriend, and it hadn't been very good. After they had broken up, she had sworn off sex until she graduated. Now it appeared that she was stuck having sex with Jason.

No, she reminded herself. *It's not sex. It's not consensual. It's rape. Always remember that. Always.*

Keira was about to give up on sleeping and try to read a little bit from one of the books when she heard a knock at her door. She looked at the clock. It was after two. No one ever bothered her this late. Alarmed, she got up from the bed and strained to listen. She was in sweatpants and a t-shirt, so she was at least somewhat decent. However, she had no clue what was going on.

The latch on the door turned, and a figure appeared in the doorway. The hallway light was dim, and she only had a small bedside lamp on in her room, so Keira couldn't really see who it was.

"Keira?" A man's voice said in the dark.

It was a familiar one, at least. One that she hadn't heard in the past two years.

"John?" She asked hopefully.

It couldn't be. She hadn't seen him since her ill-fated graduation party, though she knew he was still working tirelessly for her father.

"It's me," he said quietly.

Keira got out of bed and quickly moved to flip on the overhead light. John hadn't changed much since she had last seen him. He was in his typical black slacks and black shirt deal, but there was a look of worry on his face.

"Why are you..." She began.

There was so much that she wanted to say to him. It had hurt to think that he had abandoned her to her father, but she also knew that John's ultimate loyalty would always be to Damien Amherst.

"We don't have time for this," John told her, his voice full of urgency. "I'm getting you out of here. Tonight."

Keira's heart felt like it had jumped up in her chest. Her knees felt weak. Was she hearing this correctly? She had dreamed of getting out of this hell for so long that she didn't think it was possible.

"John..." She said, her voice shaky.

"No time," he said firmly. "Get dressed. Pack a bag. You have five minutes."

Her heart was pounding, but she immediately sprang into action, adrenaline rushing through her. It was a blur, but Keira managed to throw on underwear, a pair of jeans, and a cream-colored sweater in her adjoining bathroom. She knew it was cold outside, but she unfortunately didn't have access to any of her coats, so that would have to do for now. She also pulled on a pair of brown equestrian-style boots over her jeans.

Good enough, she thought.

Keira didn't have any luggage, duffel bags, or backpacks in her room, but she did find a large purse that was shaped like a backpack. It would have to do. She pulled a change of underwear, a few toiletries, a picture of her mother, and a few jewelry items that were her mother's. She unfortunately did not have any identification with her, but right now, she was just focusing on leaving.

By the time she was able to get at least somewhat packed, John told her firmly, "Time's up."

Before she could say anything, he grabbed her arm and pulled her toward the door.

"Don't say a word."

He led her to the door and pulled it open. There was always a security guard posted right at her bedroom door, but tonight, there was no one. Strange.

John pulled her quickly down a dimly lit hallway and down a set of stairs to the first floor of Amherst Manor. Keira still didn't see any security. What was going on?

They continued down more hallways and then out the side door that pushed them out into the cold night air. There was a man posted on the outside of that door, but he just nodded at John as they walked by him. Technically, John Stratton could probably waltz through the whole place teeming with security, and no one would say a word. As her father's right-hand man, what John said and did was sanctioned.

It was surprisingly bright out around Amherst Manor because of the many house lights that illuminated the doorways and pathways. Keira almost cried as she inhaled the cold night air. She couldn't remember the last time she had been outside.

Amherst Manor was an exquisite place: gray stone throughout the entire estate, perfectly manicured gardens, and acres of beautiful property surrounded by a high rod-iron fence. There was a huge garage for her father's car collection, housing for staff, and a stable where she used to ride constantly when she was younger. It felt like it had been a wonderful place to grow up, but now it just felt like a large prison.

They were heading toward the staff parking lot on the east end of the estate. There were butterflies in the pit of Keira's stomach as she quickly walked alongside John. Was there a chance that she could leave? It all felt surreal to her. If it wasn't for the cold night air and a slight breeze, she would have thought that she was dreaming. It wouldn't have been the first time that she had dreamed that she had escaped her father and woken up to disappointment.

Keira was beginning to get concerned about the estate's front gate. No one went in or out of Amherst Manor without being on a list. Even when she was in college, she had to schedule when she wanted to visit her own family home.

John steered her to a black SUV in the parking lot, and said in a low voice, "Get in and keep quiet. Don't do anything unless I tell you to."

Keira slid into the front passenger seat and buckled in, her hands trembling as she attempted a few times at getting the latch to the belt in properly. She was shivering a little bit from the winter night's chill, and she attempted to warm up by hugging herself.

Starting the engine, John slowly pulled the car around the long driveway out of the staff parking lot and began to head out the main drive to the gate. Keira's hands were still shaking, and she tried to regulate her breathing as the car slowly rounded a corner of highly maintained shrubbery and came out to where the main gate stood. There were at least three men at the gatehouse, one inside and two that stood next to the gate. Keira knew that they were all armed. They wouldn't shoot her, but she wasn't so sure about John.

The SUV slowly rolled to a stop, and Keira had to force herself to keep breathing. The uniformed man in the gatehouse came out and approached the driver's side of the car.

"How are you doing tonight, Mr. Stratton?" The guard asked in a conversational tone.

"Fine," John said without emotion.

The guard, who was a middle-aged man with sandy brown hair and a beard, took out a flashlight from his waistband and shined it into the car. Keira couldn't help but flinching when the light came across her eyes.

"Where are you taking Miss Amherst?" He said, his tone suddenly changing to a more hostile one.

"You heard the call," John said calmly. "It's an emergency. I'm to take her to a safe house until we figure out what's going on."

The guard didn't look too convinced, and said, "Miss Amherst is not to leave the compound under any circumstances without Mr. Amherst's expressed permission."

"It's an emergency," John said, his composure steady. "Mr. Amherst is on a transatlantic flight, and his satellite feed isn't working. Look at your messages."

The guard looked down and flipped through a phone attached to his belt. There was a long pause while he studied the screen. Then, he looked up with an odd expression on his face.

"Yes, I apologize. This is a known issue, but the order still needs to come from the next in command."

John still looked calm, his face like stone. Meanwhile, it took Keira everything she had not to lose her composure.

His voice was low when he said, "And who would that comes from?"

The guard floundered for a moment.

"Well, that would be you, sir."

John smiled and said, "Exactly. So, when I tell you that I need to move Miss Amherst, I'm expecting you to comply. Unless you want the wrath of Mr. Amherst, of course."

Suddenly, the guard looked shaken. Keira could only imagine what happened to employees who disappointed her father.

"No, of course not, sir," he said. "I'll get the gate open at once. I'm sorry."

And with that, the guard waved his hand, and the gate opened. Without another word, John rolled up the window and moved the vehicle along. Keira let out a short sigh of relief, but the ache of adrenaline remained.

They could still get you at this moment, she reminded herself as they drove along the estate's front drive and out to the main road.

It was only after a few moments that Keira realized that John's hands had been on a gun holster mounted to the side of his seat. The altercation would have been bad if he hadn't been able to talk his way out of it. She was now thankful that it hadn't come to that.

They drove on in the night. It took a long time before Keira even had the courage to speak.

"Are we safe?" She asked meekly.

John looked at her with an intense gaze, and said quietly, "No. You will never be safe until your father is dead. But for now, it seems like we are in the clear."

Keira wasn't exactly sure if she was panicked or relieved by that remark. John had always been straight to the point. It wasn't like him to mess around with anything.

They drove for another ten minutes in silence before John pulled into an unmarked gravel road off the main one that was barely visible. After a moment of the vehicle crunching through the gravel and woods, they finally stopped at a clearing. There was another black SUV there, almost barely noticeable, even with the bright headlights of John's vehicle.

When John's SUV had stopped, he told Keira sternly, "It's time to get out. Take your bag."

Keira had no choice but to follow John's directions. She wasn't exactly sure if she trusted him, but she was certain that she didn't have a choice. This was the best chance she had, and she wasn't going to blow it.

There was one glaring issue that bothered her. If John had so much power in the company, why had it taken him so long to get her out? She had rotted away in her room for over two years of her life. Why wait until now?

She followed John out of his vehicle to the other SUV. Before she could say a word, he grabbed one of her hands and placed a key in it.

"This is to the vehicle you see here," he told her. "There is a map inside and directions to an address. You are to drive to that address as quickly as possible. Don't stop. Just keep going. It's far. I understand that. Do what you can. Your father's men will be after you."

Keira could barely think. Things were going too fast. She had dreamed of an escape for years, but she never thought of it happening this way.

"You mean, you're not going with me?" She asked, her voice just above a whisper.

"No, I'm sorry, Keira. I can't," John said.

He took her small backpack and put it into the front passenger's seat of her SUV.

"Get in," he told her, his voice devoid of emotion.

Keira paused, debating what to do. She could just get in and drive away, hoping that everything turned out all right. However, if she went that route, she'd never understand what John Stratton was all about. He was separating from her, and in her heart, she knew she would never see him again. It was time to get the truth, even if it cost her precious moments of time in which she could be fleeing her father's forces.

"Wait," she said firmly, some confidence coming back into her. "I need to know why you didn't come for me sooner."

The moment that she said it, the tears started to fall. There had been fantasies of hers where Uncle John had come and carried her away over the past two years. Why had he waited until now if he cared about her this much?

John studied her for a moment, and there was a long pause before he said, "You were safe locked up in your father's home."

The answer shocked Keira.

Then, she got angry.

Safe? Safe! How dare he! She thought.

She had been dwindling in her father's clutches for years, and he had decided that she was safe? It felt ridiculous to her.

"I wasn't safe there," she spat out. "My father was killing me every day I spent there, locked in my room. And before I was locked in that room, he beat me unconscious."

"Keira, I don't think you understand," John said, some of the tough-guy act starting to crack.

She could see some emotion in his expression. It may have been the first time that she had ever seen his stoic composure falter.

"First, don't ever think for a second that I didn't want to come and get you. Second, if I had decided to try and get you, your father would have hunted us down to the point where we would have been caught. He would have killed me, and you would have been in the same damned situation, if not worse."

"Then what changed?" She asked softly.

This was a side of John that she had never seen before. He was genuinely angry at her father. The unwavering loyalty toward her father that she had once seen in him had vanished.

"I found a way out for you, Keira," he told her. "That and the fact that your father was going to try and marry you off to some asshole in his corporation. I couldn't stand for that."

This sudden show of emotion in John should have comforted her, but instead, she felt more disturbed than ever. If John was worried, then she needed to be extra worried.

"Okay," she said quietly. "I'll do what you say."

"Keira..." He floundered for a moment before he could continue. "I'm sorry for how things turned out for you. I feel responsible for your situation. I was the one who pushed you to speak with your father. When I saw what he did to you the night of your graduation party..." He trailed off, emotion choking his voice. "I'll never forgive myself for that."

She didn't know what to say. There had been times that she had been angry at John, but it was always because he had never helped her during her imprisonment, never because he had suggested to go speak with her father that fateful night. She knew that it would have all come out eventually.

"John..." Keira began, but he cut her off quickly.

"Look, we don't have time for this right now."

It was back to business with him again. The side of John who she was familiar with was now back and in control.

"Get in the car. Follow the map. It's precise. You will not use GPS under any circumstances, nor will you use a cell or LAN-line phone. Your father can and will track those things. There is cash in the glove compartment. There's also water and some food in a cooler in the back.

"Don't stop unless you need to. Don't call anyone. Don't make any waves. I couldn't get you an ID in time, so don't get pulled over by law enforcement. Do you understand all of this?"

It was a lot of information to take in at once, but Keira nodded in reply. She quickly got in the SUV and buckled in. However, she left the driver-side door open because she desperately wanted to glean a little more information out of John.

"Go left out of this place," he said. "Follow the map. And please stay safe for me, Keira."

"I will," she said, her emotions starting to get the best of her. "Thank you, John."

He looked at her with his dark brown eyes as though he were more serious than ever.

"Don't thank me until your father is dead," he said without emotion. "Now, get going. You're wasting time."

He slammed her car door shut and pointed toward where she should drive. It had been so long since she had been behind the wheel of any vehicle, but she was so full of adrenaline that it didn't matter. She hit the gas and drove off down the gravely, wooded path. The map was on the front passenger's seat, but she immediately knew what to do: she turned left.

CHAPTER 3

Damien Amherst strolled into his office at the D.C. headquarters of Amherst Global. He had just gotten back from a long flight on his private jet coming from Germany. It was early morning, and he hadn't slept well on the plane. However, there was work to be done. It took a lot of skill and effort to run a company like Amherst Global, especially when he had two sets of books to juggle. The public front of the company was very different than what was behind closed doors.

He hadn't always set out to run his business this way. When he was younger, he had promised himself that he would command respect from anyone and everyone. That meant doing things a certain way. He didn't regret the way his life had gone, but he did mourn the loss of his daughter as a potential ally. She was too young and naive to see how the real world worked. It was unfortunate, but at least he had solved the problem of what to do with her. Jason was perfect for her. She'd learn to fall in line through him, eventually.

Keira had been a problem for the last few years, and Damien had initially had no clue what to do with her, except for keep her locked away. He couldn't kill her; she was his flesh and blood. She was his legacy. But he also couldn't keep her locked away forever. After working with Jason for some time, the idea had dawned on Damien what to do with her. It would be a perfect set-up.

Damien sat down at his mahogany desk and had just opened his laptop when his phone rang.

"Amherst," he answered.

"We have a problem," said the voice on the other end of the line.

Damien received calls like this from time to time. Sometimes it was an issue that was blown out of proportion. Sometimes it ended up being a serious problem. Regardless, there was never an appropriate time in business to panic.

"Explain," he replied coldly.

"She's not in her room, sir."

A pit in Damien's stomach formed. No name was needed. He knew exactly who "she" was. There was only one female he watched constantly: Keira.

"Then where *is* she?" Damien demanded, his voice almost a growl.

"We don't know, sir."

"Then I suggest that you find her and find her quickly, or heads are going to roll." Damien hung up without another word, feeling pissed.

He said a few choice curse words.

This was not good. Everything at Amherst Manor ran like clockwork. He immediately called John. Stratton would know.

The line on the other end rang for a while but there was no answer. It went straight to voicemail. Instead of leaving one, Damien ended the call and redialed. The same thing happened. In all the years that they had known each other, John *always* picked up the phone. He had been an incredibly reliable ally.

After the third or fourth try, Damien began to get furious.

He threw his phone across the room and yelled out to his administrative assistant for the D.C. office, "What the hell is going on here? Get Jason on the line. Now!"

Yes, someone's head was going to roll. That was for sure.

* * *

Keira had been driving for over thirty hours straight without sleep. She only stopped for gas and restroom breaks, and even that had been as short as possible. She was so tired that she knew if she closed her eyes for even a few moments that she would be asleep immediately. Yet, she felt driven. She was free at least for now. Just being out of her room in Amherst Manor felt amazing even if she was exhausted.

The address that she was being sent to was in Montana of all places and looked to be out in the middle of nowhere. The drive had been going well with no issues. However, the weather had been deteriorating rapidly.

Keira was almost there and had been following the map that had been given to her closely. She knew that she was maybe ten or so minutes away from her destination, though it seemed like a million years. Snowflakes kept falling as she traveled along the road. It was around ten in the morning, though it was a lot darker than it should have been at that time of the day. She knew it wouldn't be that long until she would get to her destination, but the weather was starting to get a lot worse.

On top of that, she had no idea what lay ahead. John hadn't given her anything but an address and a detailed map. All she knew is that her destination meant safety, and so she kept on moving.

It had been a beautiful drive through the state, but Keira had barely noticed. She was tense and exhausted and just wanted to stop the SUV, curl into a little ball, and go to sleep. However, the thought of her father coming after her made her drive on.

There was also an underlying current of excitement—and a bit of apprehension. Right now, she was free. She could go anywhere and do anything. Just being on the road, putting miles between her and her father felt wonderful. Being able to see the world from outside Amherst Manor brought profound joy to her and a bit of sadness.

She had missed so much. That part of her life had been stolen, and she'd never get it back. Keira was twenty-six now with no career, despite her efforts with internships and grad school. She had no money since her father controlled her trusts.

And, of course, there was no special someone in her life. She had given up any chance with romance in her time of captivity. The only sexual relationship that she had been offered was her father trying to give her to Jason Savage as if she was a possession.

Keira sighed.

She supposed that she was just a possession to her father. He certainly didn't treat her as his daughter—or a human being for that matter. She was so incredibly happy to be away from him. However, she was worried.

She was certainly not out of the woods yet. Her father was ruthless and would hunt her down mercilessly. She had faith in John's plan—she had to since there was nothing else to cling to. This was her only chance.

Keira glanced at the dashboard of her vehicle. The fuel light had been on for a bit now. She had been stupid when she had driven right past the last gas station, but she thought that she could milk it until her destination. It wasn't that long now, but she was really worried about running out of fuel, especially now that the weather was getting bad.

Just a little bit longer now, she told herself.

Keira kept the SUV under the speed limit, since the roads were covered with snow. There was no one else on the road as it was, anyhow. A few tense moments later and she found little sign with the turn-off that she needed to go on.

As soon as she rolled onto the road, she knew it was gravel from the feel under the tires. It was hard to see from the inches of snow on the road, but she could tell that it wasn't a main road. There were trees on both sides of it, but they were becoming blurred as the snow picked up. Her destination was only a bit more to go. She needed to keep it together just for a few more minutes.

Keira decelerated to less than five miles per hour because the snow had picked up even more. Despite the headlights and the fact that it was late morning, she couldn't see much. All she could do was try and "feel" the road as she drove, but even that was extremely difficult. The vehicle was at least all-wheel drive, so she knew that it would go in the snow. She just hoped that she had enough gas to get to her destination. She was getting worried.

After few moments, she could feel the vehicle going off the gravel. There must have been a jog in the road that she had missed because of the poor conditions. Keira was having a hard time just trying to figure out where the road was. She tried to make a correction, but the SUV began to slide a bit. There appeared to be a bit of a ditch to one side of the road, and she was about to get stuck in it.

No, no, no, she told herself.

There was no way that she could get herself stuck now. She was so close to her goal. Keira gunned the engine before the SUV could fully slip off the road. The truck corrected itself and got back on what seemed was the gravel road again. However, there was suddenly a sputter and a cough from the engine, and the car shut down.

Shit! Keira thought, beginning to panic.

She turned the key to the engine, but the vehicle would not turn over. It gave out a few sputters but did nothing. She tried a few more times before finally giving up.

What exactly was she supposed to do? Keira was out in the middle of nowhere with no gas to heat her vehicle. She couldn't walk anywhere because she didn't have a winter coat. She had no phone to call out for help. Her situation suddenly felt utterly hopeless.

Keira was now mentally kicking herself for not stopping for gas. What had she been thinking? She had been so focused on her goal of reaching safety that she had taken a risk and lost.

She stopped trying to start the vehicle and considered her options.

Someone would eventually come down the road and see her, right? She thought to herself.

Keira still had some food and water in the truck. If she didn't freeze to death, she could make it for a little while. It felt like a completely stupid plan, but it was the only one she had.

She sat in her vehicle for a bit, starting to feel the temperature drop. Anxiety and fear hit her in waves as she tried to remain calm. She stared nervously out the windows, hoping to see traffic or make out any buildings. All she saw was a white-out of snow. The visibility was terrible; she could barely see a foot away in any direction.

She searched in the very back for any other supplies besides what John had pointed out, but the trunk area was empty. There wasn't even a blanket. Cursing, she stretched out in the middle row of seats and huddled into a ball for warmth.

The utter exhaustion of not sleeping for more than a day finally kicked in, and she began to close her eyes. The blackness was so welcoming that she forgot about how bad it would be when the temperature of the car equalized with the outside temperature.

* * *

Wake up. Wake up. Wake up, a voice told Keira.

It felt distant at first, but then she realized it was her own voice. She mildly wondered what was going on. There was a bit more blackness for a while.

After some time—it could have been a few minutes, or it could have been a few hours—Keira realized that she was asleep and needed to wake up. There was some important reason she needed to be awake. What was it?

Keira tried to move or even open her eyes but couldn't.

After struggling for a while, she finally opened her eyes. Her memory was foggy, and for a moment, she had no idea where she was. It was dark, and it took a few seconds for her eyes to adjust.

Once she got her bearings, she realized where she was: in a freezing cold SUV, trapped in a blizzard. Even with a blanket of snow over the windows of the vehicle, she knew it was dark out.

How long had she been asleep? Would she even be able to get out of the vehicle?

Quickly, she pulled the latch and pushed the door open. It took a moment for her to push through the snow, but she was indeed able to leave. Frosty air hit her face, and she shivered. Keira hadn't realized how cold she was until now. Pulling the door shut again to try and preserve any kind of warmth, she tried to think of what to do.

You idiot, you could have fallen asleep and froze to death out here, she told herself.

After the initial grogginess had worn off, her mind seemed a bit clearer with the little bit of sleep that she had gotten. Keira turned the key again in the wild hopes that the vehicle would start.

It didn't.

Keira did notice that the clock read 6:30. She had been asleep all afternoon, and no one had come past her to help her out.

It was at that point that Keira realized that she had to help herself. No one was coming for her. No one was going to bail her out of this one. She would literally freeze to death in her vehicle if she didn't do something. She opened the door again to frosty air, though it was already freezing in the vehicle. Squinting, she looked out toward the direction she thought the road was in. Her destination couldn't be *that* much farther away, could it?

Keira had to try something. Per the directions John had given her, she should be almost right at her destination. It was her only option to try and get there on foot. It wasn't exactly an easy decision to leave the vehicle, but her choices were limited. She could try and stay in the SUV and probably freeze to death, or she could attempt to get to her destination on foot and probably freeze to death. At lease the latter option involved her doing something about her situation. She was tired of being locked away.

Not bothering with her bag, she left the car with no coat; she just had on her cream sweater, jeans, and boots. The icy wind and chilly evening air bit at her face and hands. She wanted to cry, but it felt like her tears were freezing up before they could go anywhere. The snowstorm had died down, which was always a plus. However, it was now dark out, so visibility was still an issue. The snow was very deep as well, and almost came up to the top of her calf-length boots.

Keira stumbled along in the direction that her vehicle was pointing, hoping that she would stay on the road as best as possible. She concentrated on one foot at a time in the deep snow. Wind bit at her face, and she was beginning to shiver uncontrollably.

One foot. Then another.

Each step was painful. Her whole body was starting to go numb. Her teeth chattered involuntarily. Keira's decision to leave the safety of her vehicle seemed entirely stupid now. She was so cold that she couldn't stand it. Her eyes were half-squinted from the cold and the blowing wind.

After more trudging through the snow, Keira began to fanaticize about lying down and going to sleep. She knew the thought was crazy, but she was so tired...

It was then that she saw the glimmer of hope. There was a faint light through the distance. Since it was dark, she could now see it even through the falling snow. If there was light, that meant that there were people, and people meant help. Keira made the decision to try and get to wherever the light was coming from.

She began walking toward the faint light, freezing and tired—the thought of giving up weighing heavily on her mind. But she had made it this far, hadn't she? It couldn't be that much farther.

Keira was so exhausted that she wanted to stop. She wanted to quit. Freezing to death in the snow didn't sound so bad, right? She'd just go to sleep and be relieved of her out of control life.

No! She told herself sharply. *Keep going. Don't give up.*

Freedom from her father was within her sight. She just had to keep moving.

Her clothes were starting to get wet from the snow, which chilled her even more. Yet, she kept seeing light in front of her, and it was getting brighter with each step she took.

She moved until she could see something right front of her. What was it? She could see light that was visible through the snow. Then, she finally realized what it was: a house! And not only that, but she could see windows, which was the source of the light, and a door.

Letting out a shriek of delight, she began to try and run to the door through the deep snow. Unfortunately, she lost her footing and fell, landing in the freezing cold, powdered snow.

Keira sat there, stunned. She didn't want to move. Her shivering had stopped. Her situation felt surreal. If she just closed her eyes, she could imagine herself just slipping off into a deep sleep. She didn't care anymore, even though she was just feet away from her destination.

Pick yourself up and go! She told herself firmly. *You didn't just escape your father for nothing.*

And with that, Keira got up and kept moving. When her hands felt the door, she almost cried. Instead, she screamed.

Loud. Piercing. Primal.

After banging her hands on the door, she lost all coordination and slumped into it, feeling defeated. She was about to pass out when the door suddenly opened. Brilliant light blinded her as she felt into the warmth. Strong arms caught her.

She couldn't focus on the figure who was holding her, so instead she cried out, "Help me!"

Then she succumbed to the blackness.

CHAPTER 4

L ogan Slade had been sitting in his cabin in Montana contemplating his life. There was a lot to ponder as he was at a crossroad in his life. He was thirty-three years old and an Iraq war veteran, spending the last few years as an Army Ranger. He also happened to currently work at one of the most lucrative private military companies in the world.

Technically, he fell under the description of "mercenary," though that word did have a bit of a negative connotation.

Gray Tower, Incorporated only took jobs that kept them on the side of the good guys. That could mean anything from body guard services to bounty hunting to taking down bad guys for Uncle Sam.

The Uncle Sam stuff was completely off the books. Those assignments typically consisted of gray ops missions with no paper trails whatsoever. Everything Gray Tower did in those cases had to be plausibly deniable.

Luckily, all of the field agents were the best of the best: ex-military, special forces, the exceptionally talented, or even reformed criminals.

Gray Tower was run by Miles Bryant, a billionaire who started the company after his daughter was murdered overseas, and the killer was never caught. He was a great boss, and Gray Tower was an amazing company to work for.

Yet, Logan was burnt out. Completely and utterly burnt out.

He had spent eight years in the Army and the last three with Gray Tower. Although he loved the camaraderie he had in the Army, there was a lot of shit that still haunted him to this day.

It had been an adjustment returning to civilian life. Logan wasn't the type to marry or have children—not that the idea of a family life scared him. Deep down, it sounded good. But he didn't want the responsibility. He had seen what happened when you screwed up your kids, and Logan wasn't about to take that chance.

Without direction, Logan had spent a few months out of the Army feeling irritated, listless, and sometimes hopeless. When he had been hired on at Gray Tower, much of those emotions went away. With the company, Logan felt a part of something again. He had a lot more control of his missions and was quickly promoted to a leadership position through his performance.

Sure, it was still soul-sucking work much of the time, but it was at least work that Logan understood. However, his last mission had gotten him so frustrated that he was now contemplating quitting altogether.

For the past six months, Logan had been given a mission from Uncle Sam—strictly off the books. His job had been to go in and dig around a company called Amherst Global. It was a huge shipping conglomerate that was still privately held by a man name Damien Amherst. There was suspicion by a few unnamed top officials from government of what the company was really doing: anything from drug running to human trafficking.

It would have been hard for any government agency to investigate Amherst Global as Damien had a lot of political influences, including sway with a scary amount prosecutors, judges, and politicians. For the most part, Amherst had a free pass to do whatever he wanted.

But then, someone in the higher echelons of the government had decided that Amherst's days were numbered. That person (or persons for all Logan knew) had hired Gray Tower to eliminate Damien Amherst in any way possible. Since Gray Tower didn't do assassinations, other options had to be considered. There was a lot of scouting and a lot of research and eventually some action.

Unfortunately, Logan's efforts had seemingly been in vain. He had gained no headway whatsoever, except for a run-in with one of Amherst's higher-ups.

It had started out as a simple intel-gathering mission, a look into one of Amherst Global's possible drug warehouses. That angle had been a bust.

However, Logan had run into John Stratton, one of Amherst Global's most important men. Stratton had been on the radar, but Logan hadn't had authorization to do anything but try and take the guy in.

John Stratton wasn't like most of the Amherst's hired thugs. He had a personal relationship with Damien, and there was a history there that made him extremely loyal to his employer. They had grown up together as childhood friends that had continued later as adults.

Logan had been in the middle of clearing the warehouse, which had been unfortunately emptied of any kind of contraband. However, Stratton *had* been skulking around.

The guy was good and had been able to get the drop on Logan. It had been a solo mission, so there was unfortunately no back up. If shit had gone south, no one would have bailed him out.

Luckily, Logan had been able to get his weapon drawn, which left the inevitable face-off with guns pointed at each other. Neither man had moved.

Logan had been thinking of ways he could end the confrontation without getting killed when Stratton slowly lowered his handgun and said in a very calm voice, "I've had my eye on you for a while, Slade. You're good at what you do."

Logan had remained quiet, but his mind had been going a mile a minute. How the hell did Stratton know who he was? Logan had never been in a position where his identity could have been compromised at Gray Tower. Apparently, he had been wrong in that assumption.

"Drop the weapon," he had said, his voice had come out a little sharper than he had wanted.

"You might be the only one who can help her," Stratton continued, ignoring Logan's demands.

Logan had been debating his options. Should he shoot Stratton? The man *was* pointing a gun at him. Logan would have been justified in shooting him. Should he high-tail it out of the warehouse? If he did that, he could miss whatever intel he could get out of Stratton. Logan would have to decide and fast. However, what Stratton had just said piqued his interest.

"What the hell are you talking about?" Logan had demanded.

In response, Stratton slowly began to holster his handgun, Logan tracking his every move. If Stratton had moved the barrel of his gun anywhere but down, Logan had been prepared to kill him. It was an unfortunate part of the business: kill or be killed.

"I'm not going to fight you, Slade, and I know you won't shoot me in cold blood. I want you to know that you are the only person I can trust right now. When the time comes, I'll need your help. She needs your help."

Logan frowned. What the hell was he talking about? Stratton seemed all over the place.

"You have about five seconds to start making sense. Why the fuck would I help you? You're just another one of Amherst's thugs."

Stratton let out an audible sigh and said, "That might be, but right now, there is an innocent woman being tortured by Damien Amherst. She needs help."

Logan's interest suddenly perked up. Amherst dabbled in human trafficking, and it wouldn't be uncommon for women to be involved. The sex trade was very lucrative, and it was one of the issues that really pissed Logan off the most. This could be the lead that he needed.

Or—more likely—John Stratton was a lying sack of shit, and this was really a set up. He may have just been stalling before back-up arrived.

"Explain," Logan demanded.

"Not now. Just be prepared."

"This is a nice little chit-chat we're doing right now," Logan finally said, his weapon still aimed. "But I'm done with the vague-ass bullshit."

Stratton smiled and started backing slowly away from him.

"Stay where you are!" Logan commanded.

Stratton continued to walk backward.

"I'll fucking shoot you," Logan reminded him.

"No, you won't," replied Stratton as he continued to step backward until he rounded a corner and disappeared into the warehouse.

And with that, Logan Slade, the man who was supposed to be a mercenary badass let the bad guy go. He had no idea why.

Logan could have taken him down. Was it the look on his face? Had it been what Stratton had told him? Was it the fact that Logan had been so strung out on the last few missions that he couldn't stand taking another life? Or was it the nameless woman that was flung in his face? If Stratton had been talking about a human trafficking case, Logan wanted in on it. Nothing pissed him off more than the exploitation of women.

Nothing.

It had been a gamble, but Logan had wanted to wait and see how the confrontation with Stratton played out. Bryant probably wouldn't approve, but Logan had played fast and loose with the rules at Gray Tower before. Sure, it was risky, but if Stratton did have intel and was turning against Amherst, things could get interesting.

After the encounter, Logan had fudged the report for Gray Tower and said that it had been a complete bust with no information to gather and nothing from the warehouse. The second part was true. The warehouse had been empty, but his run-in with John Stratton had been something that he should have reported.

Logan wasn't sure if he was done with Gray Tower, or if he just needed more time to dig around Stratton to figure out what was going on. It could just be a ploy, for all Logan knew. That would piss him off more than ever.

A few months had gone by without anything to advance Logan's mission. The run-in with Stratton had been a dead-end after all. No intel. No breaks. No contact from Stratton. Nothing.

Frustrated from his lack of progress with anything connected to Amherst Global, Logan had asked for some time off. His request had been graciously granted. Bryant could have easily said no, since there was so much work to be done, but a good boss understood his employees. Logan had needed some serious time to sit and think.

He looked at the clock in the cabin. It was 1900 hours. There wasn't much for him to do this evening, since there had been a blizzard parked over the cabin for most of the day. The snowfall had slowed down a bit, but he didn't want to leave at this point. He had more than enough food and plenty of wood for the fire. Plus, he had just filled up the gas generator. He'd be fine for a bit.

However, there was a restlessness about him. He wanted to know what to do with his life: keep going at Gray Tower or move into a job that wasn't such soul-sucking work. Logan had felt like the last six months digging around Amherst Global had been a huge waste of time. Maybe it was time to move on—from everything.

The major problem was, if Logan did indeed hang up his hat at Gray Tower, what exactly was he supposed to do? How would his skills transfer over to a "normal" job? What would make up his new "normal" life? If wife and kids were out, then what?

Logan shook his head and put another log on the fire. He was hoping that a bit of time alone in his cabin would do some good. It was his time to decompress and get away from the bullshit for a while.

It was then that he heard a loud rapping at his door, which put him on full alert. He never got visitors out here, unless he was expecting them.

Logan could barely turn toward the sound before he heard a shriek from outside the cabin. Then there was a cacophony of pounding on the door and blood-curdling screams. Diving for his 1911 that was sitting on the nightstand, he ran for the door. He wasn't prepared for what he saw when he opened it.

A young woman was there, covered in snow and without proper winter clothing. Her light brown hair was soaked, and her eyes were wide in sheer terror.

She stumbled into the doorway, a bunch of snow coming in with her. Logan had to catch her, or she would have fallen to the floor. She must have been in shock and was probably suffering from hypothermia. He had to get her warm and fast.

"Help me! She cried out and then promptly passed out.

Suddenly, the quiet time of reflection that Logan thought that he was going have all but vanished as he decided his next move.

* * *

Jason Savage starred at his cell phone, reading a few business-related emails before putting it back in his pocket and sighing. At least the business end of Amherst Global was doing well. It was the personal part that was a little more complicated.

He was currently sitting in Damien Amherst's office at Amherst Manor, waiting to get more information on his runaway bride. Jason had met Damien at the manor after a rather tense phone call earlier that morning. Keira Amherst was somehow missing, despite being under lock and key.

Initially, they had thought that it was just miscommunication and that she was somewhere else on the property. But no, she was just plain missing—or, more likely she had escaped somehow. Jason really didn't care that much about her personally. He could get any woman that he wanted. However, a marriage to her would solidify his relationship with Damien, and Jason needed that if he wanted to advance his career.

Also, Jason had been looking forward to making her scream. He had been looking forward to that quite a bit. She was so helpless and pathetic. Jason knew that he could get her begging for him in a short amount of time. It just took a bit of correction on her part. That would be easy. In fact, that would be the fun part. Nevertheless, this would only work if they could find her. Both he and Damien had agreed that this had to be an inside job.

It was late evening, and they had been sifting through security footage logs personally. Initially, when Jason had arrived at Amherst Manor, Damien had been livid, almost crazed. He had just gotten back from a business trip and had gotten blindsided by the news. Now, he had calmed down and was cool and calculated as he usually was.

After some time, it was obvious who the culprit was who had sprung Keira. John Stratton was missing as well, and after some digging, they found that his name was on a sign out at the main gate for her. They'd interviewed the security guard and then disciplined him accordingly.

It was a pity that Stratton had turned on the company. He had been there from the very start and had been extremely loyal to Damien over the years. Amazingly enough, Damien was taking it a lot better than Jason had expected.

"I'm going to kill him," Damien growled under his breath.

Or maybe not.

"We'll find her," Jason assured the older man. "Stratton may have resources, but he can't hide her forever."

"Why did he do it?" Damien asked, though it was more of a hypothetical question than anything else.

Jason had his theories—so did Damien. They suspected it had something to do with Jason and Keira's engagement. Stratton had apparently been close to her throughout her life. Maybe he disapproved? Or, perhaps someone was paying him a lot of money to have leverage on Damien? Either way, Stratton was a dead man.

The "how" of how Stratton did it was obvious with some more digging. It had been a sloppy job upon a cursory look. A few security calls here. A few log manipulations there. And suddenly, Stratton could get Keira out. It looked like it had been a quick planning job as it hadn't been terribly hard to find out. Hopefully, Stratton had made other mistakes along the way, so they could recapture his soon-to-be bride.

"Thirty years he's served me! I've given him everything!" Damien shook his head. "What does that bastard do but stab me in the back—and with my own daughter!"

"That makes his betrayal all the worse," Jason agreed.

Damien shook his head. "It doesn't matter. I can get someone new. Perhaps I may rely on a new member of the Amherst family?"

A smile crept over Jason's face.

"That would certainly be acceptable."

"Good. I hope you're in for a few long nights because we will find her, and we will find her quickly."

"Agreed."

As unfortunate as it was that Stratton had turned on Damien, this may be the opportunity that Jason had been looking for. If Jason married Keira, then he could easily fill Stratton's place. That would be an even larger promotion than the one he got when he became Amherst Global's Chief Operating Officer.

Jason's thoughts drifted back to Keira, and he began thinking of all sorts of ways to punish her when she was found. That may even be the best part of all.

CHAPTER 5

There wasn't much time for Logan to decide what to do. He couldn't take this mysterious woman to a hospital in a blizzard like this. Besides, she might not make it in time, since the nearest one was almost an hour away. He had to think quickly.

Still holding her in his arms, he slammed the front door to the cabin and set down his weapon. His first task was to get her out of her wet clothes and then work on getting her warm.

Logan's cabin was basically one large room centered around a large brick fireplace cube. The small kitchen was on the right with a dining space. The living space was on the left with a bed tucked in the back. There was a cramped bathroom as well with a tub, but a hot bath would be out of the question: it would take too long for the ancient water heater to put out anything remotely hot. The only other option was using his own body heat.

Dear Lord, please don't let this girl wake up right at this moment, Logan thought to himself as he carried her over to the bed.

The last thing he needed was getting socked in the eye by a frightened female who was about to be undressed by a stranger. However, he felt like he had no choice.

He laid her down on the soft comforter and began the process of peeling off her wet clothes. First to go was a cream sweater, heavy with cold moisture, bits of ice and snow falling as he pulled it up and over her head. She had white tank top under that which was soaked as well, her bra underneath well-outlined by its dampness.

Logan pulled off the tank and hesitated at her bra. It was cream and lacey; he could see the pink tips of her nipples through the thin fabric. His mouth went dry as he watched the swell of her breasts move up and down in rhythm with her shallow breathing.

Damn, she was beautiful, he thought.

Why did she have to be attractive? Logan knew that admission was going to get him in a lot of trouble if he didn't keep his shit together.

He hesitated on what to do with her bra. For modesty's sake, he wished he could leave it on, but it was soaked through, just like her sweater and tank. As much as he really didn't want to mess with her underwear while this poor girl was unconscious, Logan wasn't sure if he had the choice.

The bra came off.

It was hard not to notice how perfect her breasts looked and how beautiful her body was. She was tall for a female; her torso was long and lean. Despite her above average height, she seemed delicate—like she would break if squeezed too hard. Her breasts weren't voluptuous by any measure, but they were perfectly proportioned to her thin frame. Her soft, pink nipples were erect from the cold.

Keep focused, he told himself.

If he didn't get her warmed up soon, she could die. It was as simple as that.

Logan worked to pull off her calf-high boots and her jeans. At least she had been wearing boots, though they didn't look like they provided much warmth in the snow. He pulled off her socks and briefly checked for frostbite, doing the same for her hands.

Her damned jeans were the hardest since they were soaking wet with melting snow and ice. He briefly hesitated on her panties, which were also of the same thin, lacey fabric as the bra. The panties were wet, and he made a split-second decision to go ahead and take them off as well. He'd probably go to hell for this, but he wasn't going to take any chances on anything sucking the heat out of her. Her skin was already pale and felt cool to the touch.

As he tugged off her underwear, he couldn't help noticing the curve of her hips and her tantalizingly long legs. He tried not to stare too much at her utterly feminine body as he peeled off his own sweater. As a concession, he kept his jeans on in hopes that he could at least minimize the violation that this would cause.

With that, he threw the blankets over and climbed in the bed with her. He carefully pushed his body on top her hers and held her.

The woman felt a bit cool to the touch. That was not good. Logan hadn't seen her shivering either, which worried him. However, the only thing that he could do was try to use his body heat to warm her up as best as he could. There was a fire going, and the cabin was warm, despite the weather, but she needed a lot more than that to try and get her body temperature up.

Logan lay there quietly for a while feeling the motion of her breathing. This was not the way he expected to be spending his evening: bare-chested against a naked woman.

No, she's not just a naked woman, he reminded himself.

She was a gorgeous, naked woman whose picture was in the dictionary under "his type." Though her damp straight hair was splayed across her face, he could see her soft facial features. She could have been a model or an actress for all he knew.

But it wasn't her looks that he was so preoccupied with. It was her body that he was *quite* aware of. Her skin felt so soft against his own. Her breasts molded against his chest. Logan's mind drifted to the mound of dark curls at the junction at her thighs and what lay beyond. As much as he didn't want to think about her like that, he was a red-blooded male. Logan was already starting to get hard when she moved suddenly, bumping into his groin.

He mentally cursed at himself, and quickly shifted his weight so that his hardening erection was away from her. As much as he tried not to, it was just impossible not get a hard-on while lying on top of a beautiful, naked woman. It didn't matter that he was trying to save her life. The adrenaline of it all was enough aphrodisiac for him, though he hoped to hell that she didn't wake up soon until he calmed his ass down.

Logan changed his focus to doing anything else he could to bring this woman's body temperature up. He rubbed up and down her arms, trying to bring some warmth into her limbs. Logan alternated back and forth between one arm and another. He rubbed her hands as well, anything that he could do to help her.

Time passed, and the fire began to die a bit. Logan wanted to get up and throw some more wood on it, but he wasn't sure if he wanted to risk getting up. The woman seemed to be doing better. She certainly felt a bit warmer, and her hair was almost dry now. Besides, he had kind of gotten comfortable lying on top of her, holding her.

He tried to remember the last time he spent time with a woman like this. It had certainly been a while. Sure, he'd hook up with women here and there when he did have some time off, but to spend time holding a woman—he couldn't remember the last time that happened. It was another unfortunate sacrifice of his chosen lifestyle.

Logan shook his head and brushed a strand of hair out of the woman's face. That was a train of thought that he didn't particularly want to go down right now.

Instead, he spent some time wondering who this woman was and why the hell she had been out in the middle of a blizzard without a coat. Why had she even been on the side road that only led to his cabin? It was odd enough that he was beginning to get suspicious. It could just be bad luck on the woman's part or maybe not. Logan had been trained to consider everything and not take anything at face value. That was what had kept him alive—that and plain luck.

The woman suddenly began to stir. She murmured something softly and moved her head so that it rested in the crook of Logan's arm. Something stirred within him—not lust this time; it was something more than that. Perhaps it was protectiveness? Maybe even possessiveness? That was strange. He didn't even know this woman's name, and yet now he felt responsible for her.

More time passed, and Logan watched her closely. She was stirring more, and he hoped that was a good sign.

The woman nuzzled into him a bit more, and her lips parted slightly. For a moment, Logan wondered what it would be like to kiss those soft lips. Then, he silently cursed at himself for allowing his mind to drift that way again.

He was trying to figure out what to do next when she slowly pulled back from him and suddenly snapped open her eyes. Her eyes looked to be either light brown or hazel; he wasn't sure in the light. There was a glazed look to her expression as if she was extremely disoriented.

She squeezed her eyes shut and kept them that way for a moment. Then she shook her head. She blinked. She stared up at him.

And then she screamed.

* * *

Miles Bryant tapped a pen against his desk as he flipped through a few Gray Tower building reports. He was working late—as always. There was a lot to get done as he was overseeing the largest transformation of his company ever.

The current phase of the Gray Tower Headquarters was going well. Most of the buildings were done with wiring, networking, plumbing, etcetera. The essential areas were online, but they had a long way to go before everything would be completed. The work was estimated to be done by next year if all went well.

Before his idea to create a central, protected location for Gray Tower's employees, most of his staff had been scattered around the country—and the world, in some cases. The new HQ would certainly be a change, but one for the better. Gray Tower was getting to be extremely profitable, and Miles wanted to begin expanding operations.

There was a knock at the door.

They hadn't installed the intercom system yet. In fact, his whole office was done sparsely. Eventually, Miles would get his office exactly how he wanted it, but there were more important issues to deal with right now.

Most of the essential command stuff was underground at Gray Tower HQ, including Miles's office and what everyone was now calling the "War Room." Everything on this level was just gray concrete walls and floors, a few pieces of office furniture, and some electronic equipment. That was it. No decorations. No nothing. Being down a few levels underground, there were also no windows. At this point in time, it was like working in a cave. Or a prison.

"Come in," he said.

Alexandria Thorn, his Administrative Assistant, came in, tablet in hand. She was always on the ball with everything. She was the best assistant he had ever had.

Miles felt guilty about making her work so many nights and weekends lately. There were many essential staff members who had or eventually would have small apartments around the compound. "Alex" was one of the first employees given one. She was essential to everything that Miles did.

Wearing a light gray pantsuit and pink shirt with pearls, she looked amazingly put together, especially for someone who had been working since seven that morning.

She was also quite beautiful. Slender and medium height with long blonde hair worn in the type of stylish waves that movie stars often did, she was a welcome sight around the HQ. Miles also had to implement a policy that absolutely none of his employees were to date Alex. She had to deal with a significant number of advances, and both she and Miles had gotten tired of it.

Alex was young for someone in her position, only twenty-four, but she was amazing. In fact, she was one of the most dependable people he had ever met. He was truly blessed to have her. She was like a daughter.

Bryant grimaced.

Like a daughter.

His thoughts couldn't help but reflect on his own daughter, Jasmine. It was a painful subject that he tried not to think about—at least not at work. That was hard some days, though, since creating Gray Tower had been in response to her murder ten years ago. It had been his idea of redemption.

Miles blamed himself for Jasmine's death. He had been the one targeted for assassination. Due to a change of plans, it was only Jasmine that had gotten on the private jet. It was Jasmine who was on the plane when it had crashed in the middle of the Atlantic when a planted bomb had exploded. Now, he was making it up to her by taking out the worst of the worst and helping those in need.

Creating and heading Gray Tower allowed him to do so unconventionally. As he had learned after the investigation into her murder, going through the proper channels didn't always get the results needed.

Miles had learned to pull the right strings and was now operating the most lucrative private mercenary company in the world. It had been his hope that he would eventually bring those responsible for Jasmine's death to justice with the resources of Gray Tower. Unfortunately, that day was probably not going to be today.

Alex smiled and handed him her tablet.

"I got the quote on appliances for the Level 3 apartments," she said with a sigh. "They can give us a discount if we buy in bulk. I'm opting for the stainless steel. These are supposed to be the nicer residences after all."

Miles nodded. It had been his wish to keep as much as his staff as possible on campus. The Level 3 apartments were the ones given to the Class A staff members, who were his most important operatives. They were the ones who got called up on a moment's notice for missions and were the ones who Miles put a lot of time and money into. Alex, though not a field agent, fell into that category.

He felt bad, though, because she was one of the few employees living in one of the apartments. They weren't even finished yet, but she was bunking there for the duration of this build. She was basically living out of boxes in a construction zone, though she always looked so put together when she came in to work.

"Agreed," he confirmed. "Get them ordered as soon as you can. I'm sure you would actually like to be able to cook and store food in your place."

She smiled slightly and grinned.

"I don't know. I was kind of enjoying eating take-out for every meal."

Miles smiled back and then suddenly frowned as he looked at his watch.

"Speaking of meals, have you had dinner yet?"

Her eyebrows raised slightly.

"Miles, I haven't even had lunch yet," she said wearily.

He shook his head and immediately said, "Stop what you are doing. We're going to get dinner. Alex, I told you to make sure that you're taking care of yourself."

She shrugged and said, "I'm fine. I just got involved with a few things."

Alex may have been his best damned assistant ever, but she also was a workaholic and had a bit of a "Type A" personality. Sure, that made for an excellent employee, but Miles considered her more than that. He was concerned about her well-being.

He stood up and gestured to the door.

"Let's go."

She looked flustered and seemed to scratch the side of her head absentmindedly.

"I'll get something in a little while. I still have a bit more to do."

"Which can wait for tomorrow," Miles cut in. "Don't make me pull rank on this one, Alex."

She sighed and shrugged her shoulders wearily.

"Fine, but you're buying," she said with a wink.

How she had this much energy this late in the evening amazed Miles. She was extremely goal-oriented and extroverted.

"Sure, let's see what the new kitchen is cooking up," he told her and grinned.

They were still working on the staff and menu. The food would get there— eventually. So would everything else, for that matter.

CHAPTER 6

Keira pulled herself out of the blackness and tried to force her eyes open. They didn't seem to be cooperating, so she kept them shut and went in and out of a dreamless sleep. She felt so cold, yet she was next to warmth. She pulled herself closer to it and felt a bit better. All around her she felt strength and heat. Maybe she wasn't out in the cold anymore. Or, maybe she had died, and this was what death was like?

No. She wasn't dead. She was just bouncing around on the edge of sleep.

Keira was finally able to snap open her eyes. It was dark where she was at, but she could make out a face right in front of her. It was a man's face. He had short, black hair, strong jawline, gray eyes that were piecing even in the dim light. Then she realized that she was pressed up against a warm, hard body, skin to skin. Keira shut her eyes and tried to comprehend what was happening. Was she still dreaming?

Opening her eyes, the man still was there, staring intensely at her.

Something felt wrong, and it only took a few more moments for her to realize that she was completely naked. And there was a strange man on top of her who also appeared to be naked.

I've been raped! She suddenly realized.

Keira had traveled hundreds of miles to escape being hurt by one man just to be hurt by another. It was a bitter irony that shook her down to her core.

Then she began to scream. And scream and scream.

Squirming from underneath the stranger's heavy body, she tried to make a swing at him with the one hand that wasn't pinned underneath his body. It was a dumb move because he slapped it down so quickly that all she could do was gasp. Before she could make too much noise, a large, calloused hand clamped down over her mouth.

"Quiet," said the low, masculine voice. His voice was calm, almost calculating. "Stop moving."

Keira continued to try and scream as well as squirm around under the man's massive weight. After a while, she felt too weak to continue, and she eventually stopped, a sick knot in her stomach. There was just no way she could get away from this man.

After a few moments of silence, he told her, "Okay, I'm going to let my hand off your mouth, and you're not going to scream. Nod if you understand me."

For a split second, Keira pondered screaming some more, but the last thing she could remember was that she had been out in the middle of nowhere in a blizzard. Who exactly would hear her if she screamed anyhow? What if she struggled too much, and he really decided to hurt her?

She nodded in defeated compliance.

"Good," he told her and slowly pulled his hand away.

Keira lay beneath him, shaking. She wasn't sure whether she was shaking because she was scared out of her mind or because she was freezing cold. Maybe it was a little bit of both?

"You are still disoriented right now," he continued. "My name is Logan Slade. You were out in a blizzard. You stumbled into my cabin. I'm no doctor, but I'm pretty sure you have hypothermia. The way we are right now? This was the only way I could get your body temperature up."

Keira let that sink in for a moment. She remembered stumbling around in the snow. In fact, she still felt freezing cold. However, she couldn't quite remember how she got out of the blizzard. She squeezed her eyes shut, thinking hard. Could this man be telling the truth?

Then it all came back to her. She had made it to a house. Someone had opened the door. A man. Was it this "Logan Slade" man that was currently lying on top of her? Something in her mind just didn't add up, though.

"You took my clothes off," she said quietly.

He grimaced and said, "Your clothes were completely soaked through. If I hadn't taken them off, I wouldn't have been able to get your core body temperature up fast enough. I'm sorry for the impropriety. I felt I had no choice."

Keira considered that for a moment. That seemed plausible enough, but she could feel the tips of her nipples brush against a dusting of hair on a hard, bare male chest. He was just as naked as she was, their bodies intertwined together as intimately as a couple after love-making. Except he wasn't her lover. He was a stranger.

"You're naked too," she reminded him, her voice barely a whisper. "You...hurt me, didn't you?"

Keira could barely choke out those words.

The look on his face hardened and a splash of anger flashed in his eyes.

"Hell, no!" Logan told her firmly.

He cursed under his breath and rolled off her; he looked pissed.

Pushing himself up on one arm so that part of his weight was off her, he replied, "Damn it. I would never...I was trying to...No! I would never do something like that to a woman without her permission."

More curse words escaped his mouth, and he moved farther off her so that he was lying beside her instead of on her.

It was then that she felt the scrape of denim across her legs. They still felt numb from being out in the cold, but she did realize that they weren't completely skin to skin as she had initially thought. How could she have missed that? How out of it had she been? Considering that she hadn't slept very much and that she had been out in the cold, maybe she should listen for a moment instead of jumping to conclusions?

Clutching the thick comforter to her bare chest, Keira stared at him and tried to decide whether to believe him or not. The look on his face seemed sincere. She shifted her body experimentally and didn't feel any injuries, except for an ever-present chill that was coursing through her.

"Okay," she said, still holding the comforter tightly to her chest. "I believe you."

There was a look of relief on his face. He blew out a long sigh.

"Damn, that's good to hear," he told her. "It was never my intention to make you think that...something had happened."

Keira nodded, not knowing what to say or do next. She was so tired and so cold that she couldn't stand it. A part of her just wanted to close her eyes and not worry about what was going on. She appeared to be safe, or at least she wasn't dying in the snow. Good enough for now, right?

"Hey, how are you feeling?" Logan asked, his voice full of concern. "You really had me worried there for a while. You've been unconscious for about two hours or so."

Keira squeezed her eyes shut, trying to process that information. She could have died out there. It had been blind luck that she had run into this man.

His expression brightened a bit as he asked, "How about I get you some warm clothes and something hot to drink?"

All Keira could do was nod. She was suddenly starting to feel like an idiot. This man had saved her life. She should be grateful to him, but she was still so weary. After what her father had done to her, it was hard to trust anyone.

With that, Logan slowly eased off her and out of the bed. There wasn't a ton of light in the cabin, but what she saw when he got up from the bed made her stomach flutter and her womb contract.

The man was gorgeously ripped.

His body was mind-blowing: large, well-muscled with thin taper down to his waist and a six-pack. There was a light dusting of dark hair across his chest, but father down, there was more dark hair that traveled down his abs and disappeared underneath his jeans. The muscles in his arms rippled as he moved, and his jeans hung on him so deliciously that her mouth went dry.

As Logan moved toward the light of the fire, she studied his face as she could see his features much better. He was incredibly handsome—almost too handsome. There was a generous growth of stubble on his face as if he hadn't bothered to shave in the last few days. His gray eyes were intense.

Keira bit her lower lip as she watched him. In a matter of seconds, she had gone from freaking out at the thought of sexual contact with him to drooling over him. What was wrong with her? There was now a small part of her that wanted him to come back into the bed.

She mentally scolded herself. Just because it had been a long time since she had been with a man didn't mean that she should start ogling strange men, especially strange men who had seen her naked. Chalk that one up to adrenaline because her emotions weren't making any sense right now.

Oh, no, she suddenly realized. *He saw me naked. The hottest guy I have ever seen has freaking seen me naked.*

Embarrassment burned through her cheeks and she pushed the comforter up to her chin. Suddenly, the whole life and death situation she had thrown herself into didn't matter. She was just a girl who felt utterly exposed. Luckily, his back was turned at the time, and he didn't see her turn bright red.

Logan pulled on a gray sweater, ruining her view. He disappeared for a moment, and suddenly, the room was flooded with light. She looked around the simple, rustic space with wood logs for walls. There weren't many decorations except for a few comfortable furnishings. She noticed a huge fireplace cube in the middle and a few couches off the sleeping area. There looked to be a small kitchen on the other side of the fireplace.

Keira hunkered down even more underneath the comforter. She was shivering and exhausted, her body still tense from thinking that she had been sexually assaulted. It was a soul-crushing tiredness that made her just want to curl up in the blankets and stay there forever.

She almost started to drift off to sleep when Logan reappeared with what looked to be a blanket and some clothes under his arm. In the brightened room, Keira couldn't help but stare at him.

Broad shoulders filled out his sweater nicely. He was tall as well, and he felt like he took up the whole space of the small cabin. Everything about him was rugged and masculine. Why did her rescuer have to be such a big, beautiful man?

I'm going out of my mind, Keira realized. *Some hot guy rescues you and you suddenly want to jump him? Get a grip on yourself.*

She had one lover in her past: a guy from college that she had dated for a bit. It had been a mistake to sleep with him; she had regretted it. The sex hadn't been what she had expected, and she hadn't gotten much pleasure from it. She eventually called things off and had stopped dating to focus on completing her master's degree. However, it had been a long time since she had been around anyone who she felt attracted to. She supposed that it would be natural for her emotions to stir up again, especially since she was in such a high-stress situation.

"Your clothes are wet, so I grabbed some of mine," he told her. "They'll be a bit big on you, but at least they are warm."

That was an understatement as he dwarfed her in size—even with her tall stature.

"Thank you," she murmured as he handed her a complementing pair of sweatshirt and sweatpants as well as a part of thick gray wool socks.

"There's a bathroom in the back. I'll give you some privacy."

As he turned away, she was a bit amused by how much of a gentleman he was now being. They had been skin to skin. He had seen her naked. Yet, here he was giving her space.

Keira changed in a tiny bathroom, shivering as she quickly pulled on the over-sized clothing. Even wearing sweats, she was still freezing cold. Looking in the mirror, she realized how tired she appeared. There were dark circles under her eyes, and her skin looked pale and hollow. All she wanted was to crawl back into the bed and try and get warm again.

When she left the bathroom, the fire was roaring, and Logan was sitting on a couch that was next to the bed with two coffee mugs.

"I'm not really a tea drinker, but I bet you could use some right now," he told her. "We'll need to keep an eye on you and make sure that you stay warm. You look tired, but I don't want you to go to sleep just yet until we can warm you up a bit more."

Keira slumped down next to him and gratefully took one of the mugs. The warm liquid was heavenly. She was still freezing cold and exhausted, but she felt okay for a moment. She felt safe.

"What's your name?" Logan asked after a few silent moments.

Keira floundered. She wasn't sure how much she should reveal about herself. She had just escaped the prison her father had made for her. She couldn't to go back. It would literally break her.

"Elizabeth," she finally told him.

Technically, it wasn't quite a lie. It was her middle name. She felt badly because she didn't want to start lying to the man who had saved her life, but she had to protect herself at all costs.

Logan stared at her intently for a moment and then said, "It's nice to properly meet you, Elizabeth. Mind telling me how you ended up wandering around in a blizzard without a coat?"

Keira began to hesitate again. She had to come up with a story quickly, or this whole ruse could fall apart at any moment

"I..." What exactly could she tell him?

Keira watched him wearily. She hadn't thought about what excuse she was going to use for her predicament. Initially, she had just been happy to be alive, but now she had to worry about what she was going to do next.

"I'm sorry," Logan apologized. "I didn't mean to interrogate you. I was just curious. This cabin is a bit out of the way. I wasn't expecting company." He smiled slightly. "You've been through a lot. Don't worry about it."

The feeling of guilt started to rise in Keira's stomach, turning it in knots. This man was being so nice to her, and all she could do was lie to him. A part of her just wanted to tell him what was going on. They could go to the police. Unfortunately, her father had so much power in the right places that it wouldn't matter. The only thing that would do is put Logan in danger.

"I was going to visit a friend," Keira finally said.

It wasn't the truth, but it was the closest that she could get.

"I must have made a wrong turn, and I ran out of gas. I got caught in the storm."

Logan stared at her for a moment as if he was deciding whether he believed her or not. Keira understood that it seemed crazy that a woman would show up on his doorstep with no jacket, freezing to death. She had interrupted his world, and she felt terrible about it.

Not only that, but Keira was putting him in danger just by being here. If her father found her with Logan, she was sure that he would be killed.

"I see," he said, the tone of his voice flat.

Was he on to her?

"Well, as soon as this storm passes, we'll get you out of here and on your way. I'd like to get you to a hospital to check you out, but it's over an hour away in good weather. You'd probably be better off staying put."

Keira nodded, taking a sip of the warm liquid. She hated that she was inconveniencing Logan so much. Not only that, but she could be risking his life by being here. Her father was crazy, and he would do anything to put her back under his control. She shuddered thinking about her father—and Jason for that matter.

She replayed what Logan had just said, and then realized that he had mentioned going to a hospital. That absolutely could not happen. Her father would find her in no time if she was admitted.

"I don't need to go to the hospital," she said a little too quickly.

Logan raised an eyebrow and studied her closely. Keira could kick herself for acting so nervous. He had to know something was wrong.

"How about we wait and see how you're doing tomorrow? It would probably be wise to stay put until morning anyhow. You're in no shape to go anywhere, and I have no idea how bad the roads are right now."

It wasn't the ideal response, but it better than Keira was expecting.

They sat in silence for a few moments, each sipping on their tea. Keira wanted to say something—anything, really—but she wasn't sure. If they got into any kind of extended conversation, then she'd have to start making up more details of her life.

Then, as the fog from lack of sleep and almost freezing to death started to lift, she thought about John and his plan for her. It seemed obvious that Logan was not her intended destination. He had no idea who she was and didn't seem like he had been expecting anyone. If that was the case, then she needed to figure out where her actual destination was.

"Sure, that sounds good," she forced herself to reply.

A yawn abruptly came upon her, and she tried to stifle it with her free hand. Logan had noticed, though, and cocked his head to the side a bit. Extreme exhaustion was getting the better of her. Keira could probably sleep for a couple of days.

"You look exhausted," he commented. "But I'm not surprised. That was quite an ordeal you went through. Ideally, I'd like to try to keep you up a bit longer to make sure you're okay. However, I don't think that you're going to last that long. Why don't you try and rest? You can use the bed, and I'll go on the couch. We'll work on bailing your car out tomorrow, and we can get you to a hospital if you're not feeling better by then."

"Okay," she said, shivering a bit.

There was a dark thought that flashed through her head. It involved Logan going back to bed with her, but she pushed that thought from her mind. Not the time. Not the place.

What was wrong with her, anyhow? She had bigger problems to worry about then an attraction to the opposite sex. Keira was ready to blame it on her near-death experience and two years of captivity.

Then, there was the problem of whether she could completely trust this man or not. He could be some creepy guy out in the middle of nowhere who was planning to gut her and use her internal organs as a chandelier or something. Hey, that kind of stuff happened, right?

Or, and much more likely, Logan could just be a normal good Samaritan. He hadn't done anything that would make her think otherwise. Besides, there wasn't much she could do. If she could last through the night and the morning until he could help her with her vehicle, she would be okay.

As she got up and moved toward the welcoming warm bed, she turned back to Logan who was cleaning up their mugs.

Say something to him, she told herself. *Thank him.*

"Logan," Keira said. "Thank you for saving my life."

His head cocked to the side, and he smiled slightly.

"Any man would have done the same."

Keira knew that wasn't true. Men like her father and Jason Savage liked to prey on the weak and helpless.

"I want to apologize for jumping to conclusions earlier too," she continued. "I feel badly for accusing you of..."

"Don't worry about it," he interrupted, walking over to her.

His height and build dwarfed her own.

Pulling the blankets of the bed back, he said, "Crawl in before you fall over. You look like you're freezing."

When she complied and sat down on the soft, queen-sized bed, he came up closer and pulled the comforter over her. Keira was still freezing cold, and she thought that she wouldn't be able to sleep. However, it was only moments later that her consciousness faded. She didn't even remember Logan leaving the side the bed.

CHAPTER 7

John Stratton sat in the dark of an abandoned warehouse with only the glow of his laptop screen as light. It was very early morning, and he was beginning to wonder if Keira arrived at her location safely. He was prepared to make contact soon, though he was still worried. She *should* have gotten there by now, but he also understood that a lot of the timing depended on Keira. If she had stopped because she was tired, then that would add some significant time. He just hoped that if she had stopped, she was staying in a safe place.

Overall, though, things were going as planned. John was still apprehensive about the future, though. He knew Damien was going ape shit over Keira's disappearance. He would use an extraordinary amount of resources to find her. John just hoped that his plan would be enough to keep her safe. It had been a complete gamble, but so far, it was paying off.

Damien had no clue where Keira was—at least from what John could gather. John still had a few inside sources in the organization as well as backdoor access through some of the Amherst Global systems, though he wasn't quite sure how long that access would last. He also knew that Damien was aware that it was indeed John who orchestrated her disappearance.

It had been a bittersweet betrayal. John had worked for Damien for years. There had been a time when they had been friends, but that had changed years ago. John had hated Damien for the longest time. The man was pure evil, plain and simple.

John knew that he should have left Amherst Global a long time ago. Just disappear. Go off the radar.

But he stayed, and there really was only one reason why: Keira.

He felt terribly for poor Keira. Lily Amherst was gone, and Damien had been an aloof father figure as she grew up. Keira had craved a real father figure and had spent a great deal of time trying to please her father.

John had hoped that she would be able to get out of being involved in Amherst Global. Damien should have known that she didn't have the personality or the unscrupulous morals to do it. He should have let her go and do her own thing. Instead, she had been imprisoned for two years with the prospect of being married off.

John could not allow that.

She'd be safe—eventually. He had a plan, though it would still take some time to completely implement. Unfortunately, time was limited. If John stayed one step ahead of Damien, his plan would work. Damien was a bastard, but he was also arrogant and over-emotional when it came to family—sometimes it was downright psychotic.

John cringed. Keira didn't know. He knew that she hated Damien for who he was and what he had done to her, but she didn't know the half of it. If John could at least shield her from the truth, then he could at least spare her that pain.

* * *

Logan was up earlier than usual. It wasn't like he had slept that much anyhow. There was something that wasn't quite right with Elizabeth, and it had been nagging him all night.

Her story didn't entirely measure up. If she were supposed to be visiting a friend, why try traveling in a blizzard? And how in the hell did she get to his cabin? The turn-off road only went to his place. She would have had to have been *really* lost to get to him.

Another thing that bothered Logan was the fact that her demeanor seemed off. He understood that she could be disoriented from being out in the elements, but when he was talking to her, she seemed almost nervous, even scared. Her answers were hesitant as well, as if she were hiding something.

He didn't want to pry too much. There could be many legit reasons why she would lie to him. She could be running from someone. Maybe it was an ex-boyfriend or abusive husband? That would explain why she didn't have a coat on. She could have just run out of her house and drove as far and as fast as she could. It also could be because he was a stranger, and wherever she was going was really none of his damned business. Logan would have loved to know for sure, but she was going to be out of his hair in a bit anyhow. What did it really matter?

Not that he wanted her to leave. He didn't mind having a beautiful woman in such an isolated place, but Elizabeth obviously had some issues going on. And Logan had a lot to work through himself. He wished that he had met her at a different point in time. She was downright gorgeous, and as far as he had seen, as sweet as could be.

Logan pushed himself off the couch and stretched. It wasn't exactly the most comfortable thing to sleep on, but he had wanted to give her space. He knew exactly what she had thought when she had woken up with him on top of her, and he didn't want her to think that of him.

He padded over to the fireplace, which had dwindled to nothing, so he needed to work on rekindling the fire. After he was finished, he was about to move on to the kitchen area to get some coffee and breakfast going when he heard a soft whimper coming from the bed. Turning, he saw that Elizabeth was curled into a little ball, and it looked as if she had been crying.

"What's wrong?" He demanded, spanning the distance between them in a few quick steps.

She looked startled.

"Oh. I'm sorry. Just a nightmare."

Logan paused for a moment, wondering if she had was having nightmares from being out in the snow, or if there was something else in her life that caused her to wake up crying.

"Well, you've been through a lot in the past day," Logan said cautiously. "Care if I make you some breakfast and maybe make you forget about all of the bad stuff for at least a little while?"

He hoped that his encouragement had sunk in at least a little bit. There was something wrong in her life, and he wished that he had the time to get to know her and find the underlying cause of it. But he was heading back out for another mission in a day so that would be impossible.

Even through a tear-streaked face, she seemed to brighten a bit.

"I would love that," she told him.

"Good. Why don't you go in the bathroom and take a warm shower? Hopefully, the pipes haven't frozen. It'll take a moment for the water heater to get going. It badly needs replaced, but it should be okay for now. There should be a spare toothbrush in the cabinet as well. Your clothes are hanging in the shower as well. They might be dry by now."

Logan really didn't want to get into the fact that he had indeed taken women up to the cabin, which is why he had spare things of everything—except clothing of course. Those times had really been nothing but a weekend deal. He didn't have the time for anything else.

"Thank you," she told him.

Her eyes seemed to brighten a bit and so did her entire mood.

He made sure the shower was working properly in the bathroom before leaving her to do her thing. Then, he worked on breakfast. He hadn't really planned to stock the cabin with a variety of things to include a guest, but he did have bacon, eggs, and toast, so that was what he prepared.

When she came out from the bathroom, she looked like a new woman. Her shoulder-length, straight hair was wet. Her skin looked a bit pinker now that she had regained some warmth, though she still seemed tired. However, there was a look of rejuvenation about her. He was glad to see her looking and hopefully feeling a bit better. He also couldn't help but notice that he had never seen a more beautiful woman without a stitch of make-up on herself. She was breath-taking.

Keep it focused, Slade. He told himself.

"Breakfast is served," he said, sliding a plate toward her on a small kitchen table.

He scooped up two mugs of coffee for them as well and set them in their respective places.

"You didn't have to do this," she said with what seemed like a catch in her throat.

"Yes, I did. You're my guest."

She smiled briefly. It was the first time that he had seen her smile.

"An accidental guest," she corrected him softly.

"But my guest none the less," he countered.

She let out a sigh, and said, "Okay, fine," as she moved to the kitchen.

Plopping down on the chair next to her dish, she dug in.

"Dug in" was an understatement. She devoured the food like she hadn't eaten in a week. When she was done, Logan was still concerned.

"Do you need more?"

She hesitated.

"No, I'm fine."

It was another lie, one that Logan wasn't going to push too much. She had an amazing body, but she was a bit thin in his opinion. He had seen a bit too much of her ribs the night before. It could be her body type, or it could be something else. He hoped it was just the way she was built because it looked like from the way she was acting that she was still starving.

"Okay, well there is more if you want it."

"Thank you," she said and tried to smile.

There was a brief pause, and she looked like she wanted to ask him something.

Finally, she asked, "Are you on vacation here?"

"Yeah, this is my home away from home. Gives me time to decompress from my job."

"It's a nice place. Very quiet and serene," she said, twirling her fork on her empty plate.

"It is," he agreed. "Just wish I had a bit more time to enjoy it."

Elizabeth fidgeted in her sear for a moment before finally asking, "What do you do for a living?"

Logan sighed. He occasionally was asked this question. Luckily, he didn't have to go into detail, especially with family. He didn't have a relationship with his parents anymore and hadn't see or spoken to his brother in years. The scripted answer from Gray Tower when he was asked was, "I work for a private security company." And that was it, so that was what he told her.

"Oh," she said quietly. "What do you do there?"

Logan was pleasantly surprised that she was interested in what he did. Maybe she was just being nice? Perhaps she was attracted to him like he was to her? It was hard to tell, since she was so guarded.

"It varies," he said.

This was also a scripted answer.

"Mostly private security for companies and individuals. Body guard services. That sort of thing."

It wasn't exactly a lie. Gray Tower did all of those things, but there was a lot more to it than that.

"That sounds interesting," Elizabeth said almost wearily.

She still looked tired, and he didn't blame her. She had certainly had an ordeal yesterday.

Logan wanted to be polite, but he also didn't want to get to know her too much. He was certain he'd end up liking her even more than he did already, and that would end up with them in his bed again—only they would both be completely naked.

And he would be buried deep inside of her.

"What do you do?" He asked, trying to shake the thought from his mind, although his dick was starting to harden.

There was an odd expression on her face. She floundered for a moment as if trying to figure out what she wanted to say.

Then she finally said, "I'm in-between jobs at the moment."

The more time Logan spent with this girl, the more perplexing she got. Perhaps she really was escaping from an ex-husband? It would explain a lot. If that were the case, he would want Gray Tower's resources to relocate her somewhere. It wouldn't be the first time that they had helped someone pro bono. He would have to do some more investigating first, though. Logan did not want to jump to conclusions and embarrass himself if those conclusions turned out to be wrong.

"Why don't you wait here and have some coffee? I'll try to get some gas in your car. Sound good?"

Elizabeth nodded and smiled slightly. She had a pretty smile, but it seemed a bit forced.

"Where do you think you left it?"

"I..." She stammered for a moment. "I don't know. It was dark and snowing heavily."

He smiled, trying to be reassuring.

"Don't worry about it. I'll go out on the snowmobile and search. Your car can't be that far out."

And with that, Logan put on his outdoor gear and left her. He had to obviously lock up his Grey Tower gear, including his guns. All he had to worry about now was finding her car and getting it gassed up. He had extra fuel just in case of this scenario.

There was a barn about one hundred yards away from the cabin that contained his truck, his snowmobile, and the spare wood that he chopped for the fire when he was up at the cabin. It was soothing to him as it was a way to forgot about his job and escape for a bit.

However, just scanning around the area allowed him to locate the car, which was a black SUV. It was within a thousand yards of the cabin too, which was probably how Elizabeth could have gotten to him in a blizzard. The vehicle was hidden partially in the snow, but he could still get to it easily just on foot. After trudging through the snow for a short trek in the icy weather, Logan brushed the snow away from the front door of the vehicle and opened it.

Logan popped the fuel cover and gave the SUV a little gas. It wasn't much, but it would get her to the nearest gas station.

Then, he climbed in the driver's seat. The keys were still in the ignition, so he started the SUV. As it spurted to life, Logan looked around. There was a cooler in the back seat with a few water bottles and a small bag sitting on the front passenger seat.

There was a part of him that was nagging to see what was going on with Elizabeth. One part of him wanted to start snooping to get to the bottom of it, and the other part was telling him to stay out of her business. It's not like he wanted to get involved in another mess. But still...

Logan opened the glove box against his better judgment to leave this the hell alone. However, curiosity was getting the better of him. He looked at the registration. If he saw that someone else owned her car, then he could see about possible domestic violence issues. He had access to many different databases through Gray Tower. It wouldn't take much to do a bit of checking.

As he looked through the registration papers, his blood turned cold.

No. No. No. No! He told himself.

This had been a damned set-up the whole time. The registration was made out to Amherst Global.

Elizabeth was a fucking spy.

She had played him the whole damned time. Who knows what information she had gained while he was out filling up her car? He searched some more in her vehicle to find specific directions to his cabin on a piece of crumbled paper.

Logan hit the gas on all-wheel-drive SUV and drove it the short distance to the cabin. Before getting out, he snatched up the registration and grabbed the bag next to him. He searched through it, but didn't find any weapons—just spare underwear, a few toiletries, and some jewelry that looked like the real deal.

He bolted out of the vehicle and stormed into the cabin. Elizabeth—or whatever the hell her name was—looked startled. She was standing at the kitchen sink, washing the breakfast dishes. Of course, she was. What had she been doing beforehand?

Logan stalked over to where she was and flung down the registration and directions paper on the counter next to her. She startled as she eyed the paperwork, an expression of panic setting into her face.

"What the hell is this shit?" He demanded, his voice a low growl. "These are the fucking directions to *my* cabin!"

Her eyes darted down to the paper, and then her face went pale. She stumbled backward, dropping the dishes that she was working on in the sink with a loud clatter.

Logan caught her by the arm and roughly maneuvered her to the bed in a few quick movements. There was a look of surprise on her face, but she didn't struggle. He pushed her down hard, pinning her arms with both hands overhead and the rest of her body with his own.

"You've been playing me this whole entire time. Haven't you?" He demanded. "What was the deal? Amherst Global paying you to get cozy with me so that you get some intel?"

"No!" She cried out.

There were tears in her eyes. She looked so damned vulnerable that for a moment, Logan thought that he had made a mistake.

But no, there was no other explanation of why a woman with an Amherst Global car would stumble into his cabin in a blizzard. Logan wondered if Stratton had put her up to this. Maybe Logan should have taken him out after all?

"Stop the bullshit," Logan commanded, hatred spewing out of him.

He was seething that he had almost fallen for the damsel in distress act. She was good—he'd give her that.

"Why'd Amherst send you here? Or was it Stratton who sent you? You'd thought you get all nice and cozy with me, huh? What was the plan?"

The color seemed to drain from her face and tears were freely falling, but she remained quiet. Why did she have to look so damned vulnerable?

Straight to business, Slade. He told himself. *She's just acting, and she's full of bullshit.*

Logan pulled her up from the bed. She struggled, but he held her firm, his strength far superior. He half dragged her back to the kitchen. She continued to squirm, but he held her firmly.

"If you keep struggling, I *will* hurt you," he told her darkly.

She suddenly felt like a rag doll in his arms. Logan kept telling himself that this was just an act. This woman was caught with Amherst Global registration; she could only be a plant, someone trying to glean information from him. He'd have to deal with her the old-fashioned way, despite her superb acting skills.

Logan pulled her along as he grabbed some rope from under the kitchen counter (you never know when you need to use it). He pushed her into a chair from the dining area and tied each limb to a leg or an arm rest. She had stopped trying to struggle. All she did was cry. He didn't know what to make of that. He had been expecting her to fight back when he had confronted her. Was this more of the ploy? He wasn't sure, but he also wasn't taking any chances.

After she was secured, he left her alone for a short period and went on the other side of the room behind the fireplace cube. There was a small, built-in cabinet with a lock that housed his weapons and his Gray Tower communications gear, which comprised of a satellite phone and laptop. It did not appear that she had gotten into it, but that didn't mean anything. Unlocking the cabinet, he grabbed the phone and dialed out for support.

For a Gray Tower asset of Logan's caliber that meant calling in to Brenden Scott. He was head of IT Security for the company, but he also was the go-to for any high priority missions and agents. Brenden was usually awake anyhow, so it worked out. The guy ran on energy drinks.

Brenden used to be a black hat hacker and an unscrupulous one at that. He was on the straight and narrow now, though. Bryant had straightened him around, and now he was one of the company's best assets.

"What?" Was the terse reply from the other end of the line.

That was Brenden. He enjoyed acting like an asshole sometimes, but he was really a nice kid deep down.

"I've got a priority issue for you," Logan told him gruffly.

He needed to cut through the usual bullshit banter and get straight to the point.

"I thought you were supposed to be on vacation, Slade," Brenden told him, boredom showing in his voice.

"I was, but I think I may have been played by Amherst Global. Tell Bryant that I need an extract."

There was a pause.

"Damn, Slade. How the hell did you get in trouble on vacation?"

"Possible Amherst operative decided to meet me at my cabin. I'm going to upload her picture shortly. I need an ID as quickly as possible."

"Her? Oh, this just got a whole lot more interesting," Brenden chuckled. "Is she hot?"

Yes, Logan answered the question in his head, but instead ignored Brenden's immature comment and said in an irritated voice, "Just get on the ID and extractions as soon as you can. I'll be working on gaining intel from her on this end. Picture is coming shortly."

It didn't take long for Logan to snap a few shots of "Elizabeth." She was still sobbing quietly, tied up and still in his sweats. He had to admit that she still looked cute and that in turn made her look helpless, vulnerable. Her eyes were red from crying, and she stared down at the floor, trying her best to avoid eye contact with him.

For a moment, he thought that he may be making a mistake, but then he reminded himself that Amherst Global was vicious. He had been poking around at them, so now they were returning the favor.

Logan stared at his captive and pushed his emotions aside. It was time to get down to business.

"Now, let's get started," he told her.

CHAPTER 8

Keira was in deep trouble. Some deep, deep trouble. What had she gotten herself into, trusting John? He had sent her to the man who literally freaked out on her when he saw the car registration to Amherst Global. Now she was tied up in a chair by that same man who looked like he would kill her with one squeeze of a hand around her throat.

She watched him talk quietly on a cell phone, trying to figure out what the hell she was going to do. Nausea was coming in waves as her anxiety hit its highest since leaving Amherst Manor. Tears were involuntarily falling down her face. At least she was familiar with her father, and what he would do to her if she got caught. This man was a wildcard.

Her weariness of him turned out to be justified: he indeed was a danger to her, though she wasn't quite sure why. The way he had reacted to the Amherst Global name made her think he was one of her father's rivals, which meant that he would be ruthless with her. But then again...

These are the fucking directions to MY cabin!

Keira had remembered him saying that and was caught off-guard by it. Did John really send her to him? Wouldn't he have known she was coming? Had this all been one huge mistake?

Logan ended the call and looked toward her, his gray eyes that had seemed so welcoming only an hour ago had turned to ice. His expression was full of anger. She diverted her eyes to the floor, waves of fear flowing over her.

"Now, let's get started," he said, his voice low and smooth.

He walked over to where she was tied up. His height itself was menacing enough. Logan had to be six feet one or six feet two by the judge of it. His well-muscled body filled out his clothes well—his black cable-knit sweater stretching across his chest nicely. He was one hundred percent alpha male. Keira no-doubt knew that he could seriously hurt or kill her without much effort.

If you keep struggling, I will hurt you.

It was what he had said to her just moments ago, and it was echoing in her brain. She knew he meant it too. Logan had said that he worked at a private security firm. What if he was just a mercenary like a lot of the goons her father hired?

Logan pulled up another chair and flipped it around so that he sat backwards, leaning his arms on the back of the chair. He was close enough that his legs were almost brushing her own.

"Here's the deal," he told her. "You're going to answer all of my questions. If I find your answers acceptable, I'll go easy on you. If you don't..." He trailed off for a moment, and then a smile spread slowly across his face. "You can use your imagination, but I assure you that it won't be pleasant."

Logan bent down and pulled what looked to be a combat knife from a calf holster that was hidden by his jeans. He began examining it closely, taunting her.

"No!" Keira gasped.

She had been right the whole time: he was going to gut her after all.

Keira could feel herself shaking, and she wasn't sure if it was from fear or from being out in the cold the night before. She pulled at her restraints to no avail. Each limb was tied to a leg or arm of the chair. She was quite immobilized.

"I have to admit that you've got the damsel in distress act down pat," he commented. "You almost had me fooled."

What was he talking about? She wondered.

Couldn't he see that he scared the shit out of her?

"Why are you doing this?" Keira choked out a sob.

"I ask the questions," he said sharply, standing up suddenly from his chair. "We'll start simple and work up from there. What is your name? I doubt it's Elizabeth."

Keira hesitated. What was she supposed to tell him? How had her escape gone so wrong so quickly? Was this really the man John had sent her to?

She continued sobbing.

"What is your name?" He asked again a little harsher this time.

Say something, idiot, or he's going to hurt you! She thought, willing herself to speak.

Keira just had to cooperate. Survive. Do whatever she had to do to stay alive and unharmed, even if that meant going back to her father.

"Elizabeth is my middle name," she told him, her voice barely a whisper.

Logan's eyebrows raised slightly as if he were deciding what she was telling him was true or not.

"Then what is your whole name?"

Keira hesitated. If he knew who she was, would he take her back to her father? But if she didn't tell him, would he make good on his promise?

"Please, just don't take me back there," she whispered. "Please."

Logan frowned and studied her closely. His features softened for a moment, and Keira got a glimpse of the gentle man who had saved her life. How had she gotten it so wrong?

"What is your name?" He asked again, though his tone was a bit softer.

"Keira."

There. She had said it as she watched him closely to see his reaction.

His frown deepened.

"Keira..." He trailed off, looking so intensely at her that she diverted her eyes to the floor. "Keira, what? Keira..."

There was a long silence, and then he said, "Amherst. Keira Amherst. Fuck."

* * *

Fuck. Fuck. Fuck. Logan thought.

How had this happened? How could Keira fucking Amherst be at his cabin right now? Damien fucking Amherst's daughter. Why was she here? How had he not recognized her immediately when she had first stumbled in last night?

Logan tried to think of the last picture he saw of her. The photographs he had seen of her were of when she had been all dolled up for fancy social functions. The casual look without all the hair and make-up could have thrown him. She also looked older from what he remembered, but it was her demeanor that had caught him off-guard. She had been so meek that he hadn't been expecting the daughter of such a powerful man.

He stared at her again, but he was not mistaken. It was her.

Logan cursed some more under his breath.

He should have known; this now changed everything.

Why would Amherst send his daughter to Logan's cabin? The undercover agent theory seemed to evaporate. Damien Amherst was too damned arrogant and condescending to get his daughter involved in something like that. Which meant what, exactly? It made no fucking sense.

She started to sob uncontrollably as Logan debated with what to do with her. Taking off her restraints might be a good start. He doubted that she was as dangerous as he had initially thought. There was still a good chance that her presence here was still nefarious, but he was pretty sure that he could handle her.

Logan moved toward her—knife out—with the intention of cutting her free.

"No!" She shrieked and jerked at her bonds.

The color seemed to drain from her face. She looked terrified.

Fuck, Logan thought.

He'd just spent the last few minutes frightening her into talking, and now she was scared shitless of him.

If you keep struggling, I will hurt you.

It was a bullshit line that had just come out of Logan's mouth. Even if she had been an Amherst Global agent, he wouldn't have touched a female. That just wasn't him; it wasn't in his character. But she didn't know that.

"Keira, it's okay," he said, trying to calm her.

It felt odd saying her name, knowing who she was. He glanced down at the six-inch combat knife in his hands and realized why she was so afraid.

"Shit," he muttered. "It's not what it looks like. I'm not going to hurt you. I'm going to cut you free."

It's not what it looks like.

It sure looked like he was a fucking monster. Logan had been so tired of his lack of progress with Amherst Global that he had been a bit overzealous. His run-in with Stratton had kept him on edge. He had been weary of the bullshit Stratton had spouted...

...but right now, there is an innocent woman being tortured by Damien Amherst. She needs help.

Stratton's words came back to him sharply, and then Logan thought back to what Keira had just pleaded with him.

Please, just don't take me back there.

The realization slammed into him: Keira Amherst was the woman Stratton had been talking about. And if what Stratton had said was true, then she was in a lot of trouble.

Logan tried to think back to what he knew about her. He remembered that she had grown up in privilege. Her mother had died when she was young in a car accident. She had gone off to college and graduated with an MBA.

Then, she had disappeared from the public eye. There had been some rumors about a drug problem and rehab. Logan had dismissed her as some spoiled rich girl and not really a person of interest to his investigation.

He stared hard at her, and suddenly, the puzzle pieces fit together.

Logan had known something was off about her and had originally guessed at domestic violence. Perhaps he was righter than he knew?

He knelt next to her and began cutting the ropes. Keira sat there, eyes snapped shut, tears staining her face. She was shaking, and Logan cursed at himself for the overreaction.

Well, how the hell did you know that Damien Amherst's daughter would wind up at your cabin? He thought.

Once he was done, he moved back and sheathed his knife back in the ankle holster. She sat there hugging herself to self-soothe. He reached a hand out to try and help her out of the chair, but she smacked it away.

"Don't touch me!"

Logan stepped away as she got up from the chair and stumbled backward. He wanted to give her some space, but he was also weary of her trying to make a run for it.

"Stay away from me!"

He held up his hands.

"I'm sorry I scared you. I honestly thought you were an Amherst Global agent."

Keira frowned but kept walking backward away from him until she tripped herself on one of the bottom posts of the bed. Logan closed the space between them in seconds, reaching to catch her before she fell and smacked her head. He was able to grab her and pull her away from danger, but she did end up falling back on the bed, pulling him with her. Logan was able to catch himself a bit, but still ended up falling over her.

There they were—once again—him on top of her on his bed, her wiggling beneath him. This was becoming a reoccurring thing, apparently.

"No! Stop!" She yelled.

And once again, his hand slammed over her mouth.

* * *

Keira struggled underneath Logan's body, his calloused hand over her mouth. She was in full panic mode, and she didn't care what he was saying. He had proven himself a violent, dangerous man. She couldn't take any more chances. Keira had to get away, even if it meant running back out in the elements.

"Damn it, Keira. Stop!" He told her firmly. "I know you're in trouble. I just need to what kind. John Stratton hinted that I might need to help you. I just didn't realize it was you. I'm sorry."

She went still at the mention of John's name. It hadn't been the first time that Logan had mentioned him, but she has assumed he was a thug-for-hire for one of father's many enemies. Was it true that he might help her? This apparently was the address John had sent her to. Had this been a huge mistake?

Logan's demeanor had softened as soon as she had said her real name. He now knew who she was, and he had untied her as soon as he had found out. Was this some big miscommunication?

Keira stared up at Logan, his gray eyes piercing into hers. There was no menace in his expression now. The violence that she had seen in him vanished, replaced by something different. Was it concern?

They remained as they were for a few heart-pounding moments, his hard body covering the length of her. At first his weight had felt suffocating, but now she was experiencing something different. A shock of sexual energy seemed to radiate down her body that went from her chest all the way down to her womb.

What is wrong with you? She mentally scolded herself. *This guy is dangerous. He threatened to hurt you.*

That was certainly true. But he hadn't yet, she reminded herself.

Logan had admitted a misunderstanding. At this point, she was going to have to trust him and trust John. It felt like a no-win situation, but at least there was the hope of a chance with Logan. She knew what would happen if she ran and her father found her.

Logan's hand slowly lifted from her mouth, and he stared down at her. He hadn't shaved this morning, and he almost had a full beard starting, which made him look both sexy but also highlighted his hard-edged demeanor.

For a moment, he just looked at her as if he were sizing her up. His lips were now dangerously close to her own. She could feel his warm breath on her. Was he about to kiss her? Would she even care if he did?

Then he pulled himself up and off her. The loss of his body weight and heat leaving Keira suddenly made her realize that she was still freezing.

"We need to talk," he told her.

She nodded. Yes, they did.

Logan held out his hand. She hesitated for a moment before finally taking it. Pulling her up from the bed, he steered her firmly to the couches in the living area section of the cabin and sat her down. He silently piled blankets on top of her and gave her a cup of coffee while he walked off and made another phone call. Keira strained her ears to try and hear what he was saying, but he spoke in a hushed voice.

She sat for a while, just happy that she was warm and safe again, though her heart was still thumping hard through her chest. The coffee smelled good, but she didn't have the stomach to drink any of it.

When Logan was done, he walked back to her and sat down on a chair across from the couch. He crossed one long leg over the other.

"Talk," he said firmly. "No lies this time, either. I'm in the dark here, and if I am going to offer you protection, I need to know what I'm dealing with here."

Keira wasn't quite sure what to say at first. Her relationship with Logan had gone from him being her savior to her capturer, and now he was back to helping her. Could John have really sent her to Logan and not informed him about what was going on? Was this really just a miscommunication after all?

"Just please promise me you will never take me back there. Ever. Please?"
Logan frowned, looking confused.
"Keira, what the hell is going on?"
And she told him. She told him everything.

CHAPTER 9

Alexandria Thorn walked quickly down hallway toward Miles' office at Gray Tower HQ. It was only nine in the morning, and it was already a crazy day. She and Brenden had been in contact with Logan and had found out that he now had Keira Amherst with him. This had taken an unexpected turn. Miles had been debating on whether to pull out of the Amherst Global case altogether from lack of progress. Now, it was priority number one.

Her heels echoed through the undecorated corridors of Sublevel 3. The lower levels felt like a tomb, and Alex couldn't wait until she could start ordering some items to try and make it look a little more welcoming. That unfortunately wouldn't be for a while, so she tried to push the depressing atmosphere from her mind.

Alex rounded a corner and walked straight into Miles' office. He was expecting her.

Miles Bryant was seated at his desk, looking at his computer intently. He looked stressed, and she couldn't blame him. There was so much work to be done and not enough people to do it. With the new compound, they needed a lot more employees, and the hiring process for an organization like Gray Tower was no picnic. There were a great deal of in-depth background checks.

Add Keira Amherst in on top of that, and things were about to get crazy.

Alex began to wait for him to finish with his work, patiently. She could have interrupted, but she didn't want to add any more stress on Miles.

He was a handsome man, medium height with a head of dark brown hair that didn't have any gray in it, despite him being fifty. His tailored suit spoke of great wealth, but he was one of the most down-to-earth people she had ever known. He was an amazing boss, and she was proud to work for him.

"I'm assuming you got my message about Logan's situation," Alex finally said, as Miles looked up from his work.

"I saw," he told her, his mouth turning to a frown. "I supposed that Logan was both extremely lucky and unlucky at the same time. I'm sure that he's not too pleased that his vacation has been cut short, but what a break in the Amherst mission! Having Keira Amherst could provide some good intel as well as allow us to use her as a bargaining chip."

Alex felt a pit begin to grow in her stomach. She hadn't thought that Miles would use a female like that, especially after hearing some of the story from Logan.

"I got an update from Logan. She apparently was held hostage by her father for years. Are you sure using her as a bargaining chip is the right move?"

Miles sighed.

"No harm would come to her. I'm springing for her to get a new identity and get away from the bastard. But we need to take Damien Amherst down as quickly as we can. A lot is riding on it."

She knew that it wasn't just about the payday the U.S. government would give them. Miles had explained at least part of his motivation for going after Amherst Global was because there was a connection between the corporation and his daughter's murder. He had been able to link a money trail that seemed to connect to Jasmine Bryant's death. Miles hadn't told her the details, but she knew that this mission was important to him.

Damien Amherst may not have been the person who ordered to detonate the bomb, but there was some culpability there.

"I understand," she said. "I've already coordinated the safe house security. They are getting ready to go right now."

It had been short notice, but Alex had been able to get it done. She had to smile at her efficiency. Sure, she had a Type A personality that was borderline crazy obsessive compulsive, but she was amazing at her job. She knew it. Miles knew it. And that was why he paid her the big bucks.

"I want Hunter to go as well," Miles told her, referring to Jack Hunter, the Head of Tactical Operations for Gray Tower.

Or, maybe the money wasn't worth it sometimes? Alex cringed at the thought of putting Jack back on assignment. He had just gotten back from a previous mission and had received almost no down time.

Also, he could be a grumpy asshole.

Unfortunately, with the break that they just got with Keira Amherst, it would be vitally important for them to put as many resources as Gray Tower could into this.

"I'll let Jack know," she said, as she swiped at the tablet she always carried with her and made a note.

"Let Jack know what?" Came a voice from outside the office.

Jack Hunter had suddenly appeared behind Alex. He always seemed to be right there whenever his name was mentioned.

He was a classically handsome guy: tall, medium brown hair, blue eyes, athletic build. Women seemed to flock to him in droves—Alex excluded. His personality was a little rough around the edges, and he wasn't really her type. Looks-wise, maybe, but certainly not personality.

Besides, Miles wouldn't like it if she tried to date anyone from Gray Tower. He had already given the warning to all the men that she was off-limits after she had started getting some unwanted attention when she was first hired.

"I'm assuming you've heard about Logan's situation," Miles stated.

Jack nodded but said nothing—a first for him. He and Logan were best friends, and Jack didn't mess around with his friends.

"The Amherst girl is number one priority right now," Miles continued. "I need you over at the Ohio safe house as quickly as you can get there."

Jack's expression looked a bit annoyed.

"You don't think Logan can handle it himself?" He questioned. "He's one of the best we have, and I'm committed to helping get this place up and running for the next year to year and a half. You already had me out on one mission that I shouldn't have been on, and now you want me on another?"

Did Alex mention that Gray Tower was a bit short-staffed?

"I know that, Hunter," Miles replied coolly. "But this is important. You understand what taking down Amherst means to me, right?"

Jack nodded solemnly. He was one of the few who knew that Amherst Global had some sort of ties to Jasmine's death.

"Understood," he said, his tone turning solemn. "I'll be on my way."

As he left, Miles glanced at Alex, and said, "Clear your schedule for the next week or so because I have a feeling that we're going to get busy."

* * *

Logan was an asshole.

After everything that Keira Amherst had told him, he literally felt like a complete jerk after assessing the real situation. She was far from an Amherst Global spy; she was a girl that had gotten caught up in something bigger than she could ever have imagined.

And she had paid for it dearly.

Keira had tried to describe what life was like for her when she was held captive at Amherst Manor. He really couldn't imagine it. Two years of her life had been gone. Two years of being out in the world had vanished when she should have been out enjoying life.

Two. Damned. Years.

Add the physical and emotional abuse that her father had placed on her, and it made Logan's blood run hot. He was pissed, and he would do everything in his power to help her.

Logan couldn't blame her for being secretive either. She had been frightened out of her mind with the looming possibility that she could be recaptured by her father. She had also been scared about getting married to fucking Jason Savage. Logan had researched the guy a long time ago and knew the man was a creep and a sadist. Keira would not have lasted long as his wife.

After she had discussed her ordeal, Logan could feel his whole mood soften. She suddenly seemed like that helpless girl he had fished out of the snow. Except, she *was* that girl. It hadn't been some act.

He felt terrible for what he put her through, thinking that she was someone else. Keira had already been through enough. She hadn't needed him to make things worse. Yet, there he had been, threatening her with violence. She hadn't deserved that.

Logan bitterly wished that Stratton had been more specific when they had met, but at this point, he was just glad that Keira was now in his custody. She would make a great asset for Gray Tower and should give them a lot of intel on Amherst Global.

However, there was another reason Logan was relieved that she was safe and with him. He was unfortunately attracted to her, which was why dealing with her was going to be tough. Logan had almost kissed her on the bed. What the hell was wrong with him? He had to admit that she was incredibly good-looking, but this was unlike him. Logan took his job seriously. He couldn't allow himself to be distracted by her. It was for her own safety and his.

What made it worse was that he could swear that she had—at least for a moment— wanted to kiss him back. Even with the fear in her eyes, he could tell.

Not good. Not good at all.

They were still sitting on his couches, though Logan had gotten up several times to update Gray Tower on what was going on and stay apprised of their extraction. Keira was sitting under blankets, visibly shaking. He wasn't sure if it was from cold, shock, or fear, but he would make damned sure that he would protect her from now on.

"First thing," he began. "I will *never* take you back to that bastard. Is that clear?"

She nodded slowly. Her face was tear-streaked, and she looked so damned vulnerable.

"Second, I'm sorry that I scared the hell out of you. I've been investigating Amherst Global for a while now. I honestly thought you were an operative. I'm sorry that I frightened you, okay?"

The apology wasn't nearly enough, he knew, but it was at least a start.

Keira nodded and looked away from him. It was obvious that she was uneasy with him now, and he couldn't blame her. She hadn't exactly seen him at his most charming.

"I didn't think John would send me to someone who wasn't expecting me," she said quietly.

"That's not your fault," Logan told her. "And it doesn't excuse how I treated you. I had been investigating your father's company for over six months now. I should have recognized you."

Keira tried to smile, but it looked forced. Her face was still tear-streaked from her talk with him.

"Keira, I'm so sorry for that has happened to you. No one should have to go through what you experienced."

"I hate him," she said quietly.

What exactly could he say? She was on the verge of being broken, and he had almost pushed her over the edge with his shit. However, what the hell was he supposed to do in his position? A random woman had shown up at his door who turned about to be affiliated with Amherst Global.

"You will never have to deal with that bastard again," Logan told her firmly. "Do you hear me?"

Keira nodded slowly.

Logan stared at her. Even without a stitch of make-up on, she was incredibly beautiful. Suddenly, now that he understood she wasn't some scummy Amherst operative, all those feelings that he had for her were bubbling back up again. He couldn't help but think back to the night before with her under him, naked and infinitely vulnerable.

Focus on the mission, Slade, he reminded himself.

He had to keep remembering that she was indeed vulnerable and didn't need to be put in a position where she could be taken advantage of.

His sat phone began to beep again, shaking him out of his thoughts.

Picking it up, he stood from the sofas and replied, "Slade."

"Slade, it's Hunter," said the voice on the other side.

Jack Hunter was the Head of Tactical Operations and oversaw Gray Tower's most important missions. He was also one of Logan's best friends.

"I need an extraction fast," Logan told him immediately. "How long are we looking at here?"

"No extraction," Jack told him solemnly. "We don't have enough resources right now, and the HQ is not up to par with security right now. The building is just not ready yet. We will have to use a safe house instead."

Jack was talking about the new Gray Tower Headquarters, which was being constructed in a rural area outside of Blacksburg, Virginia. It would eventually be state of the art facility when it was finally finished, but that would be at least a year from now. Due to the continuing construction, there were only a few areas that were completely secure.

"Where exactly do you want us to go?" Logan asked, trying not to let the irritation show in his voice. "My cabin is compromised."

There was a pause at the end of the line.

Then Jack replied, "We have a safe house in Ohio that's open right now. I can get a security team to meet you there. Then we can go ahead and debrief Ms. Amherst."

That was Jack: take charge, down to business.

"Give me the address, and we'll be there," Logan said.

At this point, he couldn't mismanage another moment with Keira. Logan had been expecting an extraction with all the resources that Gray Tower had. Now, he had to worry about getting her to Ohio on his own. He'd be willing to bet that Damien Amherst was vigorously searching for her.

"Check your messages. There will be a team to meet you there," Jack replied. "And I'm going to send a clean-up team for your cabin as well. It's just going to take some time. We'll try to take that Amherst Global vehicle and see if we can get any information from it, but that's a low priority right now."

Logan sighed.

"It's not the ideal situation, but I appreciate it, Jack. I'll get her to the safe house as soon as possible."

Jack listed off a few more details before Logan ended the call. This was about to get interesting.

Logan looked over at Keira who was still bundled up in the blankets he had given her, eyes wide and face pale.

"We need to go," he told her, trying to keep his voice as calm and non-threatening as possible. "I'm going to take you somewhere safe. I don't trust staying here. If Stratton knew about this place, then it can't be that hard for your father to find it either."

She nodded but didn't look any better.

"It's okay," he said, his voice low. "I won't allow anything to happen to you. I promise."

Nice one, dumbass, he thought. *This is coming from the guy who manhandled and tied her up.*

"Okay," Keira mumbled and tried a weak smile.

Then her eyes widened in panic. Something was wrong.

"I had a bag in the car. I need it."

"I saw it, and we'll pick it up before we leave," he reassured her.

What he didn't mention was that he had rummaged through it, but she didn't need to know that.

"You will take my winter jacket as well. It'll be huge on you, but it'll keep you warm. I have a lighter one around here that I can wear."

Logan tended to pack lightly, so it didn't take long for him to pack up the cabin and get them situated in his extended cab truck. He would have preferred to go through the process of winterizing the place since he doubted that he'd be back any time soon, but there just wasn't any time. Maybe he could bug the clean-up crew to do it whenever the hell they decided to get there?

As he pulled away from the cabin, a sinking feeling fell in the pit of his stomach. For whatever reason, he knew that his life was suddenly going to change. He wasn't sure why or how, but something was going to change—for better or worse.

CHAPTER 10

I t's two day's drive to the safe house," Logan said. "Just hang in there. You'll be safe there. I promise."

They had been on the road for a few hours, though that was the first thing that Logan had said to Keira since they had left his cabin. So far, it had been an uncomfortably silent ride.

Keira was still reeling from the events of the morning. Logan Slade frightened her with what he was capable of, yet this was the man John had sent her to. Perhaps that was for the best? She knew that Logan could handle himself, yet she wasn't sure what to think of him.

It hadn't even been twenty-four hours since she had met him, and they had gone from lying together naked—well, she had been naked at least—to him tying her up and threatening her. And now what was he to her? A protector of some sort?

Keira felt confused and scared. She was trusting a man who she wasn't sure is she even *should* trust. Sure, he had promised to keep her safe. He was now being very cordial to her, but he wasn't the same guy who had made her breakfast that morning. Logan was now extremely reserved.

In a way, she could understand. She had lied to him after all. He had been investigating Amherst Global. She wasn't quite sure why, but ever since he had found out she was connected, his whole demeanor had changed. At least they both had that in common: anger toward her father. That had to make him one of the good guys, right?

Right now, Keira was going to go with the adage of, "The enemy of my enemy is my friend." She wasn't quite sure if she could trust Logan. John certainly did. But at least he was against her father, so that would have to be good enough for now.

Keira shifted uncomfortably in the front passenger's seat of Logan's truck. She was wearing her only pair of clothes with a new pair of underwear that she had packed. Her jeans were a bit stiff from air-drying the night before, and her sweater wasn't exactly the bright cream coloring that it was when she had left Amherst Manor. She hoped wherever they were going that she could get a change of clothes.

Besides that, she was beyond tired—and cold. Keira had caught herself dosing lightly and was trying her best to stay awake. She probably needed to be checked out at a hospital for what she had been through, but that just wasn't an option right now. The only hope that she could hold onto was that she was safe for the time being.

She peaked at Logan and saw that his jaw was clenched. Even through the ever-growing stubble on his face, she could see it. He was tense and didn't look too pleased to be taken away from his vacation. Her appearance at his cabin had really screwed things up for him.

To make things worse, it looked as if John hadn't even told him that she was coming. She was now his burden.

"I'm sorry that this whole mess dropped into your lap," she finally told him. "If I would have known where I was going, I would have found somewhere else."

He sighed and shook his head. The tension seeming to drain from his face.

"That's nonsense, and you know it. Where would you have gone? What would you have done? Eventually, your father would have found you, and you would have gone right back to where you were. Stratton was smart to send you to me. I'm the only one who is going to keep you safe at this point."

Keira let that sink in for a moment.

"You keep saying that, but I don't quite understand. You said worked at a private security company, but my father has connections everywhere. And the way you interrogated me..."

She trailed off, closing her eyes. Keira had never been so frightened in her life when Logan had come back from fishing her vehicle out the snow. He had been consumed with anger, and she had been convinced that he was going to kill her.

Biting her lower lip, she realized that she was driving off to some unknown location with a man who she knew nothing about, a man who was downright dangerous. Panic began to creep through her.

Logan must have caught onto her apprehension because he told her, "At this point, you might as well know. You're already in over your head as it is. I work for a company called Gray Tower. It does mercenary work for the most part. Stuff that's off the books for the government. We also do private security contracting. That sort of thing."

Keira inhaled sharply and asked, "Not like the kind of people my father hires, right?"

Logan shook his head.

"We only do missions that are morally sound or for the greater good. Trust me, Gray Tower is *not* like the thugs your father employs."

A wave of relief washed over her. She didn't want to have jumped from the frying pan and straight into the fire with another group of bad guys.

"Is that why John sent me to you?"

"Something like that. I had a run-in with him a while back. Almost shot him too. He referred to you, though I didn't know it at the time. He must have decided that I was a safe bet with you."

"Oh," Keira said, though she still felt nervous.

Something was nagging at her. She still didn't feel completely safe with him. Then it hit her.

"Logan, if I hadn't told you who I was—would you have hurt me?"

It was a blunt question, and she regretted it as soon as it left her lips. She was probably going to anger him even more.

He visibly stiffened in his seat, and she could see him grip the steering wheel a bit tighter.

Yep, she had just made him angry. Why couldn't she just let things go? If she had just kept her mouth shut with her father two years ago, she wouldn't even be in this position.

"No," he said firmly. "I would have never..."

Logan seemed frustrated—and pissed. He scratched his jawline absentmindedly and shook his head.

"I was just saying that to try and scare you a bit. I would never hurt a woman like that. Damn it. I just wanted..."

A few curse words came out from under his breath. Not sure what to do, Keira found herself reaching out to touch his arm lightly. He stopped muttering under his breath and glanced at her.

"I understand," she said softly. "You were doing your job."

"Still, I was overzealous and ended up scaring the shit out of you. I'm sorry."

"You've already apologized," she pointed out.

Shut up. Shut up. Shut up, she thought. Why couldn't she just let things be?

To her surprise, a sad smile crossed his face.

"Yes, I suppose that I did, but it will never be enough. You've already gone through hell with your father. I shouldn't have made things worse."

Keira nodded, not knowing what else to say.

"I've got to know, though," Logan continued. "Why was it John Stratton who got you out? Why now? What am I missing here?"

Oh, where to begin?

"John was always there for me when I was growing up. He was my father's closest confidant, so he was around quite a bit. My father was always so distant that I latched onto John's guidance."

She let out a short, bitter laugh, thinking about her childhood.

"I even called him 'Uncle John.'"

Keira watched Logan for a reaction, but he only nodded in encouragement to continue.

"I had gotten extremely bitter toward him after my father had me locked up in my room for so long. I thought that he'd forgotten about me—or worse—had sided with my father and was encouraging my captivity.

"After a while, I had given up hope. And then he suddenly came and got me out of there. He said that he couldn't sit by and watch me get married off to Jason—that he didn't do anything until now because I was at least safe being locked away..."

She trailed off, trying to fight tears that were beginning to well up in her eyes.

There was a long pause before Logan said, "You know he's a bad man, right? He's done a lot of shit for your father that you wouldn't believe if I told you."

"I know," she said quietly.

It had been another revelation that discovering her father's secrets revealed: John had been doing Damien Amherst's malevolent bidding for years. The man who she had respected for so long had suddenly become complicit in her father's dealings.

They drove in silence for a while moving along the snowy highway. The weather had cleared up, and it was now a crisp but bright sunny day. Perhaps things were starting to look up for her? She still wasn't quite sure about Logan, but at this point, he was keeping her safe.

After a while, Logan said, "I'm so sorry about what happened to you, Keira."

More tears began to prick her eyes, and she fought back the urge to start sobbing like a baby.

"Me too," she said softly.

* * *

Damn it, Logan.

Jack Hunter was completely annoyed at the fact that his best friend and colleague had decided stop and rest for the night instead of moving on to the Ohio safe house. Jack had been ready to get the debriefing started in the morning. Now he'd have to wait much longer. Sure, Logan had a much longer drive. And yes, he did have Miss Amherst to deal with, but Jack had expected him to push it a little bit.

Instead, Logan had messaged him that he would be stopping for the night because Miss Amherst was "tired." Wasn't that what sleeping in the car was for?

It was late evening, and Jack had arrived at the Ohio safe house. If he wouldn't see Logan until tomorrow evening, then he could at least get as much organized as possible in anticipation. It irritated him that Logan was taking his good old time getting here, but what exactly could he say? He trusted that Logan could read a situation right. If he needed to rest with this Amherst girl, then he needed to rest.

That didn't mean that Jack couldn't sit and steam. If it had been his call, they would have pushed on. There was no time to waste, and there was too much valuable intel. Gray Tower was now in possession of Damien Amherst's fucking daughter. She had information that Jack needed to know and now.

He was one of those people who liked to throw himself into his work. He had built up too much at Gray Tower to slack off. The Amherst girl was too valuable, and he knew how badly Bryant wanted the information. Therefore, Jack was going to get it for him. It was that simple.

Jack had been with Bryant from the start of Gray Tower and felt responsible for everything that happened there.

Before he had signed on with Bryant, he had been so completely lost. Alcohol had almost destroyed his life, and it had taken a hell of a lot of work to get it back.

After six years in the U.S. Army Special Forces, the Army had decided that they had had enough of Jack's outside antics and discharged him before he could really do something stupid.

He had been a forced periodic drinker because he refused let his brothers in arms down. His missions never suffered—or so he thought—as he never drank right before or during. It had been his behavior while on leave that had gotten him into trouble.

After a string of ugly events, Jack had to give up the career that he had worked so hard to attain. He had completely and utterly blown it. Being in the Special Forces was an opportunity that was not given to just anyone, and he had squandered that chance.

Jack had shamed and dishonored himself.

Yet, even when the stakes were so high, he couldn't stop drinking. He resigned his commission and basically became hammered around the clock for a few months before he finally was able to turn his life around.

It had taken a lot to get sober, and even then, he had lost his career and his family. Bryant had been the one to give Jack the chance that he needed, and working for Gray Tower had given him a new life. Jack owed a lot to Bryant, and he would never squander the opportunity.

Tapping his fingers on the kitchen counter of the safe house, Jack looked back at his checklist. It appeared that everything was in order, except for Miss Amherst of course. The security for the safe house was in place, working in shifts. All of Jack's equipment was set up. At this point, he should probably get some sleep, but he was wired on too many cups of coffee and was generally irritable. It was a common occurrence for Jack because most people pissed him off.

He was working on that, though. Even after five years of sobriety—with its ups and downs—he still had a lot of work to do.

Sighing, he decided that he could at least do another perimeter check before trying to get some sleep. There would be a lot of work to do when Logan finally decided to get his ass here.

CHAPTER 11

Even though Logan could have driven all night if he had to in order to get Keira to the safe house, she was fading fast. He knew that she hadn't had much sleep in the last forty-eight hours. She looked pale and fragile, and there were heavy dark circles under her eyes.

Logan felt it would be best if they stopped for the evening, got a good dinner, and rested. After sending a quick message to Jack of his plans, he focused on getting them off the road and to some place safe to stay for the night.

They were a little outside Minneapolis, and it didn't take him long to find a little motel off the highway that was near some places to eat. Logan didn't feel comfortable sitting down to eat with her but picking up something and taking it back wouldn't be a problem.

He was carrying in a shoulder holster under his black leather coat as well as the built-in concealed car holster that was attached the bottom of his truck's center console. Logan could take care of himself, but the goal was to be as inconspicuous as possible. There was no need to draw attention to themselves. If Damien Amherst found them, it would be a large team that would come after them, and—despite Logan's skill—it would be more than he could handle.

"Our options are limited for food," he told Keira. "I am not leaving you alone, period. So, that leaves us with drive-through. Is that okay?"

"Sure," she said quietly.

She looked tired. Worn-out. Exhausted. And utterly beautiful.

Logan had been doing his best not to notice that, but it was hard-going. His cock had been in a state of half-mast throughout most of the drive. He hated that she affected him like that; he was now charged with getting her to safety. Gray Tower could get some much-needed intel from her.

He couldn't afford to notice her like that anymore. It wasn't professional for one thing, and it wouldn't be fair to her. Because once she was debriefed, Bryant would make sure that she disappeared into obscurity and away from her father. Logan would then go back to doing missions for the company, and that would be the end of it.

Not only that, but Logan was starting to think that he may have gone overboard with her interrogation earlier in the day because he was pissed that someone so sweet and beautiful could be an Amherst operative. Now that he had some time to stew over it, he realized that he should have just contained her and gotten back-up. Hell, he wasn't trained for interrogation. It should have never happened. He had allowed his temper to get the best of him, and he had hurt her in the process.

Keira Amherst was seriously getting in his head, and he needed to cut that shit out immediately.

Breathing out a deep sigh, Logan attempted to shift his focus to the task at hand: food and shelter. His job was to keep her safe and well—nothing more.

They ended up stopping at a burger joint drive-thru, and then headed to the motel's office to pay for a room. He used one of his many fake-IDs that Gray Tower provided. If John Stratton had found out where Logan had been vacationing, then he had to be on Amherst Global's radar too.

Once they got to the room, Logan pulled two large duffel bags from the back seat of his truck and took them in. That was all his Gray Tower gear, which included his laptop, his sat-phone, his M4A1 rife, a twelve-gauge tactical shotgun, ammo, clips, and a few personal items, including a spare set of clothes. Unlocking the door, he checked around the small room and bathroom before allowing Keira to come in.

"What's in those bags?" She asked, sitting the fast-food bags and drinks down on a small table next to an ancient TV. "They look heavy."

"Just some insurance that I get you to the safe-house alive and well," he replied as he began unpacking the shotgun. It would work the best in small spaces.

However, in most combat situations, he preferred the M4 because it was what he had used as a Ranger. It was a military rifle that had some tricky legalities to navigate through to own as a civilian. Being employed at Gray Tower did have some perks, though.

Out of the corner of his eye, he could see Keira's eyebrows raise slightly, but she said nothing. He unpacked the laptop and sent off a few messages to Jack and Brenden about their whereabouts and status, then turned to Keira, who was patiently waiting for him to finish. Apparently, she didn't want to start on her food without him.

"You can go ahead and start without me," he told her, trying to sound casual. "I might be a moment. You must be starving, anyhow"

"I would prefer to wait," she said softly. "I've eaten alone for practically the last two years of my life. I would like some company."

Suddenly, Logan felt like a complete idiot. Keira had been isolated for so long that she needed companionship, even if it was from a practical stranger.

"Ah, damn, Keira. I'm sorry," he said, putting down his gear. "I can pause for a moment and eat with you."

"No, no. You don't have to. I can wait."

Logan ignored her comment and sat down next to her, pulling off his jacket to reveal his shoulder harness and sidearm. She eyed it but said nothing.

They munched in silence for a while on burgers, fries, and soft drinks. It wasn't his usual fare he typically tried to eat as healthy as possible. He prided himself on staying in shape, but when he was on a mission, he ate whatever the hell he needed to push through.

The little table that they were eating on in the motel room wasn't that great, and it wobbled a bit. The place itself was small and run-down. There was the ugliest green wallpaper that he had ever seen, one that contorted into a dizzying sea of paisley green drool. A single queen bed lined the back of the small room. This room was all that the motel had available, so it looked as if he was sleeping on the floor tonight.

Logan studied Keira quietly while she devoured her own food. She was a classic beauty with soft skin and haunting hazel eyes. She always looked so sad, and now he could understand why. Not only had she been a prisoner for years, but her asshole father was planning to marry her off to a stranger.

After spending so much time collecting information on Amherst Global, he had dossiers on all of Damien Amherst's associates. Jason Savage lived up to his name. He had killed before, and apparently was a notorious sadist in the bedroom. Keira would not have lasted long with him.

"Thank you," she said suddenly. "For sitting with me. I know it sounds stupid, but I've craved sitting down with a meal with someone other than my father."

"It's not stupid," he told her. "You've been through a lot. More than most people ever will."

He wanted to tell her that was the main thing that attracted him to her. She wasn't just physically beautiful; she was also intelligent, sweet, strong, and resilient. He didn't know many people who could deal with what Keira had been dealt and still be hanging in there. From what he had heard of her ordeal in the snow, she should have been dead just from exposure alone.

Logan couldn't imagine someone surviving in an unheated vehicle for hours in those conditions, let alone slogging through the snow to his cabin afterward. She was certainly resilient—and damned beautiful.

Stop thinking about her that way, he told himself. *It's not going to end well for either of you. And besides, she's Damien fucking Amherst's daughter.*

It was at the point that he realized that she was still shivering. Unfortunately, she would feel that way for a while if she did have hypothermia, even after her body temperature had normalized.

"Are you okay?" He asked.

She rubbed her arms to warm herself and said, "I should probably put your jacket back on."

"I suggest that you take another warm shower. Unfortunately, it's going to be a while before you feel normal again."

"Okay," she said, getting up and grabbing her bag.

When the bathroom door closed, and he heard shower start, Logan tried very hard not to imagine her standing naked under the hot spray.

* * *

Keira stood under the shower and allowed the hot water to beat over her until her skin turned pink. She desperately wanted to feel completely warm again, but it just wasn't happening. The shower did make her feel a bit better, but it just wasn't quite enough.

The bathroom was tiny and was in poor shape—just like the rest of the motel room. She tried to ignore the grungy, old tile and concentrate on how good the water felt against her skin.

There was a small part of her that really wished that Logan would join her. She had to admit that the man was amazingly hot. It wasn't only that, though. He also seemed to be thoughtful and considerate. Ever since finding out who she was, he had bent over backward trying to make sure that she was safe and well.

Keira also understood that he was dangerous, and she was glad that they were on the same side. Perhaps that was what made her so attracted to him? Or, perhaps it was because she had been alone for so long?

One thing was for certain: she was in the middle of a lot of trouble. She wondered if it was the adrenaline that was making her so crazy. It felt like every time she looked at him, he made her aroused. She had tried to ignore him, but that was impossible. It was just the two of them, and he was charged with her safety. Not only that, but he was a large man and had such a commanding presence. Keira considered herself tall, and he dwarfed her by at least six inches.

She debated on whether she should just go ahead and settle the ache between her thighs by herself. It seemed silly and juvenile, but Keira had been alone for so long— that was what she had been used to. Besides, Logan would probably get curious if she took a suspiciously long shower, so she decided to get out instead.

When she stepped outside of the shower, she wrapped a towel around her body and began her preparations for bed, thankful that she had at least some of her toiletries to work with.

It was then that she felt something on her shoulder. She brushed the itch and felt something fall down her bare arm and to the floor. When she looked down, she screamed.

A huge cockroach had fallen from the ceiling, onto her shoulder, and now it was on the floor. After the shock wore off, she felt like an idiot.

It's just a bug, she scolded herself and began to feel like an idiot.

A few moments later, the door flew open and Logan burst into the bathroom, his handgun out of its holster, pointed to the floor but ready.

"What's wrong?" He demanded, his eyes darting around the tiny room. "Are you okay?"

Keira just stood there for a moment, baffled by what had just happened. Then she realized how the situation must have looked from his perspective. Logan had heard her screamed and assumed the worst.

Suddenly embarrassed, she felt herself turning red.

"There was a roach," she stammered, feeling her face grow hot.

He looked down at the bug that was scurrying across the floor, looked back up at her, and laughed. It was the first time that she had really heard him laugh, and it was deep and throaty and sexy as hell. If she hadn't felt like a complete moron, she would have enjoyed it.

Logan placed his gun back in his shoulder holster, walked over to the roach, and stepped on it with his boot.

"There," he said. "Problem solved. The next time you run into a bug, just come and get me. No screaming next time, okay?"

"I..." She was floundering. "I'm sorry! I didn't mean to..."

"Don't worry about it. That thing was pretty huge."

Then, he winked at her, a wry smile spreading to his lips.

If Keira hadn't been so embarrassed to begin with, she probably would have laughed. She had just acted like a big baby in front of a total badass.

Then his wry smile seemed to disappear, and he just stared at her for a moment, his eyes darkening. She looked down at herself and realized that she was in nothing but a towel. Heart pounding, she froze, not knowing what to do. It was true that Logan had seen her naked when he ended up fishing her out of the snow, yet she felt more exposed than ever.

His gaze raked across her body, male appreciation showing in his face. She stiffened, emotions swirling up through her chest. Keira wondered if he had been thinking of her in the same way, or if Logan was just acting like any other red-blooded male.

Long, agonizing moments passed, and then he finally said, "Why don't you get dressed, and I'll clean up that little critter for you?"

Keira felt herself nodding as he quickly left the room, shutting the door behind him. She cursed at herself the whole time she got dressed. There was no change of clothes for her, but she did have a spare set of clean underwear that she had thankfully packed.

She continued cursing at herself when she left the bathroom and tried her hardest to avoid eye contact with Logan. That task was hard to manage as the little motel room was already tiny. Maybe she could just pretend like the whole bathroom thing hadn't happened?

Keira decided to just sit on the bed, folding her hands in her lap and waiting for him to tell her what to do. It was depressing to think that for the last two years of her life, all decisions had been made for her. She had no control over anything, including what she had to eat, when she got to leave her room, and even what she wore. Now that she wasn't under her father's thumb, her life felt more out of control than ever.

"It's getting late, and we're going to have an early morning tomorrow," Logan told her. "I'm going to get ready for bed. Will you be okay out here by yourself for a moment?"

She nodded and clasped her hands tighter in her lap.

Logan walked over to her and gently sat down a large t-shirt and a pair of sweatpants.

"I brought some spare clothes, figuring you at least would want something a little bit more comfortable to sleep in."

Keira stared at the bundle and tried to smile. Her hand traced over the soft fabric of the well-worn cotton garments. They looked and felt like luxury.

"We can run your clothes through the wash at the safe house, but until then, I'm sure you'd like something different to wear."

"I don't know," she said quietly. "I think I might burn these clothes when I get the chance. They've already made too many bad memories."

She shuddered at the thought of being caught out in the storm.

"But you're away from your father," he reminded her. "And you're here. You're alive and well. That's something."

One of his hands reached out and gently brushed down her sweater toward her hand. When his fingers touched the bare skin at the base of her thumb, she had to keep herself from flinching as his stroke burned her skin. His fingers slowly clasped around hers, and he stood there for a moment, just holding her hand.

Heartbeats passed.

Logan eventually squeezed reassuringly and released his grip, walking over toward the bathroom and slipping inside. It was not long after that the sound of the shower came on.

Keira let out a long hiss through her teeth as she stared at the door he had disappeared into. The door wasn't shut completely; he had left it cracked, presumably to keep an ear out for her.

She forced herself to get up and get changed into the sweats he had provided before he was out of the bathroom. One embarrassing incident was quite enough for one day.

Keira quickly pulled off her sweater and jeans and pulled on Logan's spare clothes. She sniffed absentmindedly and noticed that they still smelled of whatever fabric softener he used. It was a small little pleasure as she breathed in the fresh, clean fragrance.

She spent a moment combing her damp hair with her fingers, and then she lay back on the bed and sighed, feeling clean and almost warm. Stretching out on the stiff, queen-sized bed, she could have probably fallen asleep right there. However, she began to wonder exactly where Logan was going to sleep. There was the only bed, and it wasn't that large to begin with. The room was small and did not even have a couch like Logan's cabin did.

What exactly were the sleeping arrangements supposed to be?

A wave of panic came over her. Then, the logical side of her interrupted. Logan was a professional. This is what he did for a living. He knew what to do. She was the one freaking out about everything.

Regardless, she sat anxiously on the bed until he reappeared from the bathroom.

And—of course—he was without a shirt. Just his jeans. He was running a towel through damp hair, looking like a chiseled statue. Logan really had to be the most beautiful man that she had ever seen.

A longing welled up inside of her, and she reminded herself that she only really felt this way because she had been locked away for so long. Chalk it up to adrenaline and loneliness and this is what you got.

Soft, gray eyes stared back at her, a look of concern crossing Logan's face.

"You can take the bed," he told her. "I'll grab some blankets and a pillow and go on the floor."

It didn't seem right. This man had saved her life. He was taking her out of danger from her father, and he was going to sleep on the floor of a disgusting hotel?

"No," she said firmly. "I wouldn't feel right to make you sleep on the floor after everything you've done for me. It wouldn't be a problem if we both slept on the bed."

Keira was in deep, deep trouble. It wasn't that she was necessarily worried that he would do anything. She was more concerned about doing something stupid herself.

Oh, like a night of wild, passionate love with Logan would be stupid, she told herself.

It would be in the morning when she turned back into a mission for him. That thought seemed to deflate her ego a bit.

Logan stared at her for a moment as if he weren't quite sure what to say.

Then he finally said, "I'll be fine. I've slept on worse."

"No," she said flatly. "I would feel badly."

She pressed down on the bed and winced.

"Although I'm not sure if this mattress is much better than the floor."

He continued to stare at her in silence for a few more moments and then finally said, "Okay, but only because you're insisting—that and you might need roach protection during the night."

She smiled and tried to stifle a laugh that turned into a yawn, realizing that she was utterly exhausted.

Keira slid over to one side of the bed and pulled herself under the covers. The sheets weren't exactly top quality, but at least they appeared to be clean. She watched as Logan went around the room, checking the lock on the door, turning off lights, and bringing his handgun to the nightstand on his side.

When he clicked off the last light and plunged the room into darkness, Keira's heart seemed to skip a beat when he slid onto his side of the bed. The space felt small with his size, and she was already brushing up against him. Moving over closer to her edge, she tried to give him some room.

She reminded herself that she was just indeed a job to him, and that was just fine with her. He would keep her safe; that's what was important right now. She could deal with the shambles that was her life later. If she was away from her father, then she would be okay. Keira might be on an emotional rollercoaster right now, but she was at least safe.

Despite being so close to Logan, it did not take long for her to succumb to the welcoming embrace of unconsciousness.

CHAPTER 12

L ogan couldn't sleep. He was putting the blame squarely on the soft body sleeping next to him. There was an ongoing fantasy running through his head about him rolling on top of her and taking her right then and there. He should have told her no and slept on the damned floor, but she was apparently very persuasive. Or, he secretly had wanted to be right next to her. Either way, he was fucked, plain and simple.

It was taking all his control not to make a move. He was painfully hard, his cock straining against his jeans uncomfortably, wanting to be freed.

That couldn't happen.

Keira was in a very vulnerable spot in her life. He had been the first new person that she had seen in years. Even though he had noted the same longing desire in her eyes, it would be shitty of him to try anything. He would be taking advantage of her if anything happened.

Still, though, it had been hard not to notice her all evening. And when he had seen her in that towel, he had almost lost it. For that moment, he hadn't cared that he was on a mission. He hadn't cared that she was Damien Amherst's daughter. Logan had just wanted Keira, the strong, bright, beautiful woman.

Logan shut his eyes and gritted his teeth. He needed to get his mind right and his dick in check, or his mission could go south and fast.

Keira stirred next to him, and he tried to block her movement from his mind as he drifted into a light sleep.

It could have been minutes or hours later that Logan felt more stirring. He had felt her toss and turn quite a bit, though he didn't mind. However, he soon heard a strangled cry beside him.

Sitting up suddenly, Logan put a hand to Keira's shoulder as he heard another cry slip from her mouth.

"No," was the soft words that escaped her lips.

He checked and saw that her eyes were still closed. She must be dreaming.

When another cry escaped her lips, he knew that it wasn't a dream; it was a damned nightmare, and Logan unfortunately had an idea of what it was about.

Keira started to toss and turn a little more now, and Logan tried to gently wake her up by nudging her shoulders, at first gently and then a little harder. More whimpers came from her, but she wasn't waking up.

"No!" She shouted, her eyes still closed.

Her arms began to flail around in the sheets.

Damn it, he thought. *That's all I need is more screaming and shouting from her tonight.*

"Keira, stop," he commanded. "You're having a nightmare. It's me, Logan. Stop."

Getting frustrated, he pinned her with his own body to keep her from hurting him or her own self—she had begun scratching at him a few moments earlier.

Then in the darkness, he could see her eyes open. She looked dazed and disoriented, and she let out another yelp.

Okay, enough of this shit, Logan thought. *She's going to wake up the whole damned street.*

He could have clamped down his hand again, like he had on a few other occasions. Instead, he found his head lowering and his mouth came down on hers.

As soon as his lips found hers, her whole body seemed to still. Logan kissed her hard, brushing his mouth over soft, supple lips. He was lost in her scent, lost in her taste. Hours of fantasizing about her had nothing on the real thing.

Lust shot up through his cock as it greedily pushed at the zipper of his jeans. He groaned as he realized that he needed to stop. But...

Instead of slapping him away or crying out, her lips parted slightly, and he eagerly began to explore her mouth with his tongue, thrusting into her mouth in a slow, rhythmic movement. She tasted sweet, like honey.

As he continued to explore her mouth, he found that one of her hands had moved free from his body and was now grabbing at the nape of his neck, trying desperately to pull him closer into the kiss.

Oh, hell yes, he thought as he kissed her harder until he could feel blood thundering in his ears.

Logan needed more, so much more.

He broke the kiss, only to begin trailing kisses down her neck. Keira cried out at the touch, and his name escaped her lips. One of his thighs parted her legs, and her hips bucked into him, putting firm pressure on her clit. She was so damned responsive to him, but he needed more.

His hands began to work over her body as he traced a trail along the other side of her neck, a low moan escaping her mouth. Logan's hands went down her bare arms and found the edge of her overly large t-shirt. He found the soft skin of her belly, and for a moment, traced lazy circles at the edge of the waistband of her sweatpants before trailing up her torso to her breasts.

Keira had taken off her bra, and her bare breasts fit perfectly into his hands. His mouth found hers again as he began to mold the firm mounds in his hands. He played with the taut peeks of her nipples between his fingers as his mouth devoured hers.

Still, it wasn't enough, and he pulled his body up slightly in order to begin tugging her shirt off.

* * *

Keira felt lost as Logan pulled her shirt over her head and she lay topless before him. She had woken up from a terrible nightmare to Logan kissing her ferociously. Her fears from the nightmare had immediately subsided and had been replaced by the sudden need to be comforted and to forget, even if it was for just a little while. She had been thinking about exactly this all evening, and now that it was happening, she was going to let this play all the way out.

There had been times in her past captivity that she had fanaticized about a handsome man rescuing her from her father and then making fierce love to her. Though it hadn't quite happened exactly as she had dreamed, it was indeed going to happen.

Two years of loneliness and despair seemed to melt away as Logan brought his mouth back down to her neck and began kissing down to her chest. He hadn't shaved once since she had met him, and his facial hair was starting to get long, providing a coarse, erotic shock to her skin as he seared a path down her body.

His mouth stopped at her breasts. A hand played with her right breast as he sucked her left nipple into his mouth. She arched into the aching friction as he sucked and swirled his tongue around her sensitive flesh.

Before she thought that she couldn't take anymore, Logan switched to her other nipple, lavishing attention on that peak as well. A moan escaped her lips as he sucked and then lightly nipped the tip erotically with his teeth.

His head pulled back up to her own, and kissed her deeply again, pressing the full length of his body down on her own. Without her t-shirt on, she could now feel his bare chest rubbing erotically against her own. The slight dusting of hair on his chest moved deliciously across her aching breasts. The hard muscles of his abs seemed in contrast to her soft belly.

"You taste so fucking good," he breathed between kisses.

Logan shifted his weight, and she felt the bulge of his erection against her belly through the tough fabric of his jeans. Her womb clenched and ached as she imagined that part of him inside of her, moving in the same rhythm as the thrust of his tongue inside her mouth. Her clit throbbed, and she tried to grind against his leg to relieve the ache.

She also attempted to unzip his pants, but he caught both of her arms in one hand and pulled them up over her head, affectively trapping her as he continued kissing her.

A thrill shook down her spine, followed by a sudden feeling of dread.

Trapped. She felt trapped.

Her thoughts went back to the nightmare: She had been back in her room at Amherst Manor, both her father and Jason there. Her father had stood back and watched as Jason had climbed into her bed and began to do awful things to her.

She remembered the panic and terror she had felt during the dream, and it had shaken her to the core.

Logan suddenly stopped, pulling his head up to study her, his face full of concern. His hand released her arms and trailed down to her face. He wiped a tear that—unbeknownst to her—had started to fall down her face.

"What the hell am I doing?" He asked, though she was pretty sure it was rhetorical. "I'm supposed to be protecting you, not getting into your pants."

It was the voice of reason.

He sat up, suddenly leaving her feel more vulnerable than ever. Keira pulled her arms across her chest in a poor attempt to cover up. She found her hands shaking and more tears seemed to fall. A new wave of embarrassment came over her. She knew why he had stopped. Deep down, she was grateful that he had stopped. But she still felt so exposed.

Seeming to understand, Logan silently helped the t-shirt back over her head and then surprisingly pulled her up into his arms. His muscular arms enveloped her, and all she wanted to do was snuggle down and stay there forever.

"I'm so sorry, Keira," he told her, his voice husky. "You are such a beautiful woman, but you've been through hell. I should have been able to control myself—not try and take advantage of the situation. This won't happen again. I can't protect you if I'm too distracted fucking you."

A pit settled in her stomach. She hadn't quite expected the harsh language. What they had been doing hadn't felt like the precursor to "fucking."

"Besides," he continued. "You deserve so much more than what I can give you. Once your safe, we'll part ways and most likely never see each other again. Don't ever forget that."

Keira hadn't thought about that. She hadn't been thinking at all. In all the fear and adrenaline of hiding from her father, it had never crossed her mind that her and Logan would eventually go their separate ways. Why she had attached to him so quickly, she had no clue. It had barely been over twenty-four hours since she had met him, and she was clinging to him like he was a life preserver and she was out in a storm at sea.

"Tomorrow, things between us stay professional. No more of this. Got it?"

She nodded slowly and tried to not allow the disappointment from showing in her face. That secret fantasy of some whirlwind romance with her rescuer vanished in a puff of smoke.

"Tonight, though," he continued, "I'm going to hold you just like this. Maybe I can scare away some of those demons haunting you."

Logan leaned her back down into bed, keeping his arms around her. The strong, corded muscles of his arms made her feel so safe and secure. His clean, male sent was comforting. Keira had been surprised by his last comment but didn't protest. She *did* feel much safer snuggled up next to him.

After a few moments of silence, Logan asked quietly, "You were dreaming about your father, weren't you?"

"And Jason," she added, trying not to cry again. "He was hurting me, and my father was just watching, allowing it to happen."

"Keira," Logan breathed. "Those bastards will never touch you. Do you understand? They will never even come close to you."

Blinking back tears, she whispered, "Thank you."

Keira didn't remember when she felt back asleep, but she thankfully did not dream.

* * *

"Pew, pew, pew, motherfucker!"

Brenden Scott aimed his mouse and tapped at his keyboard frantically.

He wasn't quite sure what time it was, but he didn't care. Brenden was in the game of his life right now, and he wasn't planning on stopping anytime soon. Smiling, he virtually turned a corner where a lot of players jammed up and found two more people to blast. Those Gray Tower guys might be badasses in real life, but in this game, Brenden was hot shit.

Reloading, he saw movement from the far screen of his three, ginormous monitor set-up. He turned sharply, but not before he got blasted from a player on the opposite team who was crouched in a corner, hiding. Luckily, it was not quite enough to kill him.

"Fucking camper! Bitch noob! I own your ass!" Brenden yelled to his monitors as he hammered the player with a spray of bullets.

Another kill! That was game, he realized, and he had gotten the final kill!

"Yeah! That's what I'm talking about!"

His kill streak was preserved, and he was once again back on top of the leaderboard. Some little bitch had knocked him down to second in the nation last week when work had been crazy. It had taken him the past two nights to get back to his rightful spot.

Brenden was camped out in his office at Gray Tower Headquarters, which was where he spent most of his waking hours. There really wasn't much of a reason to leave, except for grub, bathroom breaks, and some shut-eye. His system was here, and Bryant and had sprung for gigabit Internet connection, something that he could not get at his old apartment.

So, he had moved into one of the available Level 3 apartments. It was all about priorities.

His eyes flicked down at the time and realized that it was almost five in the morning. He probably should get some sleep. Besides, the game lobbies were starting to thin out a bit. There wouldn't be much good competition coming back online until the evening.

Glancing back at his screens, he noticed an in-game message. He smiled as he opened it and recognized the sender. It was Selene, an accomplished hacker and quite a decent gamer. She knew a shit-ton that went on in and was well-connected.

And she wanted to chat.

Brenden smiled.

He hadn't talked with her for a while, and he had missed the company. Despite never having seen her (she only showed an avatar), he was pretty sure that he was in love. It was only a matter of time before he convinced her that she felt the same way.

Connecting through a private group chat in the game with just the two of them, Brenden leaned back in his desk chair and grinned ear to ear.

CHAPTER 13

Keira woke up to an empty bed and the sound of the shower running in the bathroom. Light was streaming in from the thread-bare curtains of the motel room. She immediately missed the warmth and strength of Logan's body next to hers, his arms wrapped protectively around her. But it was morning now, and she knew that everything had changed. Logan had told her that last night.

She sighed and threw the sheets off her, assuming it would be a good idea to be dressed before Logan got out of the bathroom. Keira was pretty much done with embarrassing situations for the rest of her life.

When Logan appeared from the bathroom doorway, he was showered, shaved, and ready to go in his typical jeans, sweater, and shoulder-holster combination.

He stared at her intently, and for a moment, she wondered if he would comment on the previous night.

"How are you feeling?" He asked instead, his tone brisk and business-like.

It was as if last night had never happened. Keira was a bit relieved. She was good at pretending too; she had done it all of her life with her father, feigning happiness when she really felt like her life was out of control.

"Okay," she told him, though she wasn't sure.

"We have another long drive ahead, so we'll need to get going as soon as possible."

Twenty minutes later, they were packed up and on the open road in Logan's truck. She felt marginally better just being on the highway again and being able to look out at the world passing by. Even though she had been traveling extensively over the past few days, it was so much better than being shut up in a little room.

Keira snuggled down into the leather seat next to Logan's in the sweats he had loaned her. They were much cleaner than her other clothes and more comfortable to travel in.

Not that she was truly relaxed. She was anxious and tense, partly from fear of her father but partly from the words left unspoken during the previous night. Instead of worrying, she tried to focus on the scenery, which felt exciting and new since she hadn't seen much outside of her bedroom in years.

The landscape seemed to blur by as they drove. Logan didn't say much the whole time, though Keira wished that she could just sit and talk with him. She had realized that they almost had sex the night before, and she barely knew a thing about him. All she really knew was that John trusted him and that he worked for a mercenary company called Gray Tower.

She felt silly for how she felt about him. He was incredibly handsome, had an amazing body, was intelligent and strong, and incredibly sweet. He was also dangerous and passionate—and, apparently, off limits. The logical part of her thought that was for the best. The emotional part of her was something different entirely.

She knew almost nothing about him, yet she was attracted to him. He seemed to want her as badly as she did him, yet he had pushed her away. It was frustrating to say the least, but what could she do?

Of course, why should she try and even think about guys and relationships and all of that? Her main goal was getting the heck away from her father. She couldn't afford any distractions, regardless of how sexy they happened to be.

Keira's thoughts began to stray for a while. For the most part, she was just happy to be out of her father's house, so she sat back and tried to enjoy the drive as much as she could.

After many hours and a few stops for gas, they pulled off the highway and onto a road in the suburbs. Middle class homes were scattered sporadically along the road. Mostly, it was a lot of tall trees with a dusting of snow over the top of them. Keira had paid close attention to where they had been driving, and they were now in northeastern Ohio, a part of the country that she had never visited before now.

More time passed as they traveled out of the suburbs along a long, two-lane road. The scenery alternated between open farmland and woods with houses interspersed throughout the area.

Logan finally turned into a gravel driveway that was surrounded by woods. They drove up it for a moment before finally coming to a ranch-style house with rustic wood siding that sat above a pond. It was evening, and it was getting dark out, but the house just seemed so perfect, like an oasis retreat. The outside house lights were on and so were many of the inside lights as well. The home looked like an inviting little sanctuary for her.

Keira did a double take, however, when she saw at least three men who seemingly appeared out of nowhere, armed to the teeth. One walked up to the truck, and she tensed as he neared.

"We're okay," Logan spoke up, as if he knew how tense she was at the situation. "Those are my colleagues. Stay here."

She felt uneasy, but she trusted him. It was odd considering that it was only yesterday that she had been terrified of him.

Without another word, Logan got out of the truck, walked up to the man who had approached him, and started talking. Keira watched diligently from the passenger seat, wishing she could hear what they were saying.

After a few moments, Logan walked back toward the car, and Keira could feel her body tense in anticipation, a pit forming in her stomach.

However, when Logan opened her door and said, "We're good. Let's get inside," a little bit of the wave of anxiety seemed to pass.

Keira didn't even realize that she was shaking until she jumped down from the truck and walked out into the cold winter air. Logan steadied her with strong arms as she wavered for a moment. He guided her to the front doorway and into the warmth of the house. One of Logan's colleagues followed them inside.

They stepped into a foyer that was tastefully but sparsely decorated. There was a living room to the left that looked as if it was rarely used. The man that Logan had met with had followed them inside and turned toward Keira, eyeing her up and down.

The man was tall, though he looked to be not quite as tall as Logan. He was wearing a black leather jacket and a black shirt underneath that stretched nicely across a well-toned chest. Black pants matched the ensemble as well as a pair of combat boots. Keira saw at least one handgun in a holster attached to the man's belt, although she suspected there might be more.

Logan's colleague was also quite handsome in a rugged sense. He could be a male model—for a hunting and fishing magazine at least. His short, medium brown hair was styled perfectly, but the outfit he had on said badass. Deep blue eyes pierced at her in a disapproving manner.

"It took you long enough," the man said, not taking his eyes off Keira. "I wanted to get this done as soon as possible, and you took your good old time getting here."

Keira looked anxiously at Logan, fear and apprehension starting to take hold again. This man didn't seem to be friendly.

Logan's eyes narrowed as he said sternly, "It's not that easy, Hunter. I had to consider Miss Amherst's well-being. She's been through a hell of a lot, and she has a lot more to go through before it's all said and done."

"Hunter" crossed his arms and frowned. His dark blue eyes darted back and forth between Keira and Logan.

"I get that, but at this point, she's an asset to the company," Hunter said sternly. "We need to get as much intel from her as possible."

"We can get what we need without stressing her out," Logan replied quickly, settling a hand on her shoulder.

Keira tensed and started to get angry. She suddenly didn't like the fact that two people who were practically strangers to her were arguing about her as if she wasn't even in the room. Many of her father's associates and employees did the same thing, and it annoyed her to no end. Over the last two years while she had been a captive, it had been extremely disheartening. She wasn't going to allow this to happen to her again. As the two men went back and forth for a while longer, she decided that she had had enough.

"So, hey," she said awkwardly, though her MBA training and internship experience began to kick in. "I would like a say in all of this. You both are discussing that I'm an asset to your company, but I haven't agreed to anything yet."

The two alpha males stopped their argument and looked at her. Keira's throat caught for a moment as she somewhat expected Hunter to blow up on her.

Instead, Hunter narrowed his eyes and then gave a slight, wry smile, saying, "Oh, Slade. I like this one. She's got some spunk, doesn't she?"

Then he winked at her. *Winked* at her! What the hell?

"I'm sorry, Keira," Logan said, trying to mask a chuckle. "Let's get you fed, and *the three of us* can discuss what your options are afterwards."

Logan looked over toward Hunter, nodding in his direction.

"This is Jack Hunter, by the way. As you can see, his personality is a bit lacking, but since he's technically my boss, I have to put up with his shit."

"Fuck you, Slade," Jack replied tersely.

She watched as Jack turned away and started walking down the hallway without another word.

Keira cringed a little bit. She understood that it was banter between the men, but she didn't want Logan to get into any kind of trouble.

"I didn't mean to..." She began to say, but Logan cut her off.

"We're just bull-shitting around. Don't worry about Jack. He's harmless. He's also very good at his job, and he *will* make sure that you are safe."

"I understand," Keira said as she was pulled ahead toward the back of the house.

The home turned into a more open-style area with a kitchen, dining room, family room combination. It was just as sparsely decorated like the other areas of the house, but it looked comfortable enough.

Jack had sat himself down at the table in the middle of the kitchen and living space, a laptop next to him. Keira eyed several video cameras on tri-pods that were set up in the front of a set of cream-colored couches.

A moment of fear ran through her. She knew what they would use those for: interrogating her.

No, she shouldn't think of it like that. Keira's father was a high-profile suspect in a number of crimes. She may know something of importance. It would only be wise to question her to the fullest extent, even though she wasn't sure what they wanted from her.

She watched as Logan proceeded to dig up some dinner for her. It wasn't much: just some sandwiches. She wasn't really that hungry anyhow. When she was presented with the food, she picked at it, knowing that she should eat, though she couldn't stomach much.

Keira had been trusting Logan all along that he would keep her safe but meeting Jack and realizing that she was still in a lot of trouble worried her deeply. The whole time that she had been eating, Logan had barely said a word to her. Meanwhile, Jack was either busy on his laptop, on his cell phone, or talking with Logan. When she was finished with her meal, she looked at Logan for guidance.

"Let me lay out what Gray Tower would like to do for you," he told her.

He suddenly didn't seem like the same person that she had shared a bed with that very same morning, the same person who had kissed her senseless the other night. Logan was now completely down to business.

"Jack and I would like to take turns interviewing you about Amherst Global, your father, and anything else that could be relevant. If this is okay with you, we'd like to get started immediately."

Keira nodded, though she wondered what help she could be when she had been locked away for the past two years. She had little knowledge of her father's organization, and what she had found out had gotten her locked up.

"Afterwards," Logan continued still in all-business mode, "We will move you out of country to a safe location indefinitely."

"Oh," Keira said.

She knew deep down that she wasn't going to be able to stay with Logan forever, and she liked the idea of getting the hell away from her father. However, there was a part of her that wished she could stay where she felt safe. To her, Logan was safe.

"It's nothing to stress over," Logan reassured her, misinterpreting why she sounded down. "We'll just ask you some questions. Answer them to the best of your abilities. I will warn you, though, that this will take some time. Perhaps a few days. Jack is thorough as hell."

Her mood changed a bit. At least she knew what her future would be for the next few days. Even knowing that she would be sitting around this home, talking about her life for hours on end, didn't bother her. Anything that wasn't her being back at Amherst Manor was good enough for her.

Jack looked up from his laptop and said in an annoyed tone of voice, "I've been ready, so whenever you want to get started would be just great."

Keira sighed.

Jack seemed a bit abrasive to her, but she desperately wanted to get this all over with.

"Okay, I'm ready," she told them.

* * *

Logan sat in the safe house's family room watching Jack grilling Keira in typical Jack Hunter fashion. In the past two hours, Jack had already finished going through her early childhood and was moving on to the teen years. Anything to glean any information about Damien Amherst. Jack was intense when it came to his work, and he took his job seriously. However, Logan wished for Keira's sake that Jack would lighten up a bit. She had been through hell, and she still had a long way to go before she would be truly safe.

He watched her closely as Jack asked her questions. She was beginning to look at bit overwhelmed, and she was definitely tired.

Keira had just finished a question about her friends in high school when Jack suddenly cut in and stated, "At some point, we're going to need to do a detailed layout of Amherst Manor as well."

Logan could see it in Keira's eyes that she was overwhelmed and exhausted. It was time to end this for today.

"I think that's enough for tonight, Hunter," Logan cut in firmly. "It's getting late. We can start back up tomorrow. She's not going anywhere."

Jack glanced up from his laptop, his eyes narrowing. The man was a workaholic, and Logan knew that if it were up to Jack, they'd be grilling Keira all night.

"Fine," Jack said brusquely. "We'll continue tomorrow morning."

Logan glanced at Keira and noticed a definite look of relief in her eyes.

"I'll take her downstairs, and get her settled in," Logan said.

He wasn't asking either. As far as Logan was concerned, he would be the one directly responsible for her safety.

The safe house had a finished basement with an extra bedroom and bathroom. There were two escape windows, and from the perspective of trying to keep someone safe and hidden, it was ideal. There was also a den downstairs next to the bedroom with a built-in set of bunkbeds. Upstairs, there were three bedrooms for support staff or guards.

Currently, there were four guards on assignment at the house, each taking twelve hours shifts, two at a time. Logan would have liked to have more people, but that was all that Gray Tower could spare. They were in the middle of a reorganization that included the new headquarters and hiring of more staff.

"I can take the downstairs if you'd like to get some rest," Jack offered.

"No," Logan said sharply.

A strong feeling of possessiveness came over him. There was no way in hell that he was going to let Keira out of his sight. Logan knew that Jack would certainly protect her from her father. However, Jack was known for working hard and playing hard as well, especially with women. As attractive as Keira was, it wouldn't take long for Jack to make a move. The asshole act was just a facade. As soon as business was over, Jack would pounce.

Logan had seen Jack eying Keira and assumed that Jack found her attractive. What red-blooded male wouldn't?

You pushed her away, yet you can't stand the thought of her with another man, can you?

Yeah, that was true enough. Even though Logan knew that Keira wasn't his, he still couldn't stand the thought of Jack with her. Logan and Jack were best friends, but that didn't mean Logan couldn't be possessive over a woman.

"No," Logan said firmly. "I've got it."

Jack raised an eyebrow, then smiled slightly.

Eh, shit, Logan thought.

Jack knew. He and Logan had been friends for too long not to know that Logan had feelings for her. Logan supposed that the two men would have to have a talk at some point as Jack ran a tight ship.

"Fine," Jack told him, the slight smirk still on his face. "I'll take the master bedroom up here then. Get some rest because we're going to have a hell of a long day tomorrow."

Logan nodded, relieved that Jack hadn't pushed the issue in front of Keira. He did not need to get into that right now.

"Grab your bag and follow me," Logan said as he turned toward Keira.

She looked relieved and incredibly exhausted. He hoped that she would be able to get some rest tonight. She'd have another long day in the morning.

Logan and Keira made their way out of the family room and down a set of steps that led into a den with a TV, several couches, and two bunk beds that were built into the wall. Logan pointed to a door on the right.

"Your bedroom is in here," he said, trying to sound nonchalant. "There's a full bathroom attached to it as well. It's a bit nicer than that motel's bathroom. I'll be out here if you need anything."

Keira stared at him for a moment, still silent. Her hazel eyes looked greener than brown in the light. She looked so damned vulnerable and beautiful, but he reminded himself to remain professional. Things between them had already gone far enough last night.

"Thank you," she said quietly. "Thank you so much. I feel safe for once."

Anger at Damien Amherst bubbled up in Logan's chest. What kind of father would do this much harm to his daughter? Logan had seen first-hand what could happen when parents became estranged with their offspring, but what Keira's father had done to her was beyond cruel. It was plain evil.

Logan turned the door to the bedroom without looking at her and said softly, "I'm glad you feel safe."

What the hell else was he supposed to say? He couldn't make her problems go away. The only thing he had been able to do was complicate matters.

They stepped into the room with Logan hitting the light. There were no windows and only another door on the other side of the room where the bathroom was. The bedroom was done sparsely, like the rest of the house, with just a basic color scheme of beige on brown. There was also a plain dresser with spare clothing that she could use.

It wasn't exactly five-star accommodations, but it was comfortable.

Keira seemed to survey the area and then gave out an audible, "Oh."

"I know it's not the fanciest place in the world, but it will be safe for you," he told her. "There's a bathroom on the other side, and I was told that there were fresh clothes in the drawers. You might have to dig for the right size."

It was standard for Gray Tower in a safe house like this.

"I can get the clothes you brought washed as well."

There was a washer and dryer in a small unfinished part of the basement that Logan could use. He'd have to do the same for himself, so his clothes didn't get a little ripe.

"Oh, okay. Thank you," she said quietly.

Something was off with her, and Logan wasn't sure he wanted to pry.

He did anyhow.

"Are you okay?"

"Yeah, I'm fine," she said almost immediately.

Logan knew immediately that this was bullshit. No one ever said, "Fine," without having extra issues.

"Seriously, what's wrong?" He asked again.

"I just was hoping that there might be a window. Even just a small one. This room feels so claustrophobic."

Logan's chest tightened. He knew why she didn't want to spend any time in a small, windowless room, alone. She had been locked up by herself for too long.

Then Logan said something he knew that he would probably regret later.

"You're welcome to hang out in the other room with me. There are two, small windows and a television. That's the best I can do."

Her face brightened considerably, and Logan's chest tightened a bit more.

"Okay," she told him, a smile spreading across her face.

They spent the rest of that evening binge-watching one of those crime scene shows, Keira cuddled up on the couch under some blankets while Logan took some time to sort through his inventory. When he ran out of things to make him look like he was busy, he finally sat down next to Keira. It was such a domestic scene, one that made Logan uncomfortable.

It felt too damned good being next to her, doing normal things. It made him imagine another life where he wasn't running special ops, and she wasn't hiding from her father. He had to stop that line of thinking. It would only be a few more days, and she would be taken away somewhere while he was left to do continue with his job. The situation sucked, but that was the way it needed to be.

As it got later in the night, Keira drifted off to sleep on the couch. Instead of trying to move her back to the bedroom, Logan took up a bunk bed and attempted to get some sleep.

CHAPTER 14

Keira sat bewildered in borrowed clothes, which were a bit too big for her, as Jack Hunter continued to hammer through the most intimate questions that he could possibly ask: names of friends, acquaintances, boyfriends, her GPA in college, addresses she lived at, and anything else that seemed irrelevant to Keira. And he wanted the most detailed answers as well.

She sank further in the comfortable sofa, feeling frustrated.

They had been at this interview—which felt more like an interrogation to her— for the entire day with minimal breaks. Meanwhile, Keira was tired and irritable. Jack wasn't exactly the most pleasant person to be around. His personality was quite abrasive, and although she knew that he was just doing his job, she couldn't help but want this whole ordeal over with as quickly as possible.

The only thing that was keeping her going was the thought that they would have to break at some point for the evening and that would mean that she could go back downstairs with Logan.

She couldn't quite describe how much she had enjoyed herself the previous evening. Her father had kept all access to the outside world away from her and that included television. To sit and watch something with another person had meant so much to her. It meant even more that the person was Logan. She enjoyed his company, even if he didn't show much emotion.

Keira had a feeling that the whole stoic thing was an act. He had certainly been passionate that night in the hotel room.

As much as she wanted to ignore it, what had transpired in that room had rocked her to her core. The man had been amazing, and they had only technically gotten to second base. It was more than that, though.

Logan seemed like he actually *cared* for her. Despite the violent side that he had shown her, once he had been certain of who she was, he had bent over backward for her, making sure that her needs were met. She had even overheard that Jack had been pissed at Logan for stopping overnight at that motel and had wanted him to push through the night, but Logan had held firm about her needing to rest.

Keira knew that she was falling for him, but it was not meant to be. She knew that she would eventually be shipped off somewhere, hidden away from her father. But still...

She had been around a lot of mercenary, gun-for-hire types. Those were the type her father employed. Jack fit the bill, but Logan was completely different in the way he behaved.

"Miss Amherst? Miss Amherst?"

Jack's voice broke through her thoughts. Dang, she had been caught daydreaming.

"Wait, slow down," she told him. "What do you want, again?"

Jack was seated across from her in the family room, typing away on his laptop. A tri-pod with video camera was set up to the side, pointed at her. Wearing a black t-shirt with a shoulder harness and gun, Jack was incredibly intimidating.

He was also incredibly good-looking. Did this Gray Tower place hire anyone who wasn't a gorgeous thirty-something male? But then again, Jack's personality left a lot to be desired.

"I asked about John Stratton's role in your father's organization," Jack repeated firmly, a look of annoyance on his face.

"I already told you all that I know."

"Then go back through it again," Jack said, irritation showing in his voice.

Keira just wanted the questions to stop. Her head was beginning to throb, and she was having a hard time concentrating.

"Jack," came a low, quiet voice from the kitchen. "I think we're done for today."

Logan had been hanging around the area during the interview, silently monitoring what was happening. Keira appreciated that he was there since Jack had been so intense to work with.

She looked back and forth between the two men nervously. There was too much testosterone in the room. It was a silent battle between two alpha males.

"I'm going to remind you that we're on a timeline," Jack replied tersely.

"And she's not going to be able to give us anything if she's exhausted and frustrated."

More glares were exchanged.

Finally, Jack sighed and said, "We can stop."

He didn't look happy about his decision, but Keira was just grateful that the questioning would stop. Her brain felt fried.

"We have a meeting at 2200 hours," Jack continued. "Get her situated downstairs and meet me back up here. I can send a guy down to babysit."

Keira winced at the word, babysit. If given a fighting chance, she could hold up just fine.

"I don't need a babysitter," she cut in, trying to emphasize annoyance.

Jack looked at her intently and then smiled.

"My apologies, Miss Amherst. I spoke poorly. I just want to ensure your safety at all times."

She nodded, satisfied that she had gotten him to apologize. It was a snarky apology, but at least it was one. Keira had started to worry that she was being treated like a thing and not a human being. That was how her father had certainly regarded her.

Logan crossed the room to where Keira was seated, gesturing toward the steps that led down to the basement.

"Come on," he said, eying Jack as if waiting for the man to make another comment.

Thankfully, Jack said nothing.

"Let's get you settled," Logan said softly.

Keira got up from the couch, stretching her arms a bit as she went downstairs. It had been an incredibly long day, and though she hadn't done much physically, she was mentally and emotionally exhausted. She was sick of answering questions that drug up so many unpleasant feelings about her father.

She was also sick of being shut up inside. Keira wanted to be out and about. She certainly didn't want to be shut up in that back-bedroom downstairs, so she plopped herself down on the couch in the den.

Logan attempted a smile, but it seemed strained.

"I would suggest getting some rest in your bedroom, but I doubt you'll listen."

Keira tried to smile as well, but she couldn't quite fake one.

"Are you alright?" Logan asked, his expression softening.

She rubbed her temple, trying to relieve some of the tension that was built up.

"It's just hard drudging up my past, and that's all I've been talking about today."

"I understand," he said, rubbing a hand over his jaw.

He had shaved that morning, but there was a definite five o'clock shadow growing. She wasn't quite sure if she preferred him with or without facial hair. Unfortunately for her, he was way too handsome either way.

Keira noticed that Logan appeared tired as well, and she couldn't blame him. She had just interrupted his vacation, dumping a huge load of problems in his lap.

Laughing nervously, she said, "I suppose my father has done a number on me, hasn't he?"

"He's a bastard," Logan replied simply, gray eyes piercing. "But he doesn't define you."

"That's what I keep telling myself, but it's hard. He's destroyed my life."

Logan sat down next to her on the couch and tenderly took her hand in his. Their close proximity made her heart pound faster. Sometimes, his presence felt overwhelming, and it was even more so when he was next to her.

"That's not true, Keira, and you know it. You're away from him and are about to start a new life. That's something. You're strong, intelligent, and beautiful. And you're damned resilient. Don't ever forget that."

Keira felt her face grow hot from his compliments. She turned her face so that he couldn't see her blush. His fingers gently traced the outline of her knuckles. A sharp thrill ran down her spine and into her lower belly as she thought of how his hands had touched her the night before.

She turned toward him, desperately wanting more from him. But he seemed to sense that the moment had gotten too intense and pulled his hands away. He apparently didn't want to go down that avenue again.

Sighing, Keira tried to pull her attention away from the sexual attraction between them.

"So, if the U.S. government wants to take my father down, and they know the types of dealings he's into, why haven't they just arrested him?"

That certainly would have changed the last two years of her life.

"It's a little more complicated than that. Damien has a lot of power and influence—and a lot of good lawyers. We'd have to catch him with the proverbial smoking gun.

"But it's even more than that. Damien Amherst is just a cog in a larger network of even worse bad guys. By putting him under surveillance and allowing him to continue his operations for a little bit longer, we can hopefully gain important intel."

Anger welled up inside of her.

"You're just allowing my father to do whatever he wants so you can fry some bigger fish later?"

This realization bitterly dawned on her as she realized the suffering that Damien Amherst caused could have been largely prevented. It was hard not to think about what would have happened to her life if her father had been apprehended sooner.

Logan's face darkened as he leaned close to her and practically growled, "Damn it, Keira. You can't think of it like that. We'll take your father down. I swear to you that we will."

Some of her anger seemed to dissipate when she realized how passionate Logan was about getting justice for her father's atrocities.

This guy is trying to help you, and you're acting like an ungrateful brat.

"I'm sorry, I didn't..."

"Don't apologize," he interrupted. "There is nothing you need to apologize for. Just realize that if I had any idea of what was going on with you, I would have put an end to it—immediately."

Keira knew he meant it too. The look on his face told her that Logan was dead serious.

"Okay," she told him quietly.

Logan glanced down at his watch and said, "Look, I need to get back up to Jack for our meeting. I'll send a guy down to guard you while I'm upstairs. Will that be okay?"

She nodded, wishing that he didn't have to go. Logan was the only person who she felt truly safe with, but he had emotional walls up. So did she.

After two long years of isolation, she desperately wanted someone to confide in. She just wasn't sure how to anymore. And if she was really falling for Logan, what would happen when her interviews were done? She'd most likely never see him again.

As she watched him go upstairs, there was a feeling of despair. She might be free from her father, but would she still be alone for the rest of her life, hiding? It was an unpleasant thought, one that she tried to put out of her mind.

* * *

"So, what the fuck is up with you?" Jack asked pointedly when Logan came upstairs for the meeting.

"I don't know what you're talking about," Logan told him, not wanting to get into it with Jack.

Logan was under enough stress as it was. The last thing he needed was Jack on his case.

Jack leaned over the kitchen counter where he was setting up the equipment so that they could do the meeting remotely. He knew that something was up. The two men had been friends for too long.

"I call bullshit. You've been moody as hell, and we've been butting heads since you've arrived. You're going to have to tell me what's going on, or I'll have you pulled from this mission."

Logan could feel his blood pressure rising. There was no way in hell he was going to leave Keira, so he was going to have to give Jack something. Jack may technically be Logan's boss, but they were also friends. How was Logan supposed to tell him that he had fallen big time for Damien Amherst's daughter?

Luckily—or unluckily, depending on how you saw it—Jack was pretty astute.

"You've got a thing for the Amherst girl. Don't you?"

Damn it.

"It's complicated," Logan finally admitted.

Jack shrugged.

"Not complicated to me. Have you slept with her yet?"

Logan bristled.

"None of your damned business!"

"I'll take that as a 'No' then."

Logan clenched and unclenched his fits, wondering whether it was worth it to get fired if he decked his boss. He certainly wouldn't have been the first person at Gray Tower to fantasize about it. Despite their friendship, Logan sometimes had a hard time dealing with Jack's abrasive personality.

"Look, I get it. She's attractive," Jack continued. "Don't think I haven't noticed that. I'm just a bit concerned that you aren't focused on this assignment."

"I'm fine."

Jack raised an eyebrow.

"Just keep your damned head in the game. Either get her out of your system or get her out of your head. Got it?"

"Sure. Whatever."

The two men stared at each other for a moment before Jack smiled slightly and slapped Logan's arm a few times.

"Are we good?"

"Yeah, we're good."

"Great," Jack said, looking at his watch. "Because it's almost time for our meeting."

There were a few more moments where Jack continued his set up. Logan wondered briefly how Keira was doing without him but decided to push her out of his head and concentrate on the task at hand.

At the appropriate time, the screen from the other end showed Miles Bryant himself and in the subsequent screens, his administrative assistant, Alexandria Thorn and, of course, Brenden.

They were sitting at a conference table in a concrete gray room with no decorations. It would be many more months before the new Gray Tower Headquarters would be finished.

"Gentlemen," Bryant greeted them.

He was in his early fifties, average height with a handsome face and dark brown hair. Bryant commanded attention wherever he went. He wore a traditional dark suit, his hair cut close to his head, which was typical for him.

Alex stood by him in a pencil skirt and blouse, tablet in hand. She was a cute blonde who looked like a freaking movie star. Most of the guys that Logan knew in Gray Tower thought that they were in love with her, but Bryant had put her completely off-limits to any employee. Period.

Brenden, meanwhile, was sitting in a chair with his feet up on the conference room table. He wore a t-shirt that had seen better days and jeans. His hair was almost always a different color. Currently, it was light blonde with green tips.

The kid had a goofy personality, and he was a bit immature. However, he was excellent at his job, and that was what mattered the most.

"Sir," Jack and Logan said pretty much in unison.

They kept it pretty damned formal with Bryant.

"I've been going through your interviews with Miss Amherst, and there's not a whole lot that we don't know about Amherst Global or Damien Amherst already.

"That being said, having Ms. Amherst is an invaluable opportunity as a bargaining chip."

Logan tensed, suddenly feeling possessive, and asked, "What kind of 'bargaining chip' are we talking about here?"

"Nothing sinister, Slade," Bryant replied. "But I've heard chatter from a few sources that Damien Amherst is going nuts trying to find his daughter. We can use that to our advantage."

"What about the issue of Stratton?" Logan asked. "He's the one who sent her to us."

Logan had reported on what Keira had told him about Stratton—that he had sent her to his address. What he had failed to digress was his previous altercation with Stratton.

"Stratton's a wild card at this point," Bryant said. "He appears to be going against his employer—or maybe I should say former employer? It's almost as if he were invested in Miss Amherst. What she said on her interview about him was interesting. He has had an unusual role in her life."

"Apparently so," Jack agreed. "Not sure whether to trust him or not. Plus, he's been MIA since springing Miss Amherst."

Logan's throat tightened as he thought back to his first encounter with John Stratton, an incident that he neglected to report. It seemed like the right time to come clean.

"I ran into John Stratton a month ago at the warehouse bust."

Jack's eyes widened. Bryant crossed his arms and frowned.

"I don't remember reading that in your report," Bryant said.

"That's because it wasn't in there," Jack replied. "I know because I approved the report before sending it on to you."

Jack had always been a stickler for details.

"What the hell, Slade!" he grumbled, glaring at Logan.

"I was waiting to see how the situation panned out," Logan said grimly. "I'm sorry that it wasn't reported. It should have been, and there's no excuse."

"We'll talk about this later, Slade," Bryan said, his voice a bit icy.

Yeah, Logan was probably in a shit load of trouble, but he didn't seem to care anymore. He kind of figured that his days were numbered at Gray Tower, especially with how he had been feeling lately.

"Now what happened at this encounter?"

Logan explained the details without trying to think about how pissed his bosses currently were at him.

After he was done, Jack said, "Well, what he said seems to make sense now. He must have been planning to get Miss Amherst out for a while. I wonder how he got your contact info."

"I was wondering that as well," Logan agreed.

Bryant turned to Alex and Brenden, "I'm going to need the both of you to look into any breach in security here. Ever since Miss Amherst showed up at Slade's cabin, I've been concerned. There's no way Stratton should have gotten to Slade like that unless there was a leak somewhere.

"Alex, start pulling HR files. Brenden, I want a full security sweep."

"Yes, sir," they said in unison.

"That's all great and everything, but that still doesn't tell me why you neglected to report talking to Stratton, Slade," Jack interrupted.

Logan hesitated because he himself wasn't quite sure why he didn't report it.

"I suppose it's because I should have taken him down and didn't. He was a high priority target, and I did nothing."

Bryant frowned.

"Interestingly enough," he said. "We wouldn't have Miss Amherst if you would have dealt with Stratton more appropriately. However, maybe after this is all over, you should take an extended vacation, especially since this mission has interrupted what was supposed to be some time off for you. You've been burning the candle at both ends for too many years at Gray Tower."

That was true.

Logan was one of the senior level operatives at Gray Tower with a long stint in the Army before that. He was just plain mentally tired of all the shit that went on.

"Sure," Logan replied a little more harshly than he wanted.

"Good," Bryant said. "Now, we've run into a bit of a problem with securing a place for Ms. Amherst to go after her interviews are done. I'll let Alex explain."

Alex had been frantically tapping away at her tablet when she looked up and smiled. She was the best damned assistant Logan had ever seen.

"We have a spot for her right outside of Sydney, Australia," Alex said in her bright and cheery voice.

Interestingly, she had probably just put in a fourteen-hour work day, but she always stayed positive.

"Unfortunately, it's going to take a few more days to get her new identity ready," she continued

"How many more days are we talking about here?" Jack asked gruffly.

"I'm waiting two days on her new driver's license, but the passport is probably going to take three or four days," Alex replied.

Logan had an uneasy feeling. That was too long.

"Her interview is almost over," Jack said. "Are we just going to sit around here and wait, then?"

"No," Bryant said. "You are coming back to headquarters to help Alex and Brenden. Logan can stay on with Miss Amherst until she is safely settled."

Logan's throat seemed to tighten a bit. He wasn't sure if he was relieved to have a few more days with Keira, or if he was now panicked that he would have to spend that much longer with her.

"Sounds good," Jack said. "I can probably head out late tomorrow morning."

"Good," Bryant said. "I'm going to adjourn the meeting, though Logan, I do want to talk with you one on one after this is all over with."

"Sure," Logan said, his voice dry.

Bryant was either going to put him on an extended vacation or just fire him outright, probably. The sad part was Logan just didn't even care anymore.

CHAPTER 15

Keira was flopped out on her bed, alone. Again. A guard had been stationed in the room that she and Logan had been hanging out in, and she didn't quite want to spend time with a stranger.

Now she sat in the windowless room that she had barely used, feeling trapped. It was as if she had jumped from one prison to another. The loneliness was starting to creep back in. She didn't feel it when Logan was around. In fact, she felt alive when she was around him.

But it didn't really matter. They would go their separate ways as soon as Gray Tower found a place to hide her.

Keira pondered whether she should just go to bed. She was tired, but her mind was going a mile a minute. There was no chance of her sleeping until she could get her racing thoughts calmed down.

She also still felt a bit cold. The heavy comforter didn't help either. She wondered if she would ever truly feel normal again after her ordeal in the snow.

Plus, there was a feeling of isolation and despair. She had been battling depression ever since she was locked away. It seemed to be particularly bad right now, but at least there was a light at the end of the tunnel for her.

A sudden knock startled Keira out of her little pity-party.

"Come in," she said, half expecting it to be the guard who was positioned outside of her room.

She hadn't yet changed for bed and was still decent, though that only meant switching from one set of large borrowed comfy clothes she had found to another set of large comfy clothes.

Keira did a bit of a double-take when Logan strolled in. Her stomach immediately began to flutter. Why did she have to have such a strong reaction to him?

Get it together, she told herself.

She felt like she was back in high school again, though it had been a while since she had been around a man who she liked. A long, long time.

There was a troubled look on his face as he stared at her for a moment.

"Is everything alright?" She asked cautiously.

"Everything's fine," Logan said flatly. "I've got some good news and some bad news for you."

"Okay," Keira said, suddenly nervous.

He moved toward where she was bundled up in the bed. It was a small bedroom, and with tall, well-muscled body, it felt like he was taking up most of it.

"The good news is that Gray Tower has found a place for you to lie low for a while. It looks like you are headed to Australia."

Keira wasn't sure how she felt about that. It certainly was pretty much as far away from her father as she could get. However, she would also be far away from everything she knew—and far away from Logan.

"And the bad news?" She asked hesitantly.

"It's going to be a few more days before you can leave. Gray Tower is working on a new identity for you."

"I see."

Keira wasn't quite sure how she felt about that as well. While she remained in the states, she was sure that she was in danger from her father. However, that meant more time with Logan...

"Don't worry. We'll get you away from here," he told her, and he looked sincere.

She nodded and clutched the blankets a little tighter.

Logan's eyebrow raised slightly.

"Are you okay?"

Keira tried to smile, but she felt herself faltering.

"I think I'm just in my head a little too much," she admitted.

He nodded and stood silent for a moment.

"Well, if you need to get out of your head for a bit, you're always welcome to keep me company in the other room. I'm sure we could pick up our TV marathon from last night."

Her mood brightened significantly.

"Sure," she said, eager to get out of the windowless room but even more eager to spend any time with Logan.

Keira followed him out into the other room and sank down into one of the couches. There wasn't much on TV except for the news, but she didn't mind. She soaked up the information as she watched intently. Keira had been cut off to the outside world, and it was nice just to catch up on everything that had been happening beyond her childhood bedroom.

Logan sat opposite of her on the couch, watching the news in silence. She wanted to talk with him, but he had a stony expression on his face that didn't bode will with conversation.

After a while, though, she got restless and decided to strike up a conversation.

"You know almost everything about me, but I know almost nothing about you," she said, breaking the silence.

"What do you want to know?" He asked, his voice low and soft.

"Well, I don't know. Tell me about your childhood. Tell me about your family. What did you do before you worked for Gray Tower?"

Logan stared at her for a moment, and then said, "Childhood was typical. Grew up in Indiana. Mom and Dad. A younger brother. Pretty boring, which is why after high school, I ended up joining the Army."

"I see."

Keira knew that she would do anything for a typical, boring family. Even before she found out her father's secret, she never really liked trying to fit into the rich lifestyle.

"I had eight years in the Army with the last few as a Ranger. After that, I got recruited to Gray Tower, and you can figure out the rest, I suppose."

"What all do you do at Gray Tower?"

Logan shifted in his seat, as if he were uncomfortable.

"I can't tell you a whole lot. Most of it is classified. I can tell you that I helped with private security for my first year until I got promoted. After that, the missions got a bit more complicated."

"I see. Do you ever get to see your family?"

Logan frowned.

"No. I'm estranged from them."

"I'm sorry to hear that," she told him, wondering what the story was behind Logan and his family.

"Me too."

There was an awkward silence. Keira couldn't help but just stare at Logan. He was a big, beautiful man, despite his brooding demeanor. She desperately wished that they could have met under different circumstances.

"You and your mom seemed close," he pointed out.

She nodded.

"She was amazing. She was the nicest, most generous person you would ever meet. I'm still not sure what she saw in my father, though thinking back now, he was able to charm and mislead everyone I suppose."

"Damien Amherst has a lot of people fooled. Look how long it took for his true colors to come out to you."

Keira fidgeted uncomfortably.

"Yes, he did," she admitted softly. Then she found herself blurting out, "I miss her so much."

"I'm sorry about your mother."

She nodded, sadness creeping over her.

Logan had listened to her whole story throughout the interview process. He knew about the car accident that had killed her mother when Keira had been just sixteen. Her mother had been the only one in the car, and it had been a devastating loss for the family. She had been driving home in icy conditions and had veered off the road into a ravine. Her mother hadn't survived the impact, and Keira still mourned the loss every day.

"Thank you," she said quietly.

She stared at him for a moment. He stared back, his gray eyes piercing. The man was so freaking handsome that he gave her butterflies in the stomach. Keira wondered what would happen if she were to just give him a kiss on the check. You know, just to thank him for being so helpful and protecting her and all?

Her thinking was a bit warped, she knew. The memory of the other night was still etched firmly in her mind. She knew that there was an attraction between them and a need, and right now, that need was aching to be fulfilled.

What the hell! Why not? She thought.

She was tired of not living her own life. She was tired of being controlled. And most of all, she was tired of feeling lonely and trapped.

Keira slowly leaned toward him and gently kissed his cheek. It was rough from a five o'clock shadow. When she drew away, her eyes met his. Logan's eyes seemed to darken with desire.

"Thank you," she whispered again.

"You just said that," he pointed out, his voice low and husky.

"I know. I just can't tell you enough how grateful I am that you are helping me so much."

He nodded but said nothing. Their faces suddenly seemed too close together.

Her mind went blank, and she found herself going in for a kiss right on his lips.

It was just as wonderful as when they had kissed in the motel room. Keira could tell that she had taken him by surprise, but that quickly wore off as he began to kiss back.

Soft, full lips brushed hers, first softly then more firmly as Logan took command of the kiss. His tongue found hers and began gentle strokes as he deepened the kiss. One of his hands reached to cup her face, and the touch sent shivers down her body.

She let out a soft moan as his fingers gently brushed her face and moved to the back of her head, pulling her against him. A dull ache formed in her womb as his hands fisted in her hair. The need for him only intensified as his mouth claimed hers.

"Keira, we can't do this," Logan muttered into her skin as his kisses began trailing to the sensitive areas of her neck.

In response, her hands slid down to his rock-hard biceps and gripped them tight. She didn't want this to end. Being with him was the only thing that made her forget about her circumstances.

And suddenly, as soon as it had started, their passionate embrace ended.

Logan pulled his head away, breathing hard and swearing under his breath. Disappointment began to creep through Keira as he gently but firmly took her and sat her up on her side of the couch.

"No," he said, his voice low and a bit harsh. "This can't happen."

She blinked in surprise by his tone, her heart sinking a bit. His expression turned to stone.

"Look, Keira, you are a beautiful woman. There's no denying that," he told her, his voice devoid of any emotion. "There's also no denying that we find each other attractive. However, I can't do my job with these types of distractions. This right here could get us both killed."

Keira bit her lip and stared down at her fingers. Logan had mentioned that briefly the other night, but his tone tonight sounded dead serious.

"Not only that," he continued, "but you're in a fragile state right now. You were imprisoned by your father for two years, and the first new person you see ends up saving your life. This attraction is just a bunch of adrenaline. It's not anything that could last, and even if we were in completely different circumstances, I'm not the type to settle down. Sorry."

She wanted to protest that maybe she wasn't looking for anything serious. Maybe she wanted a quick fling?

But who was she fooling? He saw right through her.

Keira had always been traditional when it came with men. If she dated, it was for the long term with marriage ultimately being the goal. She was a bit out of her element with Logan as she wasn't the type to just jump into bed with a guy. Her current circumstances had blown that thinking out the window, though. Perhaps Logan was right about the danger and adrenaline?

Regardless, his words of rejection still hurt. It felt like someone had punched Keira in the gut. Logan's words stung in her ears. She understood that she had taken a gamble with kissing him, but he didn't have to let her down so harshly.

She was even more angry at herself for getting so emotionally involved with someone who wouldn't and couldn't return those feelings. It wasn't as if they didn't have chemistry. It wasn't as if he wasn't attracted to her physically. But it was now obvious that there was a mismatch in personality.

"Okay, whatever," she managed to say.

Getting up from the couch, she turned away quickly from him and began to walk back to her room.

"Keira, wait," Logan said, but she didn't listen as she opened the door and shut it firmly.

She felt like an idiot. There was a point in time when she had been confident around men. Now, she felt lost, and a bit humiliated.

Fighting back tears, she flopped on the bed. Her best efforts at trying to hold it all failed, and she began sobbing. Keira wasn't quite sure if she was crying over: Logan or at her situation. Maybe it was a little bit of both?

She didn't know why she was so emotional. He was just some guy that she had met, right? Sure, but if that were true, why did it hurt so much?

Keira curled up on the bed and sobbed for a bit. Then a bit of anger took hold. Anger at Logan, and then anger at herself.

Finally, she drifted off into an uneasy sleep. At least she was safe from her father. That's all that counted right now.

CHAPTER 16

Logan stared up at the ceiling, silently cursing at himself. He was lying awake on the top bunk in the room next to Keira's. It was dawn, and he hadn't gotten much sleep. He felt like the biggest asshole of all time.

Logan kept replaying what had transpired last night, trying to figure out what he should have done instead. Rejecting her advances had seemed like the smart thing to do at the time. He couldn't do his job if they started getting physical. Hadn't Jack warned him about all of this?

Yet, that look that she had given him when he had turned her down seemed to be etched in his memory.

He hadn't wanted to hurt her. All Logan had wanted to do was push her away a bit. They couldn't be together like that. It wouldn't be right, but he hadn't been expecting her to kiss him. Hell, he had always thought that he would be the one to make the first move as he had done in the motel room. He had never thought that she would be the one to initiate something physical.

Logan also hadn't expected a pretty heavy make-out session—one that he barely was able to pull himself from. He couldn't help but love kissing her. She made his blood run hot with lust. It had taken everything ounce of self-control to stop.

He had known that if he had continued, he would have been inside her within minutes. He also knew that a one and done quick screw wouldn't have gotten her out of his system either. The more that he was around her and the more that he touched her, the more he wanted to claim her.

It was a feeling that scared the shit out of him. He couldn't have feelings for a woman who was about to be shipped off half way around the world, nor did he think that he was capable of being a good husband or father.

Logan knew that Keira was the happily-ever-after type with the white picket fences and the three point five kids. He didn't feel right leading her on with a sexual relationship. It was that simple.

Or, it was more complicated than he could have imagined.

Logan had panicked a bit when trying to explain his position to her. He had ended up sounding like an asshole. Everything he had said turned out harsher than he had intended. He had hurt her. Badly.

He heard the shower from the other room kick on. Keira was up. He hadn't exactly been looking forward to facing her this morning. However, he did have a job to do, so he'd have to suck it up.

Rolling out of bed, he winced at some soreness in his muscles. After Keira had stormed away, Logan had ended up in the unfinished section of the basement. There was a weight set there, and he lifted until failure on most of his routine. Anything to try to get Keira out of his head for a little while.

He changed quickly into his usual attire and headed upstairs to see Jack, figuring that Keira would be okay for a few moments without a guard downstairs. At this point, it was probably best to give her some space.

Jack was packing up as Logan wandered into the combination kitchen and living room area.

"I'm headed out in five. Luke and Tyler are on duty right now if you need anything," Jack said, referring to two of the men on their security team. "I have a shit load of work to do back at HQ, and I want to get back as quickly as possible."

"Understandable," Logan replied.

There were a few more moments of packing before Jack started heading to the door. Logan followed.

Before Jack opened the front door, he paused and turned toward Logan.

"Look, I need to apologize to you," Jack said with sincerity. "I was acting like an ass last night, and that was not my intention."

"I appreciate that," Logan told him, nodding. "And I'm sorry for keeping the stuff with Stratton a secret. I should have reported it at least to you if nothing else. I'm still not sure what I was thinking."

Jack nodded, a silent understanding between the two men.

And suddenly, things were back to normal. Just like that.

"You have to admit, though, that Miss Amherst is pretty cute."

Logan tried to smile, but it probably fell a bit flat. Keira wasn't just cute; she was gorgeous. And he could have had her last night...

He shook the thought out of his head.

"Yeah, she is," he agreed.

Jack scratched his jaw absentmindedly as in deep thought and then said, "Be careful with Miss Amherst. She's a sweet girl, but she's got a ton of baggage that comes with her."

Logan knew that, and he really didn't care. Sure, she was Damien Amherst's daughter, but she was nothing like her father. Sure, she may have some emotional issues from being a captive for so long, but he admired her strength and her courage.

What really was telling him to stay away from her was the nagging feeling that he couldn't be what she needed him to be. It was that plain and simple.

"Yeah sure," Logan agreed. "I've got it under control. No issues."

"Well, I'm glad we had this little chat before I left," Jack said with a smirk. "I'm off."

Back in the house, Logan put on a pot of coffee and sat in silence as he gulped the bitter liquid. He knew that he was sulking, but he couldn't seem to snap out of it. At least he did feel a bit better with some caffeine in his system. It would most likely be another long day.

Logan's cell phone lit up and began a soft ring tone. Looking down at it, the number was listed as "Unknown." Getting an uneasy feeling, he answered it.

"Yes," he answered sternly.

"Get her out of there. Now." Came the voice from the other end.

It was a male voice that was oddly familiar, but Logan couldn't quite place it. The thing that Logan was most interested in was the reference to "her," which he had a sinking feeling was geared at Keira.

"Who is this?" Logan demanded, popping up out of his seat on alert.

"John Stratton," came the cool reply.

Adrenaline began to pump through Logan's veins as he pondered the implications. If this really was Stratton, then they were in trouble.

"Really," Logan said, trying sound casual. "How did you get this number? What do you want?"

"Logan, just shut up and listen," the man on the other end said curtly. "Your position is compromised. There are men coming right now. You only have minutes, if you're lucky. Get Keira out of there *now*."

Logan's heart started pounding hard in his chest.

"How do I know you're telling the truth? This just could be a ploy to force me to go on the move."

"Because I care about Keira more than you know. And your address is 354 Wilburne Road. If I know it, Damien knows it."

"Fuck," Logan cursed, hitting the alarm button for the guards.

"Get her out of there, and don't trust anyone in your organization. I think the same person who has been feeding me information about you is also doing the same for Amherst now."

"Who the hell is it?" Logan demanded.

"I don't know," Stratton admitted. "All communication was digital. Look, just get her out of there! Don't trust *anyone* at Gray Tower."

The line ended abruptly. By this time, the two off-duty agents were in the room, rifles in hand.

"What's going on?" One of the asked.

"I got a tip that this place is compromised. I'm moving the asset. I need you to provide cover. We have a possible incoming."

"Shit," the other mumbled.

They dispersed as Logan grabbed his bags and bolted downstairs to get Keira. He burst open the door to her room. She looked startled, understandably. Wearing the outfit that he had first seen her in when she had stumbled into his cabin (thanks to a laundry room in the house), she looked stunning. But he didn't have time to think about her like that now.

"Grab your bag. Now!" He told her with urgency. "We have to go."

"Wha...?" Keira started to say, but he cut her off.

"No time. This position is compromised. Get your bag. Now!"

Keira bolted upright and grabbed her bag. Luckily, she had listened when he had told her to stay packed no matter what. Logan took her hand and literally pulled her out of the room and up the stairs. He practically dragged her out of the house and to his truck. He knew his men were in position around the house, though they were not visible.

Logan was barely able to get Keira in the truck when he heard vehicles crunching up the gravel driveway. There was no one scheduled to arrive at the safe house on Gray Tower's end, which meant that whoever was coming wasn't friendly.

Shit, he thought as he slammed himself into the driver's seat of the truck.

Right now, it would be better to try and run than get into a firefight with Keira in the vehicle. His men could hold them off long enough to try and get away. There was a back entrance to the safe house from the woods that was not on any of the schematics from Gray Tower. Jack had purposely left it that way in case of a situation just like this one.

Logan swung the truck into reverse and spun it around toward the other direction as a group of men in black with guns appeared from the convoy of black vans and SUVs. Hitting the gas, the truck rocketed off toward the back of the house across an open grassy area. There were woods directly ahead of them which contained an off-road path that went through the back of the property.

Pop. Pop. Pop.

Gunfire, he thought as he maneuvered the vehicle over the grass and toward a barely visible dirt path. There was the distant sound of rat-ta-tat-tat, rat-ta-tat-tat.

Shit, he thought. *They brought automatic weapons.*

Sure, Gray Tower used military weapons, but they almost always used a three-round burst as it was more accurate. These guys were going for the intimidation factor.

Logan glanced at the rearview mirror as he heard more distant gunfire.

Double shit, he thought.

One of the enemy vehicles was following them: a black van with a now cracked windshield from what was undoubtedly return-fire from Logan's team. It was careening toward them, trying to find traction on the grass.

Fuck, Logan thought as his truck bounded through the opening in the woods and onto the dirt and grass path.

Of course, things couldn't be *that* easy, but at least it was only one vehicle. Plus, it was not one of the SUVs. There was a good possibility that Logan could lose them on the off-road section with his truck.

The truck twisted and turned through the wooded path, the van not far behind them. Logan glanced over at Keira for a moment and saw that she had turned almost completely white.

"Breathe," he told her.

Instead of taking a few deep breaths, she started to hyperventilate. He had to lose this tail, or Keira was going to melt down completely.

There was an abrupt jog in the trail, and Logan had to slow and turn the truck sharply, fishtailing a bit before he corrected the vehicle. When the truck straightened out, he hit the gas.

Checking his mirror again, he saw the van having issues negotiating the turn. It smacked into a tree and stalled there for a moment as the driver attempted to correct the vehicle.

Fuck yeah.

It was the window of opportunity that he needed. The van wasn't out of commission, but it would give them the lead they needed to lose the Amherst goons.

There was an opening up ahead to a rural road that shouldn't have much traffic on it. Logan gunned his vehicle toward the road, hoping to put some distance between them and the van.

The truck flew out of opening as Logan braked and turned onto the road, only to hit the accelerator when the vehicle was straightened out. Glancing back at his mirrors, the van was still not in sight.

Logan pushed his truck as fast as it could safely go until they reached an intersection. Turning right, he continued, going as fast as he dared to go. He needed the speed, but he also needed to keep the truck under control.

He kept checking the rearview mirror. So far, the van was still not in sight. Maybe they had gotten out of this after all?

There were a few more heart-wrenching moments. Then, he made a couple of quick turns.

Suddenly, they were back in the suburbs, and there was still no van.

Logan navigated through a couple more turns until they got to a main thoroughfare with more traffic. A few minutes later, and they were booking down the highway. The Amherst goons were nowhere in sight.

He let out a long hiss through his teeth. For the moment, they were safe.

INTERLUDE

12 Years Ago

Logan drove through the suburbs of Indianapolis, taking in the nostalgia of the place. He was currently on leave for two weeks before he would be shipped back out to Afghanistan for his third tour of duty in the Army. It wasn't exactly enough time to recharge, but he would take what he could get.

The section he was traveling through was upper-middle class. Large houses with manicured lawns sprawled in cutesy sub-divisions. Everything felt cookie-cutter.

Logan had grown up here, but it wasn't his scene. His parents had always wanted him to go to college and get that high-paying, white collar job. Instead, he had upset them by enlisting in the Army straight out high school, despite their very boisterous protests. It was one of just many disappointments that marked against him in his parents' eyes.

This visit to his parents wasn't exactly something that Logan looked forward to, but it needed to be done. Besides, he was looking forward to seeing his younger brother Nathan.

Pulling into the driveway of a large two-story red-brick house, he fought down a wave of apprehension as got out of his car and walked up the path. The car was a beater that he used when he was on leave. There was no sense in having a car payment for something nice when he only used it a couple of weeks out of the year. The rust and age of the four-door sedan looked out of place against the neat and orderly scene of suburbia.

His parents' home fit right in: well-trimmed hedges with a nicely maintained exterior. It was the epitome of the American Dream, but it just wasn't *his* dream.

Logan barely got to porch steps when the front door opened, and his mother popped out. Beverly Slade was in her forties, and she kept her appearance like the mom next door: medium height, slender with short brown hair that reminded Logan of a stereotypical sitcom mom.

Her personality was bubbly and bright, though his father was a lot more reserved. His parents had a bit of an "opposites attract" relationship that had suited them well for years now.

Instead of the warm welcome that he had been hoping for, she looked troubled. Logan frowned as he went in for a hug. His mom seemed tense in their embrace.

When the hug uneasily ceased, his mother called out, "Charles! Come to the door! Logan is here!"

A man who looked like an older version of Logan came to the door. The look on Logan's father was unreadable. That was common, but Logan could still feel that something was wrong.

"Logan, come in," Charles Slade said curtly, eying him up and down.

There was a look of disapproval from the older man, and though Logan had gotten used to it by now, something still seemed off. The mood between his parents appeared to be strained, which was out of place for them. They were usually a very loving and affectionate couple.

Okay, something was *very* wrong.

The inside of the home was just as beautiful as the outside. It was a colonial-style home with a large, two story entryway with steps to the upstairs. There was a living room and formal dining room on either side. Neither room was used very much, but his parents loved having a home that they could show off.

The décor was tastefully done in contemporary. His mother had chosen soft beiges, whites, and grays all throughout the home, and the pictures on the walls coordinated with the look.

As they moved to the back of the house, there was an open layout for a remodeled kitchen, informal dining room, and a family room with a beautiful fireplace with a red brick mantle. Pictures of the family were displayed prominently, though there were no photographs of Logan since he had joined the Army.

That was another way his father could voice his disapproval without saying a word. Logan ignored it, though. He was following his own dream, not his father's.

There was new furniture in the family room, though Logan wasn't quite sure what was wrong with the old stuff. His mother and father both prided themselves on outward appearances which had driven Logan nuts over the years. Their home was an expression of their never-ending goal of "keeping up with the Joneses."

"Can I get you anything?" His mother asked suddenly. "I was just about to start dinner. Is chicken casserole okay? Why don't I make you some coffee?"

"Coffee is fine," Logan interrupted before his mom babbled on.

She was on edge, but as Logan looked around the quiet home, he had an idea of why.

"Where's Nathan?" Logan asked, noticing the house was oddly silent.

Nathan had just graduated high school and should have been around. He and Logan had been extremely close before Logan had gone off to the Army. They had done everything together and were best friends. Nathan had looked up to Logan, so it had been important that Logan stay on point throughout his life. He had wanted to be a good example for his brother.

As the last three years had passed, they had unfortunately drifted apart. Logan had been away, and without his older brother to gravitate toward, Nathan had instead gotten in with a rough crowd.

From what Logan had heard from his mom during his deployment, Nathan had really gone off the deep end and barely graduated. The smart, compassionate young man was now gone, replaced by a frustrated youth who was more interested in getting high and chasing tail than going to college.

Logan had always tried to spend time with his brother every time that he was back in town, but each visit felt like they were drifting farther and farther apart. It troubled Logan, but he wasn't his brother's keeper, even though their parents blamed Logan for his brother's demise.

"He's out right now," Logan's father told him briskly.

His father had been a bit distant toward Logan since he had joined the Army, but right now Charles' demeanor was downright icy.

Besides, Logan doubted that was the whole story. Regardless of the distance between Nathan and him, Nate would always make sure that he was available when Logan was in town.

"So," Logan's father began, quickly switching the subject, "how was your flight back?"

Charles sat down on a plush beige couch and crossed his legs informally. Logan did the same on another couch opposite of his father's. There was tension in the air, but Logan let it go for now.

"Long," he replied with a weary sigh.

His mother returned with two steaming cups of coffee, giving one to Logan and his father the other.

They both sipped the hot liquid, sitting in silence for a few minutes.

Then, Logan's father said, "I know that you have signed up for another tour, but afterward, I was thinking that you could resign afterward and join the company."

Oh, here we go again, Logan thought as he gritted his teeth.

It had only a matter of time before his dad brought the issue up again, but Logan hadn't expected the older man discuss it *this* soon.

His father was co-owner of a regional chain of hardware and lumber stores. He had been nagging Logan for years to work at the company and get a business degree. Logan had never been interested. He had always wanted to do his own thing, and serving his country was his top priority right now.

"Dad, we've talked about this," he said, trying not to allow the irritation show in his voice.

"You could start some night classes while you work," his father continued as if he hadn't heard what Logan had just said. "I'll pay your way through and everything."

"Actually, I was thinking about trying out for the Army Rangers and going career."

Both of his parents looked at him with dismay. Logan knew that they had been hoping that his service in the Army was just a phase, and he'd eventually snap out of it and get a "real" job. This only made Logan want to stay longer.

There was a long stretch of silence before his mother spoke up.

"Logan, we really need you at home. Your father needs you at the business, and Nathan really needs you to be here as well."

And there was the real reason why his parents were so desperate to get him back. They basically thought that Logan was the only one able to get through to Nate. His younger brother had looked up to him for so long that they figured that if Logan was back in Indiana, Nathan would behave and get his life together.

"It doesn't work like that," Logan said firmly. "I'm not responsible for Nathan or his behavior. That's something that he's going to have to figure out on his own. I have my own life to live, and I'm happy in the Army."

Charles stood up and began pacing back in forth, looking upset.

"You just don't get it, do you?" Logan's father bit out. "You were supposed to do the decent thing and go to college and work a good job, but no, you had to skirt your responsibilities and run off to the Army while your brother struggled without you for years. Now look at him..."

"What your father is trying to say," his mother interrupted, "is that Nathan has run off."

Logan's eyes widened as he tried to process the news.

"What do you mean, 'run off'?" He demanded.

"We had a fight a few days ago, and he left," she said, her voice shaky.

"And he stole some money and a some of your mother's good jewelry," Logan's father said, vitriol coming out in his voice.

"I don't care about most of it, but he took your grandmother's broach," Beverly said, tears welling up in her eyes.

"What the hell," Logan muttered. "Why wasn't this the first topic of conversation?"

"We didn't want to spring this on you right away," his mother told him.

"Do you know where he may have gone?" Logan asked, rising from his seat, ready to drag his brother back from wherever to knock some sense in him.

His mother shook her head.

"If we knew, don't you think we would have gone after him? I'm so worried about him. He's been mixed up in all sorts of bad stuff. He was busted a couple of times this year for underaged drinking, but your father was able to pull some strings so that Nathan wasn't charged."

His father grunted and said, "I had to pay his math teacher under the table to pass him just so that he could graduate on time."

Logan snorted.

That was that type of behavior from his parents which was aggravating the whole situation. They had been enabling some of Nathan's behavior for a few years. However, at the moment, Logan decided to keep his mouth shut about it. That was sore subject for another day.

"You know," his father continued. "I wasn't going to say this, sweetheart, but I think Logan needs to hear this."

He looked Logan square in the eye.

"This is all your damned fault, you know. You go running off to fight someone else's war, and your brother deteriorates without you. You know he used to worship you, right? Nathan went from a straight A student to a habitual drug user. Do you know we caught him with some of those party drugs?"

Logan opened his mouth to speak, but he couldn't find the words. Of course, he knew that it wasn't his fault. At the end of the day, Nathan was his own person who had to make his own decisions.

"I told you that we're not going to have this conversation," Logan replied firmly.

"Because you don't want to admit you're the one to blame!" His father snapped.

Shaking his head, Logan turned back to the hallway and began to walk to the front door. He wasn't going to stand there and allow his father to berate him for something that Logan had no control over.

"Don't walk away from me, son!" His father called out.

"We can talk when you're acting rational," Logan said simply as he opened the front door and left the house.

A feeling of unease filled him as he walked the path to his car. It had been months since he had seen his parents, and it only took a few minutes for them to start on him again. Logan also worried about his brother, thinking that maybe he could spend some time searching Nathan out.

Unfortunately, Logan never found Nathan. In fact, he never saw or heard from him again. Even worse, that was also the last time that Logan ever saw his parents again either. The rift that Nathan's disappearance caused tore that relationship apart. Logan had to stay away for his own sanity.

After the blow-up with his parents that day, he made a vow to himself to steer away from the family life route and instead threw himself into his career. Logan couldn't stand the thought of making the same mistakes that his parents did, and so he stayed single and childless.

CHAPTER 17

Present

Keira felt lightheaded and dizzy. Nausea overwhelmed her. She tried hard not to throw up in Logan's truck. It had been about fifteen heart-wrenching minutes since they had gotten on the highway, and she couldn't help but keep turning her head.

Her father had found her. How could that have happened? Shouldn't she have been safe with Gray Tower?

Despite being rejected by Logan the night before, Keira had at least begun to feel safe. She had also just gotten used to her new routine—one that didn't involve her being locked away in her childhood bedroom. When her father's men had shown up at the safe house, she had been rattled to the core.

"We've lost them," Logan told her calmly. "Try and breathe."

Keira tried to, forcing air in and out of her lungs in deep inhales. However, she felt too sick. She could feel stomach acid churning in her belly.

"Please pull over," she begged. "I think I'm going to throw up."

They were luckily near an exit, and Logan exited the highway, pulling off to the side of the off-ramp. Keira staggered out of the truck and began to dry-heave. She hadn't had any breakfast, so there wasn't anything to throw up. Still, she gagged until she felt a little better.

All the while, Logan stood behind her, stoically. He placed a hand on her shoulder. It must have been his attempt at trying to comfort her.

His touch, despite being gentle and friendly, sent shockwaves down the rest of her body. She felt raw and couldn't stand the thought of anyone touching her right now, even Logan.

The wave of nausea left, and she stood, his hand releasing. Momentarily forgetting about her father and her problems, Keira couldn't help but remember how much of an asshole Logan had been the previous night. She was still pissed, and his touch reminded her of that. He had a habit of being hot and cold with her, and she was tired of the emotional rollercoaster.

"I'm fine," she said sharply, backing away from him.

Her boots crunched as she shifted on the gravel that lined the side of the road. She almost tripped as she tried to maneuver away from Logan.

"You don't look fine," he said, his voice low and soft.

His muscles flexed slightly underneath a tight black shirt. Damn him. Why did he have to be so damned sexy?

"I'll be alright," she said curtly.

After she was able to steady herself and take a few more breaths, she realized that Logan had indeed saved her life. Again.

"Thank you for getting me out of there," she told him, her voice softening.

"Just doing my job," he replied.

Of course, he was, she thought. *I am just a job to him.*

Keira tried to push the bitter thoughts out of her head. She should be grateful. He had indeed saved her life. Her father was hunting her, and she was now dependent on Logan to keep her safe.

She watched as he took his cell phone out of his pocket. He popped what looked to be the SIM card out of it as well as a memory card. Then, he placed the cell phone in front of one of the front tires of his truck.

"What are you doing?" Keira asked, suddenly panicked again.

"Gray Tower is compromised," he replied. "I'm going to have to go dark."

"Wait, what do you mean?" She asked.

A wave of anxiety washed through her. Gray Tower was supposed to be safe. They were supposed to help her. How were they going to help her if they were compromised?

"It means that we're on our own. No contact from my superiors. No help. Just us."

"For how long?"

"As long as it takes."

A new surge of panic went through her as she tried to process the information. Keira hadn't expected to stay with Logan for much longer. Wasn't she supposed to be in Australia in a few days? Now it looked like they were stuck together indefinitely.

A car whooshed past them on the off-ramp. Keira and Logan both looked at it instinctively, watching for one of those black Amherst vehicles.

"We need to get going," he told her.

"Where are we going?"

"Haven't figured that out yet."

More anxiety.

Keira had gotten so used to the fact that Gray Tower would protect her that she had never considered what would happen if that wasn't the case. It hadn't been that long ago when Logan had been discussing her new identity. Now, everything seemed up in the air.

When they got back in the truck and began to drive off, there was the unmistakable crunch of Logan's cell phone. What had Keira gotten herself into?

*   *   *

Damien Amherst looked down at his phone and silently cursed as a message flashed across the screen: *Asset at location but not acquired. Regrouping now. Have make and model of getaway vehicle.*

He was starting to get pissed. Why was it so hard to snatch one naïve young woman? This should have been routine for his people, but it had instead turned into a giant cluster fuck.

It also didn't help that the mercenary group, Gray Tower, was now involved. Damien had a few interactions with them, though nothing major. They were a large private military group, and he had even considered them for security for one point in time. However, he had realized that they wouldn't go along with vision for Amherst Global and had quickly taken them off the list of potential business partners.

How Keira had gotten to them was an interesting question. He had assumed that it had something to do with John.

Damien supposed that he should be satisfied that they at least knew this much. He had been worried that he'd never see his daughter again, but there had fortunately been a stroke of luck.

A private contractor that he used from time to time had found a Gray Tower employee with high level access who had blabbed about Keira. Money greased a lot of palms, and apparently, this Gray Tower contact needed a lot of it.

Just because she had gotten away didn't mean all was lost. Damien would find her again. He just needed to get a bit more creative.

It was already mid-morning, and Damien was in his office at Amherst Manor. He had more to do, though it had already been non-stop work for the last few days trying to track down Keira and keep a handle on his company.

He strolled over to his desk, loosening his tie.

Keira couldn't hide forever. Damien would find her soon enough. Jason would marry her, and he would eventually have grandchildren to pass the Amherst legacy down to. The stakes were very high at this point, but Damien would win. He always won.

His desk phone rang, and he frowned. Not many people had that number, and those who did were of top importance. Damien picked up immediately.

"Yes," he answered, switching to all-business mode.

"We need to talk," said a low, male voice from the other end of the line.

Damien tensed as his usual confidence seemed to drain right from him. He rarely got these phone calls, but when he did, it was usually because he was in trouble.

"Yes, of course," he replied, trying to keep his voice steady.

"You're making a lot of noise with the wrong people," the man continued. "Get your shit together, or we're going to have problems."

"Well, you see..." Damien began.

"No excuses. Fix the issue with your daughter or let her go. We have bigger issues to worry about."

"Understood," Damien replied, a pit forming in his stomach.

The phone call abruptly ended, and Damien suddenly felt on-edge. He decided to go ahead and apply a little bit of pressure to this Gray Tower employee who was providing information. Damien was going to have to find Keira and soon, or he'd have bigger problems to deal with.

* * *

Logan chucked his Gray Tower laptop in a trash can at a gas station in southern Ohio. He had taken out the hard drive, which held encrypted information. He couldn't trust anyone in Gray Tower right now, and he knew that they could be tracked through any of the electronics that he would usually take on a mission.

He had gone completely dark: no contact, no credit cards, no known aliases. He had even thoroughly checked his truck for tracking devices. Luckily, he had opted to not have any GPS for the vehicle when he had bought it.

That left a dilemma though: Where exactly were they going to stay?

Logan had cash, but not enough to keep them going long term. He had no idea how long they would have to be on the run. It could be days, or it could be weeks or longer. There were supply drops for Gray Tower operatives around the country and the world, but he couldn't take the chance to go by one as any of them could be monitored. They were on their own right now, and there weren't a ton of options.

He did have a back-up plan for cases like this. It wasn't the best option, it also really wasn't an option that he wanted to use. However, it was his only choice, so he was going to take it.

Logan glanced over at Keira who was sitting quietly in the front passenger seat. She looked exhausted and utterly beautiful. Despite panicking a little when the Amherst thugs had been after them, she hadn't done too badly as a civilian. She was certainly braver than even he had thought. Now, he just had to figure out his next move with her.

He grimaced. Logan had only been expecting to be around her for the next few days. There was now the possibility that they'd be stuck together who knew how long.

Walking over to the truck, he opened the driver's side door. Their empty fast food containers were still sitting on the center console. It was a little before noon, and it already felt like the day had dragged on forever. It also didn't help that Logan had barely slept the last few days.

Keira stared intensely at him, her mousey brown hair hanging in front of her face. Logan knew that she was scared. He could see that in her face.

However, he also knew that she was pretty pissed at him. That was understandable. He'd been an asshole the night before. Perhaps it was for the best. His top priority needed to be protecting her—not trying to get into her pants.

"Is everything okay?" She asked hesitantly.

It must have shown on his face. He was beginning to second guess the decision on where to take her.

"We're going to have to go off the radar for a while until Gray Tower can nail the leaker," he said. "I have a place we can go. It will just be a bit unconventional. Gray Tower safe houses are out and so is any place that can be easily connected with me."

She nodded but still looked worried.

Logan climbed in the front seat, shut the door, and turned on the engine. They were gassed up and ready to go, and it would be more productive to drive and talk. Pulling the truck out of the station, he quickly got back on the highway.

"So, it will be safe there, right?" Keira asked cautiously.

"It's the best option we have right now with extremely limited resources," he replied.

"Where is this place?"

Logan hesitated. She wouldn't like it, but there weren't any other good options.

"It's in a small little town on the Delmarva Peninsula close to the Chesapeake Bay bridge."

He watched from the corner of his eye as she stiffened. As a Virginia native, he knew she was well acquainted with the peninsula that jutted out on Virginia's Eastern shore.

"That's a bit too close for comfort for me," she said quietly.

"I understand that," Logan tried to reassure her. "But our options are limited, and at this point, we are better off in the dark if there is someone at Gray Tower feeding information to your father."

Logan watched as she bit her lower lip in apprehension.

"Hey, it's the best I can do," he said gently.

He knew that she was scared out of her mind. She was doing a good job at keeping it together, but everything would eventually catch up to her.

"Okay, I understand," she said quietly and turned her head so that she was looking out the window and not at him.

Conversation ended, he thought.

Trying to push her out of his mind for a bit, he concentrated on the road ahead and the extremely long drive ahead of them.

* * *

Jason Savage was up late working in his office at the D.C. headquarters of Amherst Global. His new promotion required a lot, and he wasn't going to squander this opportunity, especially since he was promised a way into the Amherst family. He wasn't worried about Damien's missing daughter. Jason was a patient man. Eventually, it would all get ironed out.

"Harder," he commanded, looking down from his laptop where one of his administrative assistants was currently sucking him off.

What was her name again? Valerie? Vanessa? It was something like that. Jason really didn't care. She had blonde hair, generous tits, and a heavenly mouth. Good enough for him.

She obliged, sucking a bit harder and taking him fuller into her mouth. He closed his eyes, a small hiss escaping his mouth. The hot, wet suction felt so damned good on his cock. It wouldn't be long until he came.

"Yes, like that," he told her as he watched her work over him with her mouth, a smile of satisfaction spreading over his face.

Jason's phone on his desk lit up. His eyes glanced at the device. It was Damien, so he would have to answer it.

"Yes, Damien," Jason greeted him as he touched the screen to answer.

Victoria never missed a beat as she continued.

"Listen very closely," said the voice on the other end of the line.

Jason immediately knew that it was not Damien's.

"You are going to tell Damien Amherst that you no longer wish to marry his daughter. Got it?"

Jason's eyes narrowed as he slapped Vivian across the face and said sternly, "Leave. Now."

She looked startled but got up quickly and left the room at a jog, wiping her face as she ran.

Jason turned his attention back to the mysterious caller as he attempted to zip up his pants with his straining erection still in full swing.

"Who the hell is this?" Jason demanded, though he had an idea. "Stratton? Is that you? You are in so much shit right now. It would be best if you turned yourself in, and we'll make your death quick."

There was what seemed like forced laughter on the other end of the line.

"You'll have to find me first," said Stratton.

Jason cursed and demanded, "How did you come up as Damien's number? Some sort of technical trick?"

"It's the only way I'd knew you'd answer," replied Stratton. "Besides, you should know by now that I am capable of anything."

"All I know is that you're a dead man," Jason growled. "You've messed up everything. No matter, though. I'm sure we'll find Keira soon enough. Then I'm going to make you both wish that you had never fallen out of line."

He chuckled.

"Though I bet Keira will eventually come to like what I've planned for her. I'll have her begging for me in no time."

"I'm warning you, Jason," Savage told him, his voice almost a growl. "If you put one finger on her, you're dead. My issue is with Damien. If you're smart, you'll get out of this while you have the chance."

Jason laughed.

"You can't touch me, and you know it."

"Last. Warning. Get out while you can," Stratton repeated.

Jason drummed his fingers on the desk. This conversation was already getting boring.

"How about you tell me where Keira is?" Jason asked, more to piss off Stratton than anything else.

"Fat chance in hell," Stratton replied.

"Then I guess this conversation is done."

"I guess it is."

Jason was about to hit the "End Call" button when Stratton said off-handedly, "Tell Veronica that I say 'Hi.'"

Staring at the phone, Jason's eyes widened as he spun around in his desk chair, looking anywhere—everywhere. Stratton somehow had eyes in his office, and the man was toying with him. Of course, the line went dead, so there would be no comeback.

Asshole, Jason thought.

He got up from his desk and tried to casually walk out of his office without seeming alarmed, though he felt uneasy. He didn't like the fact that Stratton had eyes on his office and maybe other places as well. Perhaps he could work from somewhere else for a bit? Jason wasn't the type to take chances.

And he wasn't giving up his way into the Amherst family that easily.

CHAPTER 18

Keira sighed and waited anxiously for her and Logan to arrive at their destination. It was evening, the sky already blackened by winter's early darkness.

She shifted around uncomfortably in her seat. There had been limited stops on their journey, and she was tired of being stuck in a vehicle. It was ironic that she had driven across the United States just to eventually come back to Virginia.

Though the drive hadn't been as tumultuous as her sprint to Montana, she was starting to get sick of being caged up in one place and then another. She was beginning to realize that just because she had escaped her father didn't mean that she was free.

Now, she had essentially a built-in body guard who dictated everything that she did.

Not that she wasn't grateful. She was, but she was looking forward to when this was over. Maybe then she could have some control over her own life.

If this ordeal was ever over, she corrected herself. They were not out of the woods by a long shot.

Unfortunately, she wished that her protector wasn't so damned handsome. That would make working with him a whole lot easier. Despite him being a jerk the night before, she couldn't just shut-off the attraction, no matter how hard she tried. He'd not shaved that morning, and the dark stubble on his face was trying its best to start a beard. For a brief instant, she thought back to how he had rubbed it against her skin in the motel room.

Stop it! She scolded herself. *I don't like him anymore. He doesn't like me. This is just business for him. That's all.*

"We're almost here," Logan said quietly, breaking the silence that had enveloped his truck for the greater part of an hour.

They pulled off a limited-access highway and onto a two-lane road. It was an area that was fairly rural, except for a few houses and businesses sprinkled on both sides.

A few minutes passed, and Logan pulled the truck off the highway, heading into a quaint, old town. Century homes lined the road, some of them turned into bed and breakfasts. Keira couldn't see much commercialization—most of the economic development centered around small shops and charming restaurants. She did spot a small post office with an old fallout shelter sign on it as if the town was stuck in the 1960s.

Yes, this apparently was the town that time forgot.

Peering around, she noticed that almost no one was out and about. Sure, it was winter, but there were no cars driving around and not many lights on in the houses. The place was a ghost town.

"Cape Charles caters to the summer crowd," Logan offered as if reading her mind. "Most of the town clears out after the season is done, and then only the locals are around."

Keira nodded and continued to watch their progress.

The truck slowed at an old white two-story house that looked as if it had been converted into a duplex apartment. There was a large swing on the front porch that looked as if it would be enjoyable on a lazy summer afternoon.

Logan pulled into the gravel driveway and shut off the vehicle.

"Come on," he said as opened the truck door.

She did the same, hopping out into the cold evening air.

Instead of heading toward the darkened duplex, Logan pointed to a small little ranch that sat next to it. Both buildings were a bit shabby on the outside and looked as if they could use a fresh coat of paint.

"This way," he told her.

They walked up to the small house in silence, the winter chill nipping at her face, neck, and hands. There was a light on in the front window, so she figured that there had to be someone home.

When Logan knocked firmly at the door, Keira stood and shivered as she heard footsteps from inside. The door opened, and a short, round gray-haired woman in a well-worn bathrobe peered out at them.

She frowned at first, but then a large grin spread over her face as if she recognized Logan.

"Logan! I wasn't expecting you any time soon!" She exclaimed and immediately pulled him in for a hug.

Keira could feel herself relax as she realized that this person was a friend of Logan's.

After the embrace was over, the woman turned to look at Keira and said, "Oh, my! You brought a girl with you. How rude of me for ignoring her."

She pushed past Logan and gave Keira a dominating hug. It was a surprising gesture from a stranger, but Keira felt oddly at ease.

"Keira, this is Eileen Barber, but everyone calls her 'Momma B.' Her son and I did a couple of tours together in Iraq."

Some of the pieces seemed to fall into place, but Keira still had questions. She had wanted to pry some of the information out of him earlier during the drive, but Logan had been less than talkative.

"Momma B, this is Keira."

"It's nice to meet you," Keira said, trying to smile as best she could.

"I hope we aren't imposing," Logan continued.

Momma B waved her hand in the air and said, "I was just watching TV, dear. Please, come in out of the cold."

She looked Keira up and down.

"Oh, she's white as a ghost and so thin! Let's get you fed as well."

She and Logan were hustled into the small house, which sported knickknacks and bric-a-brac galore along with prominent pictures of a young man in uniform. They cut through a small living room with floral print on almost everything to the back of the home where there was a dated kitchen and small dinette table.

Momma B gestured for her and Logan to sit.

"Let me warm up some casserole for you both," she said, scurrying around the kitchen.

As she warmed up a pan and set plates and silverware around the table, Logan asked, "I know this is super short notice, but would you mind if we crashed the duplex for a bit?"

The older woman smiled and replied, "I told you that you could drop in any time after tourist season is over, and during the summer, you can have it if you give me a few months' notice. Honestly, I kind of figured you wanted to stay there when I found you on my doorstep with that one."

She pointed at Keira.

"I was hoping that she was your girlfriend, but I have a suspicion that she's actually a client. What kind of top-secret mischief are you up to now, Logan?"

Keira was startled to hear that Momma B knew at least somewhat about Logan's choice of profession. Looking over at Logan, Keira raised an eyebrow questioningly.

He shrugged and said, "It's impossible to lie to Momma B, so I don't try."

He turned to the older woman.

"I would be forever grateful if we could stay on one of the sides, and I would also appreciate your discretion on this."

Momma B made a zipper motion across her mouth and said, "My lips are sealed, sweetheart. And you don't owe me a thing. You were like a brother to Jacob."

Keira pondered that statement for a moment and found herself blurting out, "*Were* like a brother?"

Momma B seemed to falter for a moment as she carried heaping plates of food to the table.

Logan cleared his throat and told her, "He died in Iraq on my third tour."

"Oh my, that was so rude of me..." Keira began, but the older woman waved her hand in the air, dismissing the apology.

"Not to worry, dear," Momma B said as she gently sat the food down in front of them. "It's been some time since Jacob's death. I don't think anyone ever really gets over losing a child, but time does help with the emotions."

Keira nodded, and they began to dig in to their feast. It was the first real home-cooked meal she had eaten in ages, and it was delicious.

Small talk went back and forth between them, and Keira started to feel a bit more at ease again. The adrenaline of being chased down by her father had dissipated somewhat, and now all she felt was exhaustion.

After they had finished, Logan began discussing their arrangements with Momma B.

"I'll want to park the truck in the back where it won't be seen from the road, and if the duplex doesn't have thick curtains, I'll want to put some up. The place shouldn't be occupied, and I don't want to draw unnecessary attention to ourselves if we don't have to."

"There's a covering in the back that's empty right now because the golf cart is being repaired, so you can park there with no problem."

"Golf cart?" Keira asked, mildly amused.

Momma B shrugged.

"The tourists like the tool around in it, and I like to use it for short trips around town."

Keira wriggled her nose and smiled at the thought of Momma B cruising around the quaint little town in a golf cart.

"As for the windows," Momma B continued, "I already have extremely thick curtains up. I kept getting complaints that it got too light too early in the morning by some of my guests when I first bought the place."

"Good," Logan said, nodding.

"Let me get the keys, and I'll show you to your place. Does it matter which side you want to be on?"

"Closest to where the truck is parked works best," Logan replied.

Momma B smiled and said, "Okay, then. Let me show you to your humble abode."

* * *

Miles Bryant stared at the report and silently cursed at himself. How could this have happened? The Ohio safe house had been ambushed. Bryant had a leak somewhere in his organization, and it pissed him off to no end. Not only that, but one of his employees had been seriously injured in the fire fight.

When the call came in, Jack had immediately turned around and went back to the house. By that time, the Amherst people had already left, and he had to deal with critical injuries. There was no time to chase off after them.

Jack had been the one to call in the ambulance, while Miles had a clean-up crew working the area. Local authorities had been told to stay the hell out of it. Miles had some friends in high up places in federal law enforcement. The mess would be dealt with discreetly.

Miles' phone lit up, and he answered it immediately. It was Jack's number.

"How are we doing?" Miles asked, trying not to let the anxiety show in his voice.

This had been the first real clusterfuck since Gray Tower had started. Most missions went smoothly. Most clients were happy, and even the ones who weren't satisfied were usually the ones who would never be pleased no matter what.

"I still haven't heard from Logan since I got the "okay" code in a text," Jack said, his voice tense.

He was finally on his way back to headquarters, since he had to deal with clean-up most of the day.

"But I still haven't heard anything since. Wherever he's at, his phone is off."

"I'm assuming he went dark," Miles replied. "And that's probably a smart move, considering that Amherst apparently has a mole here. When you get here, report to me immediately, and we can go from there."

"Sure, I'll see you in a couple of hours."

The line went dead, and a twang of guilt went through Miles. It was already late evening, and Jack would probably be exhausted when he got here. But the guy had also been Special Forces, and he could handle himself in stressful circumstances. Besides, Logan and Miss Amherst were in danger, and Miles would pull every resource possible to get this mole taken care of. Then he would go after the bastards that infiltrated his organization and gotten one of his men hurt.

Damien Amherst's time was now limited because Miles would come down so hard on the man that the pompous bastard wouldn't see it coming. The Amherst Global mission was now priority number one.

Picking up his phone again, he dialed for Brenden.

"What's up, boss-man?" Came the voice from the other end.

"I'm pulling you off any kind of operative duty support. Your main goal right now is to plug that leak. Figure out who and how. That is the number one priority. I have faith in Logan to protect Miss Amherst. In the meantime, I'll deal with clean-up."

"Sure. Okay," Brenden replied, ending the call.

Miles shook his head as he stood from his desk to get another cup of coffee, but he was startled to see Alex standing in the doorway with a large coffee mug in each hand. She smiled wearily.

"I thought you might like some," she told him, looking exhausted.

"You must have read my mind," he told her as he strolled over to take the steaming mug from her.

"I figured that if I'm tired, you must be as well," she said simply.

He nodded.

"You need to get some rest," he told her, scanning her weary posture.

"If Jack is going to be up working all night, then I should be there too."

Miles shook his head.

"Jack was Special Forces, Alex. That's what he does. You, on the other hand, need some sleep. Go at least take a cat nap for me, alright?"

She attempted a smile and said, "Fine."

Before she left, she handed him her mug of coffee as well saying, "You're probably going to need this one as well."

CHAPTER 19

Momma B unlocked one side of the duplex and led Logan and Keira into the home. Keira surveyed the place and thought that it was rather nice. They had come in around the back into a small but nice kitchen with white cabinetry. There was a full bathroom next to it, decorated in blues and whites.

Keira also noticed a built-in booth in the small dinette space right beside the kitchen. It had red leather cushions that reminded her of a retro diner.

The kitchen and dinette opened into a living room with a well-worn leather couch and a small television that hung on the wall. A narrow set of stairs dissected the space between the living room and kitchen. The place was decorated with nautical touches: pictures of sailboats, sea-shell knickknacks, and a soft blue tone on the walls.

It was a cozy little space, and Keira wished that they were there under better circumstances. The place would have been perfect during the summer season.

She watched as Logan went from window to window, pulling curtains, as well as checking the locks on the doors. Meanwhile, Momma B put some food in the refrigerator, checked on necessities like toilet paper, and did some dusting.

"I'll do a better clean tomorrow and get you some more food," she promised Keira. "The place was cleaned when the last guests of the season left, but obviously there has been an accumulation of dust and whatnot."

"There's no need..." Keira began to say, but Momma B cut her off.

"You're my guest, even under these circumstances, so I'm going to make sure that you have a nice stay—all things considered.

"Oh! It's going to take a moment for the place to warm up. I only keep the furnace going enough to keep the pipes from freezing."

Keira nodded, watching Logan traverse the narrow staircase to go upstairs. A few moments later, he was back down, his expression was all business-like.

"Do you mind keeping Keira company, while I get my bags?" Logan asked the older woman.

"Of course, I don't mind!" Momma B replied. "Come, Keira, let's see if we can make some tea. I think it's probably too late for coffee."

The two women went through the process of making tea, while Logan came in and out of the house with a bunch of large bags. After he was done, he began unpacking and checking the items on his bags, weapons included. Keira watched him as Momma B chatted on about how she wished that they had come during the summer so that they could visit the beach.

Keira nodded and tried to follow the conversation, but she felt her mind drifting off. A mix of emotions seemed to overwhelm her as she found herself glancing over at where Logan was at in the living room. The last few days had been chaotic, and she just wanted the day to end. She was exhausted, but she was also still pissed.

Damn him, she thought as she watched as Logan went through his preparations.

She almost thought that he was doing it just to waste time, so he didn't have to talk to her. He seemed hell bent on avoiding her at this point, which should have been okay with Keira except for the fact that she was still really attracted to him.

Really, how could she not? The man was gorgeous, and it was hard not to stare at his chiseled jaw-line, piercing gray eyes, or completely ripped body.

Keira sighed. She might not be happy with the current situation, but at least she was away from her father, which at this point, was the best scenario for her.

"I should go," Momma B said. "I'll check on you tomorrow morning, and we'll see if we can't get this kitchen stocked properly."

"Okay," Keira said as Momma B got up and walked to the back door.

Keira followed.

Before Momma B left, she squeezed Keira's arm and said, "It'll be okay. Logan will take good care of you."

"I know," Keira said, and she meant it.

She knew deep down that regardless of any sexual tension between her and Logan, he would protect her at all costs. He had already shown that he would, and she never doubted that he would do it again if necessary.

Suddenly alone with Logan, she turned around and eyed him from across the room. He was checking the handgun that he usually wore on his shoulder holster. A rifle sat next to him on the coffee table as well as a few magazines. She wasn't quite sure if this was what badasses like Logan Slade did, or if he was still stalling. Perhaps it was a little bit of both?

Logan suddenly turned toward her and said, "Look, I'm sorry that things have turned out this way, but it's the only option that I have right now. We're completely cut off from Gray Tower."

Keira walked into the living room and began to bite her lower lip absentmindedly.

"I'm just very grateful that I am away from my father right now," she told him. "But it's been a long day, and I'd like to turn in for the night."

"Sure," he said, looking back down at his weapons.

As she began to navigate the narrow steps—a characteristic of an older home—she heard him call out, "Take the back bedroom next to the bathroom."

"Okay, sure," she mumbled as she headed upstairs.

The back bedroom was small and had just a twin bed, a nightstand, and a dresser. There was the smell of mustiness as if the house had been shut up for a while. Keira noticed that there weren't any sheets on the bed, so she went in search of linens.

It didn't take long to pull a set of twin sheets and a comforter out from the closet, so she did up the bed. Wondering if the other bedrooms were like hers, she went off to see their condition.

The two other bedrooms—the other smaller one next to hers and what looked to be the master bedroom in the front—also did not have sheets. She wasn't sure which bedroom Logan would choose, so she started putting linens on in the smaller room and then to the master.

She was almost done pulling the comforter over the queen-sized bed in the master when she felt a presence behind her.

"I thought I told you to take the bedroom in the back," Logan said, his voice icy.

He stood in the doorway, his expression darkened. His large frame filled up the entryway, giving Keira a feeling that she was trapped. For a moment, Logan frightened her. This was the man who had tied her up and threatened her with a knife not that many days ago. She dropped the comforter and took a step back.

"Keira, damn it. You need to listen to my directions."

She huffed and shook her head, trying to hold back tears.

"I was just putting on sheets for you," she mumbled, avoiding eye contact with him. "I'll go back to my room now."

She tried to push past him in the doorway, but he caught her arm with his hand.

"Keira, wait," he said, his voice much softer now.

"Let me go," she told him firmly.

She was tired of not having any control over her life, and she wasn't in the mood to deal with a grumpy Logan right now. He already brooded enough without him being pissed at her. She was beginning to think that even though he might be attracted to her, he didn't actually like her.

Logan stared at her, his expression unreadable. A shiver ran down Keira's spine as his grip on her arm seemed to burn her skin. The man could certainly be intense when he wanted to be, and she hated that she had such a reaction to him.

"Keira..." he said again, trailing off as he loomed over her.

He didn't look angry anymore. There was some other expression on his face that she couldn't quite read.

"I'm sorry," he said huskily. "I didn't mean to jump down your throat. It's just that today when those men came to take you...I don't know what I'd do with myself if you were captured or if that Jason Savage bastard had his hands on you."

She blinked in surprise. This wasn't how she expected this conversation to go.

"I thought that I was just a job for you," she said softly. "Just a distraction."

"Then I'm sorry if I let you believe that for a second," he said, stepping closer so that their bodies barely brushed together in the doorway. "I was actively trying to push you away because I honestly thought that it would be best to get you on your way and to your new life. I didn't want to complicate it, but I guess I probably just made things worse."

Keira stared at him, not sure what to say. She was still pissed at him. Or was she? She had no idea anymore.

"So, I'm not just some fragile girl?" She asked pointedly. "I'm not allowing adrenaline to run my emotions, then? And are you still not the type to settle down?"

A flicker of emotion splashed across his unshaven face. He looked upset, maybe even regretful.

"That's not what I meant. Damn it. I'm sorry," he said bringing his free hand to touch her other arm. "You're the most amazing woman I've ever met. You've endured so much, and yet you've always pushed on, without complaint—I might add. I didn't want to pursue anything physical with you because deep down..."

Logan trailed off and shook his head.

"Deep down?" Keira whispered.

"Deep down I knew from the moment that you stumbled into my cabin that I..." He stopped midsentence and shut his eyes.

Releasing his grip from her arms he backed away.

"Never mind. Go get some rest."

Keira stood in the doorway, not sure what to say or do. What had he been about to reveal? Her emotions felt raw right now, and she decided to leave while she had the chance.

"Good night," she said, her voice barely as whisper as she fled to the sanctuary of her own room.

* * *

Logan stared up at the ceiling in the room he had chosen for himself—the smaller bedroom right next to Keira's—and tried to figure out what the hell was wrong with him. This morning's events had apparently made him crazy, and he had almost let it slip his true feelings for her.

The fact of the matter was that he was in love with her.

He had made this revelation while driving her to Virginia. Logan had spent most of that time beating himself up for not being able to protect Keira like he should have been able to. He had no idea how he could have lived with himself if something had happened to her.

Logan had realized that he cared for her more than he could have imagined. Keira had somehow gotten to him in a way that no woman ever had, and it scared the shit out of him. He knew that he wasn't the type for a family; his time with his parents had beat that out of him. Keira deserved so much more than he could offer.

Yet, he couldn't stand the thought of letting her go after this was all over.

That was *if* they survived all of this.

The situation was dire, and Logan had been nervous about coming to Momma B's doorstep. If they were found out, there could be serious consequences for their hostess as well. He hoped that they wouldn't have to stay long, but he was running out of options. If he could wait long enough and keep it in his pants, Gray Tower might be able to find the leak and get them to a safe place.

That was wishful thinking, though, so Logan was planning on hiding as long as necessary.

Logan tossed to his side as his thoughts went back to Keira. He couldn't get her out of his head, and the massive hard-on that was straining against his boxer-briefs was a testament to that. The fact that he knew she was attracted to him didn't help, but he also knew that she was pretty pissed with him—something that Logan completely understood.

Still, he knew that there was a shit load of chemistry between them. Did it even matter that there was no way they could ever end up together? He had certainly never considered this with any other woman he had casually bedded. But none of those women had ever come close to Keira—not in looks, intelligence, class, or character.

A soft noise from beyond the wall to Keira's room broke his thoughts. Logan sat up straight in bed and listened closely. Another sound came, but this time it was much louder and sounded like she was crying out.

He bolted from the bed, not bothering with pants, and crossed into the hallway in just his underwear. Her door was shut, but not locked as he quickly twisted the knob and swung it open.

The room was lighter than his as Keira had pulled the curtains in her room back to let in some moonlight. She was in bed and apparently still asleep. Nothing appeared to be wrong, except that she was beginning to toss and turn. A moan escaped her lips, and she cried out again.

Another nightmare, Logan thought, as he walked to the bed and sat down next to her.

"Hey," he said softly, trying to sound non-threatening. "Keira, wake up, sweetheart. It's just a dream."

She tossed and turned a few more moments before her movements in the bed turned more violent. Logan reached out and caught her body, pulling her up so that she was sitting up in his arms. He held her for a moment until her eyes open, and she let out a gasp.

"Logan," She whispered and stilled instantly.

"It's okay," he told her repeatedly as his hand stroked her hair.

She leaned against him and began sobbing onto his shoulder, hot tears falling carelessly onto his bare skin. His arms wrapped around her and held her tightly, the feeling of her being nuzzled against him making his chest tighten with emotion. He cursed silently at her father for doing this to her. Keira tried to keep it in and make it look like she had it all together on the outside, but Logan knew that it was a front. She was scared, and she certainly had reason to be.

Logan held her for a long while, just allowing her to cry it out. More than anything, he wanted her to feel safe, and he'd do anything to keep her that way, even if that meant laying down his own life.

He blinked at that unexpected thought and stared down at her. The notion wasn't just because of his position in Gray Tower. Right now, he didn't care about his job there. He just wanted to make sure that Keira stayed out of harm's way.

Not only that, but he wasn't intending on leaving her any time soon. Fuck wherever Gray Tower sent her. He'd be right by her side.

For the first time in a long time, Logan stopped playing out the future in his head and concentrated on right now. And right now, he had a gorgeous woman in his arms who was...

Fuck, he thought as he looked down at her.

She was braless in a thin white tank top that she had been wearing underneath her sweater. She also had no pants on, covered only by lacy panties, the same ones that he had pulled off her the night that she stumbled into his cabin.

His body seemed to involuntarily react to her, his heart racing while his dick strained against the material of his underwear. Logan was suddenly thankful that there was a button snap that covered the front, or he would be in bigger trouble than he already was.

Keira shifted her body closer to his and must has felt his hard-on because she pulled back suddenly, tear-streaked face confused. Logan felt his hand involuntarily brush the tears away from her face. He cupped her face with his hands and bent his head, barely brushing his lips against hers.

Logan was tired of fighting this attraction. Mainly, he was just plain tired. Regardless, when he pulled away, he watched her closely for a reaction. Even in the dim moonlight, he could her eyes darken with desire.

He was now a goner, Logan realized. He was totally and completely fucked—his control lost.

Logan bent his head again, but instead of a gentle kiss, his lips claimed hers in a fierce and passionate embrace. Keira responded with a soft sigh and parted her mouth to deepen the kiss. She tasted amazing, and Logan found himself drawing his tongue into her mouth in slow, methodical thrusts. He found himself savoring each kiss as they enjoyed each other, but damn did he want more.

Lust shot through him as he deepened the kiss, his hands griping the back her head. He took his kisses away from her mouth, first to the shell of one of her ears where she let out a gasp at the sensation. Logan kissed further down her ear, biting at her earlobe before he moved down to her neck. She gave him access, turning her head and sighing as he continued his onslaught.

Then, his hands found their way to the hem of her shirt. They slipped under quickly as he found her soft breasts.

They were firm and fit nicely in his hands, and she let out a little moan when he cupped them. His thumbs peaked her nipples as his kisses continued on her neck.

He still couldn't quite get enough of her.

"Shirt. Off," he mumbled into her skin.

Logan began pulling the soft cotton tank up her torso, and Keira complied by raising her arms. Her tank was flung to the floor, and for a moment, Logan could only gaze and admire her beautiful body which was accentuated by the moonlight.

"You're so damned gorgeous," he told her, his voice low.

He laid her gently down on the bed and spent just a moment on admiring her perfect breasts. His cock was rock-hard and straining to be freed from the confines of his boxer-briefs, yet he just wanted to savior this moment. How much time had he spent fantasizing about seeing her like this again? If he hadn't been so bull-headed, she would have been his much sooner, he realized.

Keira's beautiful dusty pink nipples were begging for attention, so Logan hovered over her and lowered his mouth to one sensitive peak. She moaned and arched her back into him as he sucked and laved. Then, he did the same to the other breast. Keira bucked into his body, and he could feel the folds of her sex rub against his erection.

Damn it, if she kept that shit up, he was going to come right then and there.

Her fingers began to slowly slide down the ridges of his body, first down his encircling arms and then along his chest to the edge of his underwear. She began to tug at the fabric, but he caught her hands. Logan felt his breath hitch and his dick strained to be released from the confines of his underwear.

"You first, sweetheart," he told her as he reached down to the edge of her underwear and began to tug.

Logan pulled her panties down across her creamy thighs and along her perfect, long legs. A soft triangle of curls guarded her sex. His mouth went dry as he slowly slid his fingers inch by inch up her legs and to her inner thighs. He heard her breath catch as he slid his fingers ever so gently across the folds of her sex and to her clit.

His fingers circled lazily around the sensitive bud as he lowered his head and continued to suckle her breasts. She arched into him, parting her legs for better access, a low moan escaping her lips. He lazily moved his fingers around her clit and then down to her pussy, feeling hot, slick moisture. She was certainly ready for him, but he found himself wanted to prolong this moment.

He lifted his head to watch her expression. Her eyes were closed, her mouth parted as another soft moan escaped her mouth. Her hands gripped his biceps tightly as she grinded her mound against his palm, seeking release.

Oh, he would give her that release, alright. Just not yet. Logan wanted this to be special for her. He couldn't predict what tomorrow would be, but for tonight, he could make things perfect.

Logan slowly inserted a finger into her, and she let out a soft sigh. Her inner muscles clenching around him, her pussy soaked with arousal.

Damn, she was tight. His dick strained with anticipation, but it wasn't quite time yet. He wanted so badly to taste her. He wanted this to be so good for her.

Logan trailed his kisses lower across her smooth, flat belly and down to her mound. He kissed around the soft folds of her sex as his finger gently thrusted into her in slow, methodical motion. His lips met her clit as he gave it the softest of kisses before he began to suck and lave at it.

Keira gasped and arched against his mouth. Her flavor was ambrosia to his tongue. Logan could get lost in her.

He relinquished his finger from her pussy and stroked his tongue down her soft folds, invading her entrance with his mouth. She gasped, and her body strained against his mouth.

Damn it, he couldn't hold out any longer. His cock was straining, and if he didn't bury himself in her pussy soon, it might be all over before anything really got started.

CHAPTER 20

Keira was lost in the sensation of Logan's mouth on her pussy. Electric sensations moved across her womb as she worked closer toward her release. His mouth was magic, pushing her toward the edge.

More. She wanted more. She wanted all of him.

His mouth just wasn't enough. Her pussy ached to be filled, and suddenly she needed him to fill that emptiness.

It wasn't even just a physical void but an emotional one as well. How long had she been isolated from the rest of the world? How long had it been since she had been around someone she could trust? Keira trusted Logan, and she wanted him so badly it hurt.

When she had woken up from another one of her nightmares about her father to have Logan's arms around her, she had felt herself come undone right then and there. She felt safe with him. All her worries and cares disappeared when she was around him. Keira supposed that it was silly since she only had known the man for a few days, yet she couldn't deny how she felt about him, even if he had been pushing her away from the start.

"You taste so damned good," he murmured into her, his voice low and husky.

The whiskers of his unshaven face rubbed erotically against her thighs as he continued to suck and lick his way around her pussy. Her hands grasped his strong biceps as he worked, sensuous pressure building in her womb.

"Please," she whispered, arching against him. "I need...more."

She didn't quite know how to verbalize that she wanted him inside of her without sounding desperate or awkward.

His gray eyes flicked up to hers. They darkened with desire as he finished one more slow, agonizing stroke of his tongue across her clit.

Keira felt her face grow hot as he gazed intensely at her. She hoped that she didn't have to beg.

Logan stood up suddenly from the bed and slowly shucked his underwear. His cock sprang free, and Keira felt her mouth go dry as she studied his big, beautiful body.

Strong, broad shoulders and a well-defined chest ran down to a six pack and a stunning erection that stood almost to his belly button. The light dusting of hair that fell across his chest and belly highlighted the ruggedness of his body.

His penis strained upward, extending from a mat of dark hair at his groin. Logan's shaft was veined and thick as well as long. His testicles hung heavy and large from the base. Solid legs and thighs extended down, dusted by black leg hair.

He was purely male and radiated testosterone. She had never seen a more handsome man, and at least for tonight, she knew he was hers.

Logan moved toward the bed again and slowly climbed on top of her. His body should have felt incredibly heavy over hers, but he used his arms to prop himself up over her. She could feel his silky erection against her skin, and her womb clenched with anticipation.

Keira reached down and stroked the smooth shaft up to the tip of his head where she felt a droplet of precum and back down to the base. He made a low grown and stared at her like she was the most desirable woman in the world. At that moment, she certainly felt that way.

"Keira," he breathed, "if I don't get inside you soon..."

She pulled his head in for a soft kiss, tasting the essence of herself on his lips. It was erotic and heady, and her mind started to wonder about how he would taste.

"Logan," she moaned into his lips as she embraced his kiss.

Keira felt his body hover over hers. He wasn't pressing his entire weight on her, but she could feel his massive form cover her body. It wasn't an oppressive feeling; it made her feel delightfully secure and safe.

She could feel his penis pressing at her entrance, waiting to penetrate her. A sudden grip of fear jolted through her. How long had it been since she had had sex? It had been years, and she had only had one partner, an encounter that had been a mistake. Being the young, naïve virgin, Keira found the experience to be uncomfortable to say the least. She had then focused on her academics since that time. Would it hurt this time like it had the last?

Keira grimaced at the thought of it.

"What's wrong?" Logan asked, his expression full of concern.

His body was so warm against hers, but she could feel a sudden strain through his muscles that seemed to spread from his arms all the way along his torso, down to his legs as he hovered over her.

"It's nothing," she said, suddenly embarrassed.

She could feel heat burn through her face, wondering if he could sense of inexperience.

"There's got to be something," he told her. "Is this something that you want?"

Yes. Yes. Yes. Yes.

Keira couldn't think of anything she wanted more than this.

"Yes," she said, trying to boost some confidence in her voice. "It's just...been a while for me."

Duh, of course it has. She had been locked away for two years. Why did she feel the need to state the obvious?

"I know it has, sweetheart. That's why we're going to take this nice and slow."

She found Logan's promise at least somewhat reassuring, although he was probably thinking two years of abstinence when it really had been much, much longer.

"Is that okay?" He asked.

"Yes."

Logan planted the gentlest of kisses across her forehead, a move that sent shivers down her spine. She would have never thought that Logan Slade, the badass, would be a considerate and gentle lover. Keira hadn't quite known what to expect, but he certainly had surprised her.

With that, his body lowered closer to hers and his cock pressed tightly into her entrance. She let out of a gasp as he slowly entered her, filling her womb inch by inch until she could feel nothing but fullness. There wasn't any pain this time, but he had taken his time.

Then he pressed forward one final time as he entered her fully. She let out a small cry, not one of pain but of absolute pleasure that the fullness of his cock created inside of her. For the moment, she would have been just satisfied with them staying just like that.

"Damn it, you're tight," Logan groaned as he trailed kissed down her neck.

He pulled one of her legs and hooked it across his tight, muscled ass and slowly ground his pelvis into her clit, driving deep. She cried out as pleasure radiated in her womb.

Then, he slowly withdrew and repeated the deliberate and unhurried stroke again and again. The man knew exactly what he was doing.

Keira felt lost in the sensation as she gripped Logan's large biceps, trying to keep herself steady from his strong, slow thrusts. Nothing had ever felt so good, and she wanted this moment to last forever as she felt her orgasm build slowly in her womb.

"Do you know how fucking good you feel?" Logan said huskily into her ear as he began to nibble on the lobe.

She wasn't sure if he was asking or if the question was rhetorical. Regardless, she could only moan in response as he continued to pump into her.

"Do you know how long I've been fanaticizing about this very moment?" He continued. "Ever since you stumbled into my cabin, I've wanted to do this."

Me too, she thought, remembering back to the first time she had seen him without a shirt.

He had been sexy as hell then, and now he had her body humming with pleasure with each agonizing stroke.

The pressure in her clit built up to the point of no return, and Keira's body clenched and tightened, spiraling over into wave after wave of pleasure. Logan held his position, pushing all the way into her pussy as he let her ride out her orgasm.

He kissed her lightly on the lips while she got her bearing straight. Keira stared up at him, breathing hard, her body glowing with pleasure. She had sadly never orgasmed with a man, and now she was wondering what the hell she should do. Her pussy and clit seemed suddenly ultra-sensitive, all the while

"Hey, are you with me?" He asked, his voice low and incredibly sexy.

She nodded slowly, not sure what to say or do.

Luckily, she didn't have to decide. Logan took control immediately, beginning fast and deep, almost desperate thrusts. Keira gasped at the sensation, her libido, which she thought was spent, now revving back to life.

Instead of the long, lazy movement of before, Logan now plowed into her with such strength that it nearly took her breath away. The speed and force of his thrusts created new sensations in her pussy that she had never felt before.

"Oh!" She cried out as he continued his onslaught.

Logan bent in for a fierce kiss on the lips as he continued. Blood drummed through Keira's head as she felt *another* orgasm building.

"Come for me again, sweetheart," Logan said, almost growling.

Her nails dug into his biceps as she let go for another time, but this time, as Logan pushed harder. As her orgasm began to subside, she suddenly felt him pull out completely from her and then felt hot semen spray across her belly. Then his body shuddered a bit and collapsed next to hers.

It took Keira a moment to realize what was really happening because she was so elated from a second, unexpected orgasm. Then she crept back to reality: he hadn't worn a condom. Not just that, but she had known to begin with and hadn't cared. What the hell had she been thinking?

She hadn't been thinking. That was the problem.

At least Logan had had the insight to pull out, but still...

"Hey," Logan said, his voice soft and low.

Keira's attention snapped back to the incredibly hot man lying next to her, and she pushed her worries to the back of her mind.

His head bent down to gently kiss her lips, and her heart fluttered, despite the intimacy that they had just shared.

"I'll be right back," he murmured against her lips when the kiss finished.

She watched as he got up from the bed and padded butt-naked across the room in the low light. Logan seemed unabashed as his muscular body moved out of the room, his penis hanging heavy, still slightly erect.

A few brief moments later and he reappeared with a damp washcloth in his hands. Logan knelt beside her and wiped his seed from her belly. Setting the washcloth aside, he moved in and kissed her again softly.

"I'm sorry that I didn't use a condom. I'm an idiot, and I put you at risk."

"It's alright," Keira told him.

"No, it's not. I'm more responsible than that. I mean, I'm clean, but I could have gotten you..."

Keira reached out and touched a finger to his lips, hushing him.

"I don't want to think about the future right now," she told him. "I just want to think about now."

Logan looked hesitant but finally nodded.

"Sure."

Keira nuzzled into his arms, feeling him relax at her touch. She was getting drowsy, post-coitus, and felt her eyelids get heavy.

"You should sleep, if you can," Logan said softly. "I have no idea what tomorrow brings."

"Okay," she said softly, her eyes fluttering shut.

It didn't take long for sleep to overtake her. And for once, Keira felt safe and secure.

* * *

Alex rubbed her temples and tried to concentrate on the HR reports on her desk. She had been sifting through person after person, trying to figure out if they had a disgruntled employee in their midst. So far, she hadn't seen anything, but that didn't mean that she should stop trying. This was a slow, tedious process, and so far, she hadn't been getting any results.

It didn't help that Miles was playing this one close to his chest. Only he, Alex, Jack, and Brenden were in the loop. They certainly didn't want to scare of whoever was leaking the information, so support staff weren't going to be able to help.

That made Alex think of how they were going to go through the IT side of operations. Just having Brenden go through everything wasn't going to cut it. Perhaps she could hire in a consultant, but who could Gray Tower hire who would be trustworthy enough with that much sensitive data?

Alex continued to rub around her head, including her eyes which were growing bleary from looking at so much text for such a long period of time. She needed more coffee, but she was already feeling jittery from her last cup. It felt like she had been given an impossible task, and what she really needed was some help.

Some help...

An idea formed in her head that Alex began to like the more she thought about it. She did indeed know someone who could help them out and who was completely trustworthy.

Alex had a friend who she had known since high school. Katherina Langely—or Kat, as she liked to be called—was one of the smartest people Alex knew when it came to IT. Alex wasn't one hundred percent sure what field Kat specialized in, but she thought it might be network security. Kat worked mostly contract work for big companies. Her expertise was sought out, and it might be possible for Gray Tower to hire her for this project if Kat wasn't swamped with work for another company.

Flipping through her contacts, Alex worked quickly to find Kat's number. She might as well check to see if her friend was even up to it before broaching the subject with Miles.

Alex hit the dial button on her screen and hoped that it wasn't too early for Kat. The last time that they had talked, she had been on a weird schedule because she was working with a global company that had Kat up at all hours. Alex certainly could relate as she yawned and reached for her coffee.

"Hey," said the voice from the other end of the line after a few rings. "This must be serious because you never call me this early."

"Hi, Kat," Alex replied. "Yeah, this is a business call."

"I figured as much. What's up?"

"I have a contract offer for you, if you're up to it," Alex said.

"Oh, what are the details? Something fun?"

Alex rubbed her temples, thinking of the huge mess they were trying to sort out at Gray Tower.

"Depends on your definition of fun," Alex replied with a sigh.

"You sound tired. This must be serious." Kat noted.

"Unfortunately, it is," Alex agreed.

She spent some time filling Kat in on the basic details of what was going on. When she was through, Kat's tone had changed considerably.

"Look, I'll take it. I'm in between jobs right now. And you know I'm good enough that I will find out if someone is monkeying around on your network."

"Good," Alex said, feeling a bit of relief. They could get somewhere with Kat looking into things. "I'll forward you all of the contract stuff once I get this all approved. It shouldn't take long, though. This has to move fast if we want to stop this leak."

"I understand. Can I remote in or would you like me to come there?"

"Come here, please. We'll get you transportation immediately. This is highest priority for us."

"Okay then. Well, I guess I'll see you when I see you."

Alex breathed a sigh of relief.

"Thank you, Kat. It will be good to see you in person again. It's been too long."

"Yeah it has," Kat agreed.

By the time Alex was done with her phone call, she was feeling better with how things were going. Kat was amazing. She could do what others just couldn't.

There was a little pang of regret when Alex thought of Brenden. She wasn't sure how he'd handle being given help as he was pretty cocky about his skills. Hopefully, he could be a team player and help Kat. In the meantime, Alex tried to figure out how to break it to him gently.

CHAPTER 21

Logan slept deeply for the first time in a long time. He was certain it had something to do with the warm body lying next to him. As the early morning hours crept by, he dozed, content with the world for at least that moment. But as more time passed, he started to wake and felt restless. It had nothing to do with the danger that they were trying to dodge. It had everything to do with the naked woman sleeping next to him.

Keira slept next to him, using his left bicep as a pillow, her long and lean body slung against him. Neither of them had bothered to put on clothes, so he was able to admire her gloriously naked body.

Logan felt a bit guilty as he watched her sleep, knowing that he wanted more from her as soon as possible. His dick was already hard from morning wood, and it was growing harder by the second as his gaze went down her naked form.

He felt even more guilty when his mouth met hers and began to kiss those wonderous lips. There was no response at first, but after a few moments, he could feel her breath change as she woke up to his kiss.

She began to respond with a soft sigh as he kissed her deeply, allowing his tongue to begin to explore her now open mouth. Keira reacted, moving her tongue against his in a long, slow kiss.

When he pulled back, he watched her eyes flutter open.

All Logan could say was, "Hey."

"Hey," she said back, smiling and then nuzzling into his neck and along his chin, where his beard had begun to grow.

Logan stared down at her. She was the most beautiful woman he had ever seen: a classic beauty in every way. The fact that he had been inside her the night before only heightened his view of her.

"What if I said that I needed more of you?" Logan asked, his voice low.

Keira nuzzled against him closer and pressed her body against his. She must have obviously felt his growing erection.

"Yes, please," she mumbled into the skin of his neck.

Logan rolled over her, dick throbbing. Lying on top of her, he felt powerful, lustful, and almost giddy with excitement. Keira was the embodiment of the perfect woman for him, and he wanted to have her in every way possible.

"I should go get a condom," the logical side of him blurted out suddenly.

The look on Keira's face wavered for a moment, then looked more confident.

"No," she said softly. "I want all of you."

Ah, damn it, he thought.

This woman was going to be the end of him.

"Are you sure?" He asked.

Sure, there were alarm bells going on in his head, but currently, he didn't care. He wasn't concerned about the future. He just wanted the here and now.

"Yes," she said and raised her head to kiss him.

Ah, damn, damn, damn, he thought again.

Logan wasn't exactly sure if he could make this time as special as their first. Last night had been amazing, and he wasn't sure if he could recreate that moment. There was an underlying urgency to this morning that he was aware of. They had to get up. They had to face the day. Momma B would be coming by soon.

And yet, all he wanted to do was be lost in her.

That was exactly what he did.

His fingers traced her body slowly down, down, down, until they felt the wet folds of her pussy. One finger found her clit, while another pushed into her, testing her readiness. He was happy to find that she was hot and wet and ready for him. Just for fun, he plunged his finger back and forth into her, mimicking what he would be doing do her in just a few moments.

Small moans escaped her mouth, and she bucked into hands, trying to find her pleasure. He smiled, knowing that he could give her that satisfaction.

When he pulled his finger out, he moved on top of her, readying his cock at her entrance. It only took a few movements before he was inside her. Tight, liquid heat surrounded him, and he became lost in the pleasure of thrusting into her.

He tried to go slow, rubbing his pelvis against her clit when he could, which made her clench and moan beneath him. However, he didn't think he'd last too long. She felt too fucking good.

Moving like a piston, he pumped into her until she was whispering out his name. And then, he continued harder until he felt her release around him. Then he plowed into her until he could feel his release tighten in his balls. Pulling out quickly, he ejaculated over her lower belly and collapsed beside her.

After a moment of silence, he heard her say, "Mm..." The sound of her trailing off into contentment.

"Are you alright?" He asked softly.

"Yes," she whispered and nuzzled into his torso.

"Good," he said, a smile slowly crossing his face.

He bent down to kiss her deeply, his heart pounding as their lips met. Even after having sex with her, Logan couldn't quite get enough of her.

Once their kiss ended, he quickly got up to grab a towel from the bathroom and wiped her stomach clean.

When Logan laid back down against her, he knew it was time for some serious talk.

"Everything just changed between us," he began. "You understand this, right?"

"I do," Keira said, closing her eyes for a moment, weary to the world.

"I don't know how my effectiveness at protecting you has changed at this point," he continued. "Everything is all screwed up."

"I know," she said softly.

"I'll do my best, though. Do you understand?"

Keira nodded slowly and then wrapped her arms around him. They lay there like that for a moment in silence before she spoke up again.

"I want you to tell me something about yourself that I don't know," she said. "I feel like we've been intimate physically, but you've been distant in every other angle."

Logan sighed as he began to realize that he wasn't going to get around his past with Keira. She was too smart to ignore his defensive measures when it came to all of that emotional shit.

"What do you want to know?" He asked, wondering what trouble he was about to get himself in.

"I don't know. Just tell me a little bit about yourself. Anything, really."

Logan shifted his weight, feeling uncomfortable. He hadn't opened up to anyone in years, and he wasn't sure what to say.

"Well, I've been working for Gray Tower for a few years now as you know," he began. "And I'm sure you've figured out by now that I was in the Army before that. So...yeah."

What else exactly was he supposed to say?

Keira snorted and laughed.

"Seriously, that was awful. I meant your likes, dislikes, hobbies, family. What do you do in your spare time? What makes you tick? Do you secretly have a wife and kids?"

Her mouth opened for a moment and then clamped shut.

"Um, you don't secretly have a wife and kids, right?"

She instinctively pulled a sheet up to cover her breasts.

Logan laughed.

"No."

"Ex-wife?"

"No."

"Crazy, abusive, homicidal father? Or, is that only me?"

"I don't think anyone can top your father on that one."

Keira wrinkled her nose and lay her head upon Logan's chest, heaving out a long sigh.

"No, I suppose not," she said wistfully. "I suppose you have normal parents, right?"

He shifted uncomfortably, bitter memories floating in the back of his mind.

"Well, not exactly," he began hesitantly.

Keira's expression changed to one of concern, and one eyebrow drew up as if questioning what he had just said.

"Oh? Well then, I'm sorry for bringing it up."

Logan sighed heavily and shook his head.

"No. Don't be. I just didn't want to bother you with any of my problems. You've got enough going on."

She frowned.

"Well, I want to hear about it anyhow. Just because your experience wasn't as horrible as mine doesn't discount it."

Sighing, Logan reach over and planted a kiss on Keira's forehead.

"You're absolutely right," he told her.

She smiled and nodded her head encouragingly.

"You could say that my family seemed pretty normal," he began. "It was just my parents, me, and my younger brother. Everything was okay until I decided to go into the Army instead of college. My dad flipped out. He wanted me to get that business degree, so that I could end up working with him in the family business."

Keira sighed and shook her head.

"I know how that goes," she said softly.

"When I didn't cave, it caused a bit of a rift, but I thought we had smoothed things over before I had deployed. While I was gone, my parents really came down hard on my brother, Nathan. He basically lost his way. Got into alcohol and drugs. He barely graduated high school.

"Parents blamed me, of course. Since I was the one who left, it must have been my fault. I even blamed myself for a little bit until I really dug deep and assessed the true situation. The fact of the matter was, I wasn't responsible for my brother's behavior. Sure, I did my best to try and be a good example for him, but he was his own person.

"If anything, it was my parents who caused a lot of the problems. I apparently didn't fit my dad's plans, so he moved his expectations over to Nate, and the kid just couldn't handle it."

Keira nodded and frowned.

"So, where is your brother now?"

Logan gritted his teeth and shook his head, old, bitter memories coming back to him.

"I have no idea," he told her. "He ran off at the age of eighteen, and no one has seen or heard from him since. I went out looking for him many times, but never made any progress. Honestly, I'm not even sure if he's alive or not. For all I know, he overdosed years ago."

"Oh, Logan! I'm so sorry," Keira told him.

Her fingers curled around his biceps, and she nuzzled her head on his chest. Logan's heart began thudding hard in his chest. He couldn't remember that last time he had talked to anyone about this.

"It's fine." It really wasn't. "It's been years now. I've gotten over it." He hadn't.

"My parents and I had a huge blow up over it when Nate first went missing," Logan continued. "I haven't really spoken with them since."

She frowned and said nothing.

There was a long period of silence, and then they both jumped as the sound of knocking at the back door echoed through the quiet house. Both Logan and Keira sat up, sheets falling around them. Judging by the time, it was probably Momma B, but Logan wasn't going to leave anything to chance.

"Stay here," he told her as he jumped out of bed, pulled on the pants that he had shucked to the floor, and grabbed his handgun.

Gun at the ready, Logan headed down the narrow steps and to the door in the back that led off the kitchen. The back door unfortunately had a window with just a sheer white curtain obscuring the view. In this case, though, it confirmed what Logan had been hoping: the partially obscured figure of a small, pleasantly rounded woman. He relaxed a bit and fumbled with the latches to the door.

It was dark out still as he met Momma B's gaze. She eyed his shirtless appearance, giving him a once over as she walked in the house, carrying stacks of food storage containers.

"Good morning," she said cheerfully as she pushed past him and sat down her load.

"Morning," Logan told her, trying to sound casual. "Need any help?"

"No, dear. I have it," Momma B said as she shuffled around the small kitchen and started packing the refrigerator with all of the containers. "I have breakfast items for you two and more coffee. Plus, there's lunchmeat, cheeses, and bread for sandwiches later. I've also thawed some meatloaf for you. I hope you like it."

"I'm sure it will be fine. Thank you."

It was at that point that Keira poked her head down from the steps. She was thankfully dressed, but her hair was disheveled. It wouldn't take a rocket scientist to figure out what had been going on.

Momma B looked up, noticing Keira's presence. One graying eyebrow raised slightly, and the older woman smiled knowingly.

"Oh," Momma B blurted out. "Yes, okay. Hello, Keira. It looks like both of you had a good night."

Keira froze at the middle of coming down the steps. She self-consciously began combing her fingers through her messy, I-just-had-sex hair as she suddenly seemed incredibly frustrated. Logan had to admit to himself that the situation was less than ideal, and Momma B never missed a thing.

"I'm sorry, dear," Momma B apologized. "I didn't mean to embarrass anyone. Sometimes, I run my mouth too much."

Keira began to chew her bottom lip as she finished descending the steps, obviously uncomfortable.

"I'll make coffee," she volunteered, finishing her last-ditch effort to fix her hair.

Logan tried to ignore the current situation and focus on more dire issue of dealing with the leak at Gray Tower. Sure, they were in a stable position for now, but they weren't going to be able to stay in Momma B's vacation rental forever. Plus, being cut off from all information was unnerving. Logan wanted to at least give Jack some sort of heads up. Jack was the one-person Logan could trust completely. He was Logan's best friend and a guy who didn't beat around the punch.

Shaking off the awkwardness, Logan went upstairs to secure his handgun and pull on a shirt. He'd unfortunately have to send Momma B out for supplies, and yes, he did feel a tad guilty for asking her to run errands for him. However, there was no way he was going to leave Keira alone. He also wasn't going to parade her around on a shopping trip.

Logan found a notepad and pencil and began writing down his supply list. The most important thing on it was a burner cell phone, but it also had things like spare clothes for himself and Keira. He had no idea how long they were going to be there, but it may be for a while. They may have to settle in for the long run if the issues at Gray Tower weren't resolved soon.

Walking back into the kitchen, he found Momma B and Keira wiping down countertops and doing general clean up. Since the place hadn't been used in months, it had accumulated some dust.

"There are dishes in the cabinets and cleaning supplies under the sink," Momma B stated in a mater-of-fact voice. I'll have to check on toiletries and all of that. I'm not sure what I have left over from the tourist season. I'll run to the store and get you whatever you need."

"I was hoping that you'd pick this up too," Logan said, handing her the list.

Momma B glanced down at it and nodded.

"No problem, Logan," she told him. "I'll run out this morning."

Logan handed her some folded bills from his wallet, but Momma B waved it away.

"Don't worry about it, dear. I've got it."

He pushed the money back in her hands.

"You've already helped enough. Please. I insist."

Momma B smiled and took the money, tucking it into a pocket in her jeans.

"Okay, then," Momma B replied. "I'll run out this morning. But first, I want to get you guys settled in. This place needs desperately needs cleaned."

Keira stopped wiping countertops and put her hand on Momma B's shoulder.

"I can do it," she offered. "It'll take my mind off of things."

Momma B looked hesitant, but then said, "Okay. Sure. I'll leave you two be then and get your supplies, Logan."

It wasn't long after that Momma B left the house, leaving Logan and Keira alone once again. The mood had changed, though. The strong intimacy had suddenly left, and it was back to business with the two of them.

Keira began cleaning like crazy, and Logan left her to plan his next move. Everything was up in the air without any contact from Gray Tower, but he could at least plan a few contingencies if they were to be on their own for a while.

* * *

Brenden sat at his desk, heart racing as he stared at the message from Selene. He was in such deep shit right now, and there was no easy way to get out of it. Unfortunately, he was beyond fucked.

The whole ordeal had started innocently enough when she had messaged him about some outside work. He often took work from her whether it be miscellaneous hacking or whatever. The pay was always good, and he needed all of the money he could get.

His mother had racked up numerous medical bills from a cancer diagnosis a few years back. Although she was in remission, the bills from treatment remained. Brenden had been trying to help her pay for them over the last year, but even his generous salary at Gray Tower wasn't enough.

It was also around the last year that Brenden has started taking side work. His acquaintance, Selene, acted as a broker for many of these jobs. They had never met in person, but she had always come through for him, and they typically met through the several in-game text chats for a couple of Brenden's favorite PC games.

No one at Gray Tower had any idea, and he preferred to keep it that way as he didn't want to be accused of conflict of interest even though most of it was harmless. Plus, he didn't want Bryant to think he was straying back to his old life of hacking where he never gave a flying fuck. His mother's illness had softened his heart a lot since that time, and it felt good to make her proud doing legitimate work from a respectable company.

Unfortunately, the last couple of jobs he had done weren't respectable or harmless.

Selene had contacted him about another job, and the pay had been great. The job itself hadn't been good, but Brenden had convinced himself that it was worth it to get the money for his mom.

She knew he worked at Gray Tower, so he had sometimes given out information here and there—nothing important. This time, though, she had been specifically looking for intel on that Amherst chick's whereabouts. All he was supposed to do was let Selene know where Gray Tower was hiding Keira Amherst. Amherst Global was just supposed to snatch her, and then everything would be fine.

Except that's not how it all went down. People got hurt, and it hadn't just been the guys from Amherst Global. There had been serious injuries to a few Gray Tower employees. One guy was in critical condition from what Brenden had heard. It wasn't supposed to have turned out this way. It was supposed to have turned out differently.

And now Brenden's situation had gotten worse. Much, much worse.

Selene had contacted him again and told him that he wasn't going to get paid for the original info because the Amherst people thought he was playing both sides and had tipped off Gray Tower. This wasn't true, of course, but try explaining that to a group of pissed off clients who had no qualms about murdering people who got in their way.

Not only weren't they paying him, but Selene had told him that Amherst Global was demanding more information—or else. She was quite clear that he had to come up with more intel, or he'd have the brunt of Amherst Global on him.

Brenden was totally fucked.

He had backed himself into a corner. He couldn't tell anyone at Gray Tower, or he'd be in serious trouble for the injuries. However, he also couldn't do anything for Amherst Global because the fact of the matter was: he had no idea where Logan and the Amherst girl were. Logan had gone completely dark.

So, where exactly did that leave Brenden?

He had to do something. Selene had told him that Amherst Global was *not* messing around, and that they would take action. Brenden knew that they didn't mean give him a stern talking to. He had to do something, but what?

Brenden's fingers tapped nervously on his desk. Then, an idea popped in his head. It wasn't the best plan he had every come up with, but at least it was something.

He'd hack into Logan's contacts and send them over to Amherst. Most Gray Tower employees used a central address book that could be accessed anywhere, so it didn't matter if Brenden had Logan's phone or not. Someone on that list had to know where Logan was at. Heck, he might even be at one of those spots. And, in the meantime, it would give Brenden a little breathing room.

Clapping his hands together, Brenden got to work.

CHAPTER 22

L ogan watched from the kitchen as Keira curled up on the couch in the living room and shut her eyes. It was late evening, and they had spent most of the day cleaning and organizing. Momma B had come through on the burner cell phone, and Logan had made one text message to Jack: *Your pizza is ready for pick-up.*

Jack would know what that meant. It was a check-in signal.

Then, Logan promptly popped the battery out of the phone. He'd do a similar text tomorrow, but he also wanted to make sure that they weren't tracked. It was better to be safe than sorry.

Logan stared at Keira who now looked to be asleep. After dinner, she had been watching TV and had curled up on the couch. She was wearing a new black sweater and pair of jeans that Momma B had picked up, and it was nice to see her feeling comfortable.

Unfortunately, the intimacy that they had shared earlier this morning had vanished for most of the day, and it had gone straight to business-mode. That had been fine with him for the most part. He needed to concentrate on keeping them alive.

But still...

It was hard not to let his mind drift to earlier this morning when he had been inside of her. Hell, she had been so responsive to his touch. How could she not be on his mind all day?

Not only that, but Logan couldn't help but think about some possible future where he and Keira were together. Nothing like cleaning, eating, and organizing their little place together to start believing that they could have a future. He had been watching her relax that evening and had enjoyed their little domestic scene.

If they both got out of this alive, he wanted more of this, but right now he needed to focus on the present task. Sure, they were about as safe and secure as they could be right now. However, that could change in an instant, and Logan needed to be prepared for that.

Still...

He couldn't just ignore how cute she looked over there all snuggled up on the couch.

Walking over to where Keira lay, Logan grabbed a blanket and draped it over her. She shifted her position and opened her eyes.

"I'm awake. Just resting," she told him.

Logan nodded.

"Understandable. You've had a long couple of days."

"I've had a long couple of years," she corrected him.

"True."

Keira say up and patted the empty side of the couch.

"Take a break," she said. "I wouldn't mind company."

Ah, hell, Logan though as he sat down next to her.

He knew exactly where this was going to go if he spent any time with her, but at this point, he didn't care. The fact was that he loved her.

Loved.

That was a word that Logan didn't use often. Sure, he had had his fair share of flings and whatnot, but he had never used that word before toward any woman ever. Keira was special in more ways than one. She was smart, strong, beautiful, and resilient. And, at least for the moment, she was his.

Logan began massaging the back of her neck. She sighed contently and snuggled closer to him. He spent some time and worked the knots out of her neck and shoulders, trying to rub away the tension of the last few days.

Well, in her case, it would have been the stress of the last few years. It still angered him that she had been treated so poorly, and he was looking forward to when her father finally got busted for his crimes.

They sat there for a while just like that. It was the first time that Logan had felt tranquil since he had met her. It was a weird feeling—being relaxed. He hadn't even been this chill when he was alone at this cabin. Keira made him feel at ease.

She sighed and looked up at him.

"Take me to bed," she said softly.

Logan stared at her, both terrified and relieved at her statement. Sure, every ounce of his body had been waiting in anticipation for this, but he also knew that each time they made love, he was in deeper and deeper in trouble.

"Yeah," he said, his voice low.

Without another word, Logan scooped her up and walked her upstairs.

* * *

Damien Amherst smiled at the latest report. Things were finally turning around for him and not a moment too soon. Pressure was coming down from above that would surely ruin everything that he had worked for. But now there was a good chance he'd have his daughter back and everything could get back to normal.

He now had this Logan Slade's list of contacts, and he would have his men go and check out every single one of them. They had already started. It was just a matter of time.

Keira couldn't hide from him forever.

The door of Damien's office opened, and Jason strolled purposefully.

"Please tell me you've found her," he said to Damien gruffly.

Jason was usually smooth and put together, but the last week had been rough on them both. Only Jason knew the real stakes.

"Not yet, but we will," Damien replied. "Shut the door."

Once they were situated, he continued, "I've got teams across the country checking on the addresses that we received. We'll find them."

"Good, but what about Stratton? He's been a bit of a thorn on our side."

Damien shook his head. He was still trying to get over the fact that John was a back-stabbing traitor. Not only that, but John had his fingers in the entire Amherst Global organization. He knew *everything*. And from what Jason had reported yesterday with the surveillance breach, it would take a long time to sever him from the inner-workings.

Well, unless Damien caught the bastard and killed him. The sooner the better in this case. John would soon understand what it was like to betray Damien.

Hell, if he could do it to his own wife, he certainly could do it to John. That bitch had had the gull to try and leave him. She even wanted to take Keira away from him.

Lily had no sense of loyalty. She had told him that she couldn't handle his business dealings. She *should* have stuck by him no matter what. Instead, she had sealed her own fate, and Damien had to get rid of her.

Obviously, the apple hadn't fallen too far from the tree with Keira, but Jason could get her under control, eventually. It would take time, but she'd become the daughter she should have been.

"So, what do we do now?" Jason asked, sitting in one of the soft leather chairs facing Damien's desk.

"Right now, we wait. I have a feeling that everything will work its way out very soon."

Jason snickered.

"I understand. Now, is it too early for a celebratory single malt?"

"I like the way you think, Jason," Damien said, laughing.

* * *

Katherina Langely tapped her fingers nervously as she was escorted into an ominous-looking elevator by two non-descript looking guards. This Gray Tower complex was a little more intimidating than what Alex had described.

She could tell the company was seriously expanding. The complex looked large, but not much of it was finished.

The entrance, which was a large atrium with huge windows and a stunning view, had plastic thrown over the furniture as workers were installing light fixtures. She had noticed that the area around the compound was tore up from heavy machinery coming in and out. The place was definitely a construction zone.

Kat had been hustled through the area and checked in, which was a whole ordeal in and of itself. Then, she had been brought to an elevator that had begun its descent—*underground*—to its destination.

A bit of anxiety was creeping up through her. This Gray Tower company was intimidating as she knew that they did private military work for all sorts of groups. She had never been in a place quite like this before.

Kat had done a lot of jobs for many companies, but almost all of that was remotely. When she did have to come in for work, she certainly didn't have to walk around armed security.

To make matters worse, she didn't even really have much in the way of professional clothing. She had one outfit that she used when appearing in person for work, and she had neglected to get it dry cleaned the last time she had worn it. So now, she was wearing jeans and a hoodie, looking like a complete bum.

When the elevator door opened, there were more concrete gray hallways. Kat shifted her laptop bag on her shoulder and began to follow the escort guards down more hallways. After some time, she was beginning to wonder if she'd ever reach her destination when Alex popped out of a room.

"Kat!" Alex exclaimed.

She quickly shortened the gap between them and gave Kat a big hug.

"I'm so glad you could get here so quickly," Alex said, dismissing the guards with a wave of her hand.

"Well, it was easy when you booked me a first-class ticket here on the next available flight and had a driver waiting to pick me up."

"I'm still glad you could come," Alex replied with a weary smile. "We're in some trouble here. Let me fill you in."

Kat pushed her big black-rimmed glasses up farther on her nose and followed Alex through a few doors.

Alex was chattering away as they entered a large conference room complete with a big round table with chairs in the middle and huge monitors along the perimeter.

"Nice set up," Kat said, admiring the room.

Her voice echoed a bit, mostly due to the huge size and minimal furniture and decorations.

She froze when she saw two men standing toward the back of the room. One was medium height with dark brown hair and a meticulously tailored suit. The other was younger. He was tall and well-built with brown hair. He sported a black t-shirt that stretched across his arms nicely, jeans that emphasized strong legs, and a definite five o'clock shadow.

She stared at him and stood in place, unmoving, suddenly feeling awkward and out of place.

The man was incredibly handsome and wonderfully masculine. He looked like he was one of Gray Tower's military guys, but he also looked like he could be on the cover of a magazine, selling manly stuff like guns or protein powder or something.

Her heart started pounding.

Get it together, she told herself. *Be professional. Don't start drooling.*

Then again, it was hard to feel professional when she looked so disheveled. Her dirty-blonde hair was in a messy ponytail. Her outfit, although comfortable, was kind of sloppy for the job, though Alex assured her that she'd fit right in the IT department. Kat didn't wear make-up, and the huge glasses she wore made her suddenly feel like a dweeb.

Meanwhile, Alex was standing next to her, completely put together, in her cute pantsuit and pristine hair and nails. Talk about feeling like the ugly duckling of the pair.

"Holy shit. They made more of them," the gorgeous man said, laughing.

Kat froze. Wait, what?

Alex shook her head and asked in an irritated voice, "Made more of what, Jack?"

"Jack" gestured his hand toward Kat.

"Made more computer geeks. Just like Brenden."

And suddenly, Jack didn't seem as attractive as Kat had initially thought. The word "abrasive" came to mind, and something told her that she wasn't going to like working with this guy at all.

"Oh, get over yourself, Jack," Alex said, shaking her head.

Both Kat and Alex made their way over to the two men. Kat was now incredibly anxious, and she began to wonder if her deodorant would hold out for a little bit longer.

"You must be Miss Langely," said the older man politely. "I'm Miles Bryant, founder and CEO of Gray Tower. This is Jack Hunter, Head of Tactical Operations."

"You can just call me 'Kat.' I'm pretty informal."

"You don't say," Jack Hunter said, giving her a once-over.

His gaze studied her intently. There was a smirk on his face that made her face feel hot, and she could feel herself start to sweat.

Okay, now she felt under-dressed.

Don't look directly at him. Don't look directly at him.

Kat couldn't help but stare right at him. He was scrutinizing her, looking to see if she held up to his standards. She probably didn't.

Suddenly, she wished she wasn't tall, so she could shrink away.

"Jack," both Alex and Bryant said in unison.

"Kat was gracious enough to come in so quickly," Alex continued, glaring at Jack. "She's the best of the best, and we're lucky to have her."

Jack nodded and luckily said nothing else.

"Yes, we're very happy that you could come on such short notice," Bryant confirmed. "Alex had nothing but glowing things to say about you."

Kat nodded, trying to focus on business, and said, "Is it possible that I could get set up right away? I'd like to get started as soon as I can."

"Absolutely," Bryant told her. "Alex will get you set up with anything that you need. I'm going to have you work with our tech security guru, Brenden. Hopefully, together you can get this problem figured out."

With that, he shook Kat's hand, thanking her again for coming so quickly. Then, he left with Jack who still looked amused at her expense.

"Sorry about Jack," Alex apologized. "He has a bad habit of running his mouth too much. He does it with everyone. I hope he didn't upset you."

"No," Kat lied. "I'm fine. He seems like a real peach."

Alex laughed and said, "That he is."

Kat followed Alex out of the room and around a few hallways before they reached a room with a closed door. When Alex opened it up, Kat's mood improved greatly. There were multiple large-screened monitors in front of a messy desk. A man in a thin t-shirt with green hair sat in the middle of it all in an office chair that probably cost a couple grand.

Apparently, Gray Tower spared no expense.

"Hey, Brenden," Alex said. "Kat's here. I'm going to get her set up in your office if you don't mind."

He turned his chair around slowly and when he spotted Kat, he immediately sat up. A sly grin crept on his face.

"Hell-o there, beautiful," he said. "Brenden Scott at your service. You must be the extraordinary Katherina Langely who I've heard so much about."

Oh, no. Not one of those guys, Kat thought.

She had dealt with her fair share of IT guys over the years who had thought they had found a unicorn when dealing with a decent looking female in the same field. It was highly annoying.

"Hi," Kat replied, trying to show disinterest in him.

"Brenden," Alex said sharply. "What did we talk about earlier?"

He saluted her and smiled.

"I'll be on my best behavior. I promise," he told her.

"Okay, then," Alex said and turned to Kat. "Let's get you settled."

CHAPTER 23

Keira lay next to Logan, her heart pounding out of her chest, yet she was oddly relaxed. They had just finished their second round of sex for that night, and she was beyond exhausted. Her body was humming with pleasure, but her limbs felt like rubber.

They lay there together in the front master bedroom for the simple reason that the bed was bigger. Keira had certainly appreciated the extra room as it had allowed them to do some interesting things in bed. She smiled at the thought of what they had just done.

"Hey, are you okay?" He asked softly, kissing down the side of her arm.

"Yes," she told him. "I'm just exhausted. And a little sore to be honest."

"Damn. I'm sorry. Sometimes I forget that it's been a while for you."

She wrinkled her nose and said, "Probably longer than you think. I only actually had one other sexual encounter with a man during undergrad."

Logan's eyes widened.

"You're serious?"

Feeling awkward suddenly, Keira sighed and said, "Yeah. Does that make me some kind of academic nerd or something?"

He laughed a deep, sexy chuckle that gave her goosebumps. She loved it when he laughed.

"No. That means that you're all mine."

He leaned over, kissing her deeply. She couldn't quite get enough of his kisses. Heck, she couldn't get enough of him. He was the kindest, sexiest, most badass man she had ever met. Sometimes she forgot about the past couple of years when she was with him.

Sometimes.

Of course, everything came back to her when she slept. She had been dealing with horrible nightmares, and they had gotten worse with time, especially after she had escaped. There was a looming feeling that everything was going to come crashing down soon. She felt like she wasn't supposed to be happy.

"I wish that we could just stay like this and not go to sleep," she said. "I hate trying to sleep, even though that's what I did a lot during my captivity."

"Bad dreams?"

"Horrible ones," she agreed.

"When all of this is over, we'll have you checked out for PTSD."

Keira stared at him, confused.

"Wait, huh? I thought that was just for soldiers or something."

"Sure, you hear about it a lot regarding soldiers and war, but anyone with past trauma can have it. Your situation would definitely count."

"Oh, I guess I hadn't thought of it that way."

"You really should try and get some rest, though. I can't predict what things will be like day to day, and we're not going to stay here forever as tempting as it sounds. I don't want to stay in one place for too long just in case anyone does catch on."

That certainly didn't make her feel any better, but she understood Logan's concern. They were still in danger, no matter how cozy they made their new home.

"Okay. I'll try and sleep, but I want to take a shower first."

"That sounds good."

Feeling suddenly spunky, she looked at him and attempted the most mischievous smile she could muster.

"How about you join me?"

Smiling, Logan told her, "You don't have to ask twice, sweetheart."

* * *

Logan stood under the spray of the shower with Keira nuzzled next to her. For the moment, they were both just enjoying the hot water beating down on them, though Logan's cock was already straining and ready to go. Even after having sex with her again and again, just being around her made him horny as hell, especially when her naked body was against his.

He found some shampoo and poured a bit into his hand. She let out a soft moan as he began massaging it onto her scalp, working it into a lather. He did feel a bit guilty for making her sore. How was he supposed to know that she was inexperienced? All he had known was that she was great in bed and responsive as hell. Perhaps it was just time to allow her to relax for a bit?

After finishing with her hair, he worked on her body, lathering soap all over her and trying his best not to stay too long between her legs. Of course, that was impossible, and he immediately began playing with her clit.

Okay, so maybe he wouldn't penetrate if she was hurting. He'd just give her orgasms this way.

Logan rubbed, messaged, and flicked the sensitive bud until she was pressed so tightly against him that he could feel her nails biting down into his skin. His cock was straining against her belly, but he kept on his pursuit until she found release against the palm of his hand.

"Logan," she whispered. "You've got to stop doing that."

He chuckled.

"Doing what?" He asked innocently.

She smiled lazily at him and then suddenly got a devilish look in her eye.

"Doing stuff like this," she said as her hand went down to his cock.

As she tightened her grip, he let out a small hiss. She moved her hand up and down in torturous strokes that left him insane.

Damn, did she know just how to fire him up.

"Oh, like that? That's nothing."

"Liar," she said.

Then she suddenly came to her knees on the floor of the shower and took his cock into her mouth.

Logan breathed in sharply as the hot moisture of her mouth filled around his dick. When she began to move up and down in slow, methodical thrusts, he knew he wouldn't last long. She looked too damn sexy with him in her mouth, the spray of hot water beating down on her, her breasts jiggling as she took him in again and again.

She was the sexiest woman he had ever seen, and he wasn't sure how long he'd last. This woman was going to be the end of him, he realized.

It wasn't long before he pushed her away. He couldn't stand it any longer. A sort of primal lust filled him. He had to be inside of her. For the moment, she would just have to deal with a little soreness.

Confused, she looked up at him.

"What's wrong?" She asked.

Without answering, he grabbed her and stood her up. He pushed her against the side of the stall and entered her from behind.

"Oh," she moaned softly as she gripped the wall of the shower.

"You better tell me if I'm hurting you because if not, I'm not stopping."

"Please. More," she begged.

And so, he went, pounding into her amidst the steam and spray until they both were seeing stars.

* * *

Kat shook her head and rubbed her temples. She had been looking at network security logs for hours, and she really wasn't seeing much besides the usual. Gray Tower had a decent network, but it wasn't exactly how she would do things if she was in charge.

Checking her laptop screen, she noted it was almost five in the morning. Time had apparently gotten away from her.

She was exhausted from being up all night, and her eyes were starting to get heavy. Kat wondered if she could find somewhere to crash for a bit, even if it was just a short nap.

Brenden suddenly started talking to himself *again*, and she rolled her eyes and shook her head.

It didn't help that her new counterpart was about as obnoxious as they came. He had felt more like a hinderance than a help at this point.

She glanced over at him and sighed when she saw him spinning around in his desk chair, loudly slurping on an energy drink. Even with the generous amount Gray Tower was giving her for this work, she couldn't help but ponder whether they were paying her enough to put up with this.

Kat shook her head and continued her work.

Some time passed when she saw something out of the ordinary. She frowned, puzzled.

"Hey, Brenden."

"Yes, my sweet."

"First of all, stop calling me that. Second, why do you have this network port open?"

Brenden squinted at her laptop that sat at the make-shift desk she was at. Then, he smiled mischievously.

"Oh, that's so I can play Call of Heroes when I need to relax."

Kat stared at him in disbelief.

"You have a gaming port open on a supposedly secure network? Really?"

"Hey, I've got things under control," he said defensively.

"Really? Because if you did, I wouldn't be here."

Brenden snorted.

"I keep telling you. It's an HR problem. There's nothing wrong with security on my end."

Kat shook her head and sighed.

"I need a break," she said wearily.

"Me too," Brenden announced. "Want to play some Call of Heroes? It's oddly relaxing. Do you game?"

"I do," she told him. "I prefer single player myself."

She didn't have the heart to tell him that she favored single player specifically to avoid people just like him online.

"Aw. You're missing out. Here, see how awesome this game is. It'll totally change your mind."

She wanted to tell him, "No," but he was already booting up the game. Perhaps if she just let him play for a while, he'd keep quiet?

That was, of course, not possible as Brenden talked just as much when he gamed, only this time, he was even more obnoxious.

"Boom! Got you, mother fucker! I fucked your mom, you little bitch."

Kat was about to put on noise-canceling headphones when she heard a sound that didn't sound like the rattle of in-game gunfire. She turned to look and saw a message alert blink at the top of Brenden's screen.

Sitting there for a moment, nothing really registered. People message each other in games all the time. Why did she care?

Then it hit her, this was an unmonitored platform in which someone could send messages in and out of Gray Tower's secure area. She had been told that all communications here were monitored, including the usual suspects like email and phone calls. No one had mentioned that Brenden had a port open so that he could play a stupid online game.

"Hey, Brenden," she said, trying to sound as casual as possible.

"Hey, what, my sweet?"

"Stop calling me..." She stopped herself.

There was a possibility that she might need to be on this guy's good side if she wanted to get this information out of him. She gritted her teeth and tried to be as nice as possible.

"Are you the only one who is into online gaming at Gray Tower?"

"There are guys who are into consoles, but they play in their quarters above."

"That's on a separate network, isn't it?"

"Uh, yeah. Another guy oversees that."

"Yes, so I was told."

But no one can bring Gray Tower work up to the apartments above, she thought. *They check too.*

Kat had to jump through some serious hoops to bring her own personal laptop down here, and she apparently wasn't allowed to take it anywhere until she was cleared. They mentioned something about classified information.

"Does anyone play down here?" She asked innocently. "Like in their offices?"

"Nope. Just me. Bryant wouldn't allow it. I get away with it because I'm on call twenty-four seven, so he looks the other way when I want some down time in my office."

"I see," she said, a sinking feeling beginning in the pit of her stomach.

"Why do you ask?" He said suddenly, his voice sounding suspicious.

"Oh, I—uh—just thought it was really cool that you got to play during work," she lied, hoping that would quell his suspicions.

"Ah, yes. It *is* cool, isn't it?"

"Very," she told him.

Kat had to do this carefully. She didn't want to accuse someone of doing something when she was this unsure, but it didn't leave her feeling right. Perhaps she could get him away from his computer with the game still logged in. Then, she could do some quick checking to see if it warranted any suspicions. She was afraid that if he got alerted to her suspicions that he'd start clearing out his account.

"Hey, Brenden," she said in the nicest voice she could muster.

"Yes, my sweet?"

"Could you pause your game for a moment and get me a cup of coffee? This place is a maze, and I keep getting lost every time I leave your office."

Brenden grunted and said, "Well, I can't really pause an online game, you know."

"Please," Kat said, getting up from her chair and putting a hand on his shoulder.

He had bombed out of the match so quickly that she was afraid that he'd shut the whole game down. He didn't, though. It was just at the title screen.

"Who cares about the game, anyhow? Let me go get you your drink, my sweet. What do you take in your coffee?"

She was about to say that she preferred it black, but she thought giving him a complicated order might give her more time.

"Two sugars, two creams, and see if they have any of that frou-frou coffee syrup or something."

"For you, anything, my sweet."

He left the room. Once the door had closed, Kat waited a few moments to make sure he wasn't coming back, then darted to his computer.

She clicked around until she found the in-game chat feature, then started going down through the list. The first couple didn't warrant much thought. Just a few back and forth messages between online friends. But one of them gave her pause. It was from a person named, "Selene."

It only took a moment to scroll down through the messages, and her heart sank. There it was: the evidence that Gray Tower had been looking for. The leak was coming from one of their more trusted employees. And...

Crap. He had handed over an entire contacts list to this person.

Kat had to do something and fast. What was the extension to Alex?

Before she could even get up and out of Brenden's seat, she froze when she heard a very upset voice from behind her.

"What are you doing?" Brenden demanded.

Kat turned around slowly to see a red-faced Brenden, looking like he was going to explode with rage.

"I was just about to ask you if you wanted vanilla or hazelnut syrup, and I come back to see you snooping around like some sneaky little bitch."

The words hit her hard, but she tried to keep cool.

"Look, Brenden. It's over. I know everything."

Brenden slammed the door shut and stalked over to her.

Be calm, she told herself. *He's like a hundred and fifty pounds, soaking wet. What's he going to do?*

Kat tried to make a move toward the phone to call for help. She had barely picked up the receiver when she heard the distinctive sound of a gun's slide being racked.

Oh, shit.

"Drop it. Now," Brenden commanded.

She let the receiver drop to the table it was on and slowly turned around to see him pointing a small handgun at her. How he hell did he get that? She wondered. Wasn't this level supposed to be secured?

"Fun's over," he told her. "This wasn't how I had expected it would go, but it's my only choice. You're not going to keep your mouth shut, so I guess we'll have to do this the hard way."

He moved over to her and grabbed her by the arm, pointing the gun at her temple, finger on the trigger. Waves of fear fell over her as he pushed her to the door.

"Don't do anything stupid," he growled, maneuvering her out the door.

The gun then settled in the small of her back as they began walking down the hallway. Kat wished desperately for a guard or something to come, but then again, what were they going to do? Would he shoot her if there was a confrontation?

They walked alone for a few tense moments before Alex rounded a corner, looking fresh-faced and put together, tablet in hand.

"Good morning, guys!" She called cheerfully. "Please tell me both of you got some sleep."

Her smile quickly faded as Brenden brought the gun back to Kat's face. Fingers flying over a few buttons on her device, she stepped back, steadying herself.

"Brenden, what are you doing?" She stammered.

"I'd leave now, Alex, before you get hurt too," he retorted.

The moment between the three seemed like forever, but it was probably actually only a handful of tense seconds before Kat heard the pounding echo of footsteps coming up the hallway. Her eyes darted hopefully to the sound to see—of all people—Jack Hunter and three other men running toward them, guns in hand. Two appeared to be guards, but the other guy who was sporting a neatly trimmed beard, was dressed as casually as Jack.

"Oh, what in good hell is going on?" Jack demanded, anger radiating from his expression.

"Brenden's the leak," Kat managed to blurt out.

"Shut up," Brenden growled, pushing the barrel of his gun harder into her face.

"Damn it, Brenden!" Jack exclaimed. "You've got to be shitting me."

"Let us pass, Hunter," Brenden demanded. "Or this bitch is going to end up with a bullet in her brain."

CHAPTER 24

Jack Hunter kept his gun aimed steadily at Brenden as he tried to plan out his next move. Of all people, Jack had least suspected Brenden as being the leak. It was fricking Brenden, for crying out loud. Jack had assumed the kid couldn't harm a fly, despite his past as a nefarious hacker. Perhaps the kid had never truly reformed as everyone had thought?

Luckily, Jack had been with his friend and another Gray Tower badass, Gabriel Marshall. This obviously wasn't the best situation, but he was lucky to have Gabe at his back.

"How do you want to play this, Jack?" Gabe asked.

"Let me talk to the kid. Maybe I can knock some sense into him."

"I'm not a fucking kid, Jack," Brenden retorted. "You always treat me that way, but I know what I'm doing. Now, move out of my way, or I swear I'll kill her."

Jack watched as the blood seemed to drain out of Katherina Langely's face. She looked beyond scared, and it pissed Jack off to no end that she was being used this way. Kat had nothing to do with any of this. As soon as she had entered Gray Tower headquarters, she was supposed to be under Jack's protection, and look how far that had gotten her.

"How'd you get the gun, Brenden?" Jack asked, trying to calm his voice.

Brenden sneered.

"Smuggled it in piece by piece in computer cases. I'm a lot smarter than I look, Jack."

"No. You're obviously a fucking idiot if you think you're going to walk out of here like this alive. Put the gun down."

"Or what, Jack? You aren't going to risk this bitch getting shot under your watch."

It irritated Jack that Brenden would call someone like Kat a bitch. She might look like a bit of a nerd, but she seemed like a nice person.

Jack did have a few choice words to describe Brenden, though. "Bastard" and "asshole" came to mind.

"We can work this out," Jack continued, trying to remain calm. "Everyone can get out of this alive and well. But if you think I'm going to allow you to hurt her, you're even dumber than I thought."

Brenden seemed to hesitate for a moment, gun dropping just a bit along Kat's face. Jack hoped the kid would make the right decision, but he was prepared to do whatever it took to shut down the threat.

Unfortunately, the kid made the wrong decision.

Jack watched as Brenden brought the gun back up to Kat's head. She let out a small whimper, and Brenden shook his head.

"No," he answered, his voice dead serious.

However, in that moment, the kid had taken his finger off the trigger. Jack made a spilt second decision, aiming right for Brenden's head, which was the only body part that wasn't obstructed by Kat's slender frame.

The sound of Jack's gun reverberated through the empty hallways. Brenden crumpled to the floor, a hole now in his head, his gun dropping from his lifeless hand. Blood splatter had sprayed across Kat's face, and she stood there in shock, visibly shaking.

Jack stood there feeling numb. It was unfortunate that it had to happen that way, but he would have done it again in a heartbeat.

"You made the right call," Gabe confirmed from beside him.

"I know," Jack agreed. "Still didn't make it an easy one."

* * *

Kat was frozen. She wanted to run, but her legs felt like they were glued in place. Her eyes were fixed on Jack, who was holstering his weapon. Brenden was on the floor, and she was free. Why wasn't she booking it out of here?

Move. Do something, she told herself.

However, she just stood there, stunned.

Jack walked toward her, concern on his face. His demeanor had changed since the first time she had seen him. He wasn't that intolerable guy who had made fun of her appearance. He was now a protector, someone safe.

Before Kat knew it, she was in his strong arms.

"Hey, you okay?" He asked her softly as wrapped his arms around her and hugged her tightly.

She wanted to say something, but she couldn't speak.

Apparently understanding her predicament, Jack continued, "It's alright. It's over. You're safe."

It was then that she realized that she was shaking uncontrollably. Jack brushed a bunch of hair that had pulled out of her pony tail in the shuffle back from her face. He then pulled her glasses off, which she then noticed had blood spatter all over them. In fact, she felt the warm liquid all over her face and in her hair.

She began to cry. It wasn't just a cry. It was only of those ugly cries that you never wanted anyone to witness. She would have been embarrassed, but she just didn't care right now.

"Hey, you did good," Jack told her. "You did really good."

"He's dead," she sobbed into his shoulder.

"Yeah," he agreed. "He died as soon as he pulled that gun on you. He just didn't know it."

More sobs escaped from Kat, and she cried for what seemed like an eternity.

"Alex?" Jack called out.

"Yeah," her friend said.

Alex had apparently backed away from the fray during the confrontation but was now back, looking the most frazzled that Kat had ever seen her.

"Get her cleaned up and checked out," Jack said. "I've got to deal with this mess. This is going to be a shit ton of paperwork."

Kat felt Jack's embrace loosen, and suddenly, Alex was there, leading her away from all of this. She couldn't see much without her glasses on, but perhaps she didn't want to see any of this. She just wanted away as quickly as possible.

Then she remembered.

"Wait!" Kat exclaimed and stopped walking with her friend. "They have all of the contacts!"

"What contacts?" Jack demanded.

"The contacts of one of your guys. Last name was Sade, maybe? I can pull it up for you."

There was cursing coming from multiple people in the hallway.

"We are so fucked," Jack mumbled.

* * *

Damien Amherst had gotten the call at about five thirty in the morning as he was sipping his morning coffee and reading how to international stocks had been doing.

"We found his truck," said one of the team leaders. "He's in Cape Charles."

"Good!" Damien said gleefully.

The Gray Tower contacts list was a long shot that had apparently worked out nicely. It had cost Damien a lot of his support guys, but it had been worth it.

"How do you want us to proceed?"

"Carefully. Remember that my daughter is with him. She is not to be hurt. And if you can nab this Slade character alive, do it. I want to see what he knows about Stratton."

"Understood."

Damien smiled as he returned to his coffee. Today was going to be a good day.

* * *

Logan woke up from a dreamless sleep. Keira was snuggled next to him still fast asleep. Something felt off, and he couldn't quite pinpoint what it was. Had he heard a noise? Unsure, he gently shook Keira's arm.

"Huh? What?" She asked, only half awake.

"Get up. Get dressed," he ordered. "Something's wrong."

She sat up immediately and began reaching around for clothes. He did the same, finding his jeans on the floor, though he didn't have time for a shirt. His handgun was on the nightstand, and his shotgun was sitting on the floor beside the bed. Logan's rifle was unfortunately downstairs as he liked to keep at least one weapon on every level—just in case.

"Stay right here," he ordered. "I'm going to check downstairs. Take my handgun, and shoot anything that's not me. Do you know how to use it?"

She nodded, fear flashing in her eyes.

"Good girl. Hopefully, I'll be right back."

Logan moved softly in bare feet across the floor and out of the room, shotgun aimed, checking corners and blind spots as he went. After he cleared the upstairs, he began his decent to the bottom floor.

He had just begun to clear the kitchen area when he heard a window breaking from the backdoor area. Ducking behind the center island of the kitchen, Logan both heard and saw a flash bang grenade go off. Temporarily stunned, he hunkered where he was at for a few seconds, but that was apparently a few seconds too many.

When his vision cleared, he saw shadows moving to his left. Ears still ringing, he aimed the shotgun as best as he could and hoped that he would hit something as he began firing.

Logan got off about two shots before he had to return to the cover of the island. Gunfire returned to his location, busting up pieces of wood along the cabinetry. He returned two more shots before he returned to cover. There was movement from the other side as well. The bastards had gone through the front door of the duplex too, apparently, and he was effectively pinned.

More fire returned his way, this time hitting the top of the stove and microwave above it. A sharp pain pierced his side, and for a moment, Logan had thought he had tweaked his side from how he was positioned.

However, his left hand fell from the gun to his side to find it warm and wet. Apparently, one of the bullets had ricocheted, and he had been hit.

More gunfire came his way as he silently cursed at himself. This is exactly what he had been afraid of happening. He had been so fixated on Keira that he had let his guard down, and now he was surrounded and wounded. Logan had failed her, and it was all his fault.

To his dismay, his vision began to go fuzzy. His hand felt around the wound, and he realized it was a lot worse than he had initially thought. Logan's vision went black and then came back into focus.

More gunfire. More cabinetry bits flying everywhere.

He blacked out again, and when his vision came back into focus, a shadow was standing over him, gun aimed at his face. He heard gunfire upstairs. Then, there was the distant scream of a woman.

The realization that Keira was going to be captured hit him hard. He didn't care about dying at this point. He just didn't want to fail her, and he had.

His vision clouded again, and this time, the blackness stayed.

* * *

Miles Bryant shook his head as he watched Brenden Scott's body being hauled away in a black body bag. Jack stood beside him, stoically. The man didn't seem rattled at all by the turn of events, though Miles knew it would eventually catch up to Jack.

"It's a damned shame," Miles said. "I don't believe he duped me for this long."

"He fooled all of us for a while," Jack replied. "I'm just glad Miss Langely caught it when she did."

Miles nodded.

"She got done in less than twelve hours what no one else could in days," he agreed. "And of all things, he was trading information back and forth in a *video game*. We looked at his in-game conversations and found out that his mother had cancer. He was doing side jobs to pay for her medical expenses.

"I wish he had gone to me first, instead of selling out the company for money. I would have helped him. He should have known that. I'll have to do something to help his mother out now."

Jack grunted in reply. He was hard to read in these types of situations. Even though he had just killed a man, Miles doubted that Jack would show any emotion.

"So, what's the plan now?" Jack asked. "Amherst has Logan's personal contact list, and Logan may be at one of those locations."

"Or not," Miles countered.

"True," Jack agreed. "But without a lot of resources, Logan may have had to call in some favors. We can't discount the fact that his position might have been blown."

"You've been in contact with him," Miles pointed out. "Did he give a hint where? Has he answered your recent texts?"

"No, and no. It's got me uneasy."

Miles sighed and felt his cell phone vibrate in his pocket.

"Hold that thought," he told Jack and hit the green button to receive the call.

"You're a hard man to get ahold of, Mr. Bryant," an unfamiliar voice came from the end of the line.

Miles looked at the caller ID, but nothing was showing.

"Who is this?" Miles replied calmly.

"John Stratton. You know, it took me a long time to dig around for your direct cell number."

"Stratton," Miles said, mostly so that Jack knew who was on the other line.

Jack's face showed a hint of surprise.

"You've been causing me a lot of trouble lately, Mr. Stratton," Miles continued calmly.

"For that, I apologize. Unfortunately, I was out of options, but I do promise that it will be rewarding for you in the end."

"How so?"

"I have more information on Damien Amherst and Amherst Global than you could imagine. I will give you all of that information if you help me out."

"That sounds interesting, Mr. Stratton, but I'm not sure what I can do for you. I'm not even sure if I want to help you."

There was a pause on the other end of the line.

"Your man Logan Slade is down, and Keira has been captured."

Miles' heart sank.

"No," he mumbled. "Is he dead?"

"I'm unsure at this point, but I desperately need your help to get Keira back. I will give you all of the Amherst information if you and your men help me get her back."

"At this point, I'm going after Amherst regardless for Logan's sake. How do you propose we do this?"

"Damien spread out his resources across the country, trying to find Keira. His mansion's security is vulnerable right now, and I know everything there is to know about its weaknesses. I just need a small team of your best to work with me to get in."

Miles wasn't quite sure if he liked this idea, but it might be the best option he had. Local authorities were out as most were in Amherst's pocket, and the ones who weren't might end up spooking him into hiding.

"How do I know that I can trust you?" Miles asked pointedly. "Why do you even care about Keira Amherst in the first place?"

"Because she's my daughter."

CHAPTER 25

Keira's head felt fuzzy as she crawled out of a dreamless state of sleep. Disoriented, she looked around, and her heart sank. She was back in that awful room: her bedroom at Amherst Manor. A wave of panic fell over her. Shaking her head, she tried to concentrate.

No, this wasn't right. This was another nightmare. She had these kinds of dreams all the time. Hadn't she just talked to Logan about this?

All I must do is just wake up, she told herself. *Wake up. Wake up. Wake up.*

Her thoughts drifted back to Logan, and then it all came rushing back to her.

Gunfire. An ambush. Her returning fire on the men that had come to her room. Logan lying on the floor, bleeding. A needle pushed into her neck. And then nothing.

No, this wasn't a dream, she realized. This was reality.

A long cry escaped her mouth as her panic deepened into utter terror.

No! How could this happen? She had been so sure that she had been safe. Logan had made her feel so safe.

Logan...

Where was he? She closed her eyes, and her memory flashed back to Logan on the floor.

They killed him. He had been on the floor bleeding as she had been pulled out of the house, kicking and screaming. Logan was dead.

Then, the revelation hit Keira hard: it hadn't been just "they" who had done this. Her father had killed him, plain and simple. She had been worried from the moment she woke up in Logan's cabin that her father might come after him for helping her. Sadly, she had been right the whole time.

The loss was crippling. More cries escaped her as she tried to process what had happened. Right now, she didn't care if she had been captured. She'd give up her freedom in a heartbeat if it meant that Logan could be alive and well.

Keira loved him. She knew that deep down. In fact, he was the only man that she had ever loved. His death hit her deeper than anything.

She wasn't sure how long she sat there on her bed, feeling numb and hopeless, but at some point, the door to her room opened. Turning her head, she saw Jason Savage standing there in the doorway, a smug smile on his face.

"Ah, you're up," he said brightly, though there was an underlying tone of mockery. "I thought you would sleep all day. I have something for you."

He strolled toward her, wearing an expensive business casual ensemble. There was something gold and shiny gripped in his hand.

"Stay away from me!" She cried and tried to get up from her position.

Dizziness swept over her, and she had to sit back down. Whatever they had injected her with had apparently not worn completely off yet.

"Oh, no, sweetheart. You don't get to call the shots anymore. I do. You are my wife after all."

Wait, what? Keira's mind swirled with confusion.

"We're not married," she said defiantly.

"Actually, we've been married for the past week. Your father and I had a few officials paid off to get the paperwork submitted. Unfortunately, you missed the wedding, so we'll have to go straight to the honeymoon part."

"No!" She screamed and tried to get up.

She stumbled around, her legs not seeming to work quite right. Meanwhile, Jason closed the distance between them and grabbed her arm roughly.

"No need to get all upset. You haven't even seen your wedding presents yet."

Jason smiled but it looked more like a snarl to Keira.

"Look what I have here," he growled and pulled her head, so she could look at the gold object in his hand.

It was a gold collar, like a dog collar, with a place that a chain could attach to on one side.

"Do you like it?" He asked. "I had it especially made for you. Look here."

He pointed to one side of it, where several large diamonds were set in the gold.

"I put your engagement diamonds in it, since you didn't like the ring I gave you. I felt this was better suited to you, since you're so defiant."

"No!" She cried as he opened the collar on his hinges and clamped it down on her neck.

She pulled at it, screaming, but it wouldn't reopen.

"Oh, no," Jason replied happily. "This one locks shut. Wouldn't want you running around without your wedding present on."

Keira felt trapped, like a caged animal. She began to panic and began to hyperventilate.

"Take me to my father!" She blurted out between breaths, though he wasn't quite sure what that would accomplish.

He was not the person she really wanted to see, but maybe he could stop this madness. Maybe she could plead her case? She had to do something, anything to get away from his horrible man.

"Oh, I'm not going to do that. He's pretty mad at you right now, so he left you in my care for now."

His hands ran slowly down her neck to the new sweater Momma B had bought her. Jason's fingers lingered around her breasts. Her body went stiff, and she felt nauseous.

"Please, don't," she pleaded, her voice starting to get hoarse from screaming.

"No yet, but soon," Jason told her. "I have one more present for you. Come with me."

With that, he yanked Keira to her feet and led her forcefully out the door.

* * *

Pain seemed to radiate from out of the darkness until Logan couldn't take it anymore. Blackness turned to gray, then gray turned to blinding light as he opened his eyes.

His looked around the room, taking inventory of the situation. There was a bright light on him, and he was lying down on a cold floor. He was shirtless with just his jeans, and he was starting to get cold. His left side hurt like shit, and he peered down to see it bandaged, which surprised the hell out of him. Then, he noticed that his hands were bound above him with thick rope.

Okay, so not the best situation, but he was indeed alive and not currently bleeding out. One step at a time.

Logan looked around the room. The walls were stone, and there were no windows, though he wasn't sure if he was underground or not. There was no furniture in the room, but there was one man standing there with a gun, watching him.

The man took a radio out from his belt and said into it, "Tell Mr. Savage that he's awake."

There was a pause and then a muffled voice at the end that Logan couldn't quite hear.

"Oh, okay. He's coming down? I'll get this guy ready then."

The man put the radio down and walked over to where Logan was lying.

"Sorry, buddy," the man apologized as he began to pull a rope that Logan realized was attached to his hands.

The rope pulled, and Logan could feel himself painfully coming off the floor, his side stretching agonizingly as first his arms, his torso, and then his feet finally lifted from the ground. He was now hanging in excruciating pain an inch or so from the floor, his bare feet almost but not quite touching the ground.

His aching side stung like hell, and he was having a hell of a time trying to breathe. There was certainly an urge to panic, but he kept his mind calm and tried to focus on his surroundings instead of the pain.

The rope was cutting into Logan's wrists, but he swore he could feel himself slipping just a bit as if the rope wasn't quite tight enough. This was something that he could work with.

After a few moments of tugging, he could almost get one of his big toes on the ground. But then, he was interrupted by the door opening. Logan's gaze traveled to the noise, and his heart sank when he saw who appeared in the doorway.

Jason Savage strolled in, wearing what looked to be a designer button down shirt and khakis. In his hand, he held a chain, and on the other end of the chain—no, it couldn't be—was Keira.

Her face was tear-streaked, her hair a mess. She was wearing the same clothes she had carelessly thrown to the floor the last time they had made love. Only this time, she was wearing a new accessory: a gold collar around her neck that was attached to chain.

The damn bastard had her chained like a dog.

Rage flowed through him freely. He was going to kill the bastard. Right here and right now. Jason Savage would not leave this room alive, Logan had decided. He just needed to get free...

"Logan!" Keira cried out when she looked up to see him.

"Yes, your lover is alive and well," Jason said and yanked the chain hard, sending Keira stumbling in the room farther. "Don't think that my men hadn't noticed the state you both left your bed at that house you were hiding in. I know you've been fucking him, and that's a damned shame. But not to worry, the last thing he'll see before he dies is me violating you."

More anger swelled up to the point that Logan was seeing red. He tugged harder at the rope, and his hands slipped just a bit more to the point where both toes were touching the cold, stone floor.

Savage yanked hard on the Keira's chain, dragging her toward where Logan was hanging. As she got closer to the bright light shining on Logan, he could see exactly how terrified she was. Panic and despair shown across her face. She certainly had reason to be scared. Her father was evil, and Savage was even worse.

Then, the thought crossed Logan's mind that perhaps Savage had already touched her.

Something dark swelled up in Logan that he had never felt before. An odd sense of calm crept over him, and all the pain that was radiating down his side seemed to disappear. Logan had only one goal now, even if it destroyed him: He would kill Jason Savage.

"Sorry about the shoddy repair job," Savage told him, pointing to the wound on his side, which was now starting to bleed through the bandage.

If Logan had gotten stitches, he had certainly pulled them.

"We couldn't just let you die in Cape Charles," Savage continued. "I wanted you up and well, so I could kill you myself—slowly and painfully—for daring to touch my woman."

"No!" Keira shrieked and tried to run to where Logan was hanging.

Savage yanked Keira's chain so hard that she flew backward. He took his backhand to her face, and she stumbled back to the floor, stunned.

Still, Logan stayed calm. He was working carefully on his hands. There was more support as he was able to hold most of his weight now. He could breathe easier now. But more importantly, Savage hadn't noticed.

"Leave us," Savage told the guard. "Shut the door, and don't worry about the screaming."

When the door shut, Savage turned his attention back to Logan.

"Now, where were we?" He asked with a demented grin on his face.

Walking up to Logan's position, he balled up his fists and sucker-punched Logan right in the chest.

Logan wheezed as the blow temporarily knocked the breath out of his lungs. It wasn't much longer after that until Savage landed another blow.

"Stop it," Keira pleaded from the corner. "I'll do anything. Just let him go."

Her words almost broke him. She hadn't really meant it, had she? Did she really want to sacrifice her freedom and her spirit for him?

"Tempting," Savage retorted. "But, no."

Another punch, and Logan tried to gather his breath again. He was certain ribs were broken now, but he couldn't think about that now. He was waiting.

Another punch.

More pain. But he was still waiting.

Another punch.

Waiting.

Another punch.

Then, it was time.

Savage had been enjoying himself so much that he had lost his footing a bit with the last blow and had gotten too close to where Logan was hanging. It was exactly the moment Logan had been waiting for.

With all his might, Logan lifted his legs as far as he could muster and latched onto Savage's torso. With his balance off, Savage toppled. Logan still had his legs firmly around the other man, and it was enough force to pull his hands right through the ropes, though it burned his skin like shit when he had pulled free. He fell right to the floor, but unlike Savage, he had been prepared.

Logan used all his might to steady himself and push the other man straight to the ground. Savage knocked his head on the stone ground, and lay there, dazed. In a few heartbeats, Logan straddled him and began punching his face.

Rage flowed through Logan as he continued his onslaught.

He hit again and again, blood began gushing from Savage's face. Logan continued viciously pummeling the man's face until it was a swollen to a pulp. As Savage attempted to get up, Logan's hands then grabbed his head, pushed down on one of his shoulders and snapped the other man's neck.

Logan sat there on top of the dead man, breathing hard, not seeing anything or hearing anything. He just sat there. His vision was clouded, and there was a shrill ringing in his ears.

Then, reality came back to him, and he heard Keira sobbing where she sat on the floor. Logan blinked and got up, not noticing at first that he was covered in blood and that his hands were swollen and numb from the blows he had given Savage. He didn't notice that he was limping from the wound in his side and that could barely breathe from the broken ribs he had sustained. The only thing that mattered was getting to Keira.

When he reached her, she seemed to recoil from his touch at first. He wasn't sure if it was from the blood, from shock, or even from Savage hurting her.

"Hey, it's okay," he told her softly. "It's okay. I'm not going to hurt you."

She blinked and reached for him.

"Logan," she sobbed and grabbed at him, pushing against him in a tight embrace.

"I thought you were dead," she whispered.

"I know, sweetheart. I know."

Then she looked up at the body of Jason Savage and started shaking.

"Is he dead?" She asked.

"Yes," Logan confirmed and held her tighter.

Her hand brushed her neck to where that sadistic collar sat around her neck. Then, she started to panic.

"Get it off me! Get it off me!" She cried, tugging uselessly at it on her neck.

"Hey, it's okay," he reassured her. "It's okay."

Logan looked down at it, inspecting how it was secured. It was technically locked, but the construction wasn't that great. He took his swollen hands, grabbed the opposite sides of the collar and pulled, snapping the joint and breaking her free. He chucked it to the side and allowed it to clatter to the floor with a final echo.

Keira slumped down against him and heaved a heavy sigh. They sat together for a moment until the severity of the situation came back to the forefront.

"We've got to get out of here," Logan said, grunting as he shifted his weight. A lot of the initial adrenaline had worn off, and he was now feeling like shit. "Do you know where the hell we are?"

"The basement of Amherst Manor," she told him. "I have no idea how we're going to get out of here."

It then that the door of the room opened, and a man holding a rifle stepped inside.

CHAPTER 26

Jack was ready to move out with his team as soon as the van stopped. They had just arrived at the rendezvous point in full tactical gear, ready to go. Jack was still a little worried that John Stratton wouldn't hold up his end of the bargain. This whole deal seemed risky, but at this point, he would do anything to avenge his best friend.

Yeah, he had been beyond pissed when he had found out about Logan, but he had to push that out of his mind right now. Gray Tower had a mission, so that took precedence.

Jack did know that another team had been sent to the place Logan and the Amherst girl had been hiding to do clean up duty. They didn't find any bodies, thankfully, but that didn't necessarily mean anything, though.

He popped out of the back of the van, while the rest of his team stayed put. They consisted of Gabe Marshall, Mercer Cade (another one of Gray Tower's badasses), and a new guy, Ryan Hale who had just joined Gray Tower a few months beforehand. It was a small group, but they could get shit done.

Jack wanted this over. He was tired of this whole ordeal, and not only was he pissed about Logan, but he was extra pissed about what had happened to Kat. It still bothered him the way she had looked at him when Brenden had that gun to her head. She was an innocent. She didn't deserve that.

Shaking her out of his head, Jack looked around for Stratton in the quickly darkening woods beside Amherst Manor. It was cold as shit, but at least it wasn't snowing or raining, though Jack could see his breath.

A few moments later, John Stratton walked out of the deep of the woods in similar tactical gear with what looked to be an Israeli Tavor of all weapons. Jack had his M16A4 pointed down in a low ready position.

"Are we good, Stratton?" Jack called out.

Stratton came forward slowly, and Jack vaguely wondered if the older man had been telling the truth about Keira Amherst being his daughter. Maybe there was a resemblance there after all?

Or, the man was full of shit. Who knew in this case?

"I'm not going to shoot you, Mr. Hunter," Stratton replied. "I need you too much. Plus, that's not really my style."

"Well, then. The feeling's mutual," Jack said. "Are we ready to do this or not?"

"Absolutely."

Jack gave a signal, and his men filed out of the vehicle, ready to go.

They all certainly looked sinister enough. Cade had scarring down one side of his face from a roadside bomb in Afghanistan. Gabe's beard made him look like he was perpetually frowning (maybe he was for all Jack knew). Ryan was the youngest at twenty-nine but had a ton of military experience under his belt already.

"Masks up," Jack told them as they all reached to pull the black fabric over their lips so that just their eyes were showing. "Uncle Sam has approved this mission, but I don't want anyone IDed. Gray Tower was never here. Got it?"

Everyone nodded.

"Now, where is this access tunnel at, Stratton?" Jack asked.

"About a half a klick away. Then it extends under the property for some time before it dumps out into the basement."

Jack shook his head. This whole plan seemed too simple to him.

"Are you seriously telling me that Amherst just left this thing wide open, and we can just waltz right in? That makes no sense."

Stratton cleared his throat.

"As I was telling your boss, I told Amherst years ago that I had the thing collapsed and inaccessible. Only I didn't."

"Years ago? How long have you been planning this little revenge scheme, Stratton?" Jack asked incredulously.

"Since the day he killed the woman I loved," the older man replied softly.

"Okay. Okay. I got it. Soap opera stuff. Love triangle. Intrigue. Keira Amherst is actually your daughter."

"I don't expect you to understand, Mr. Hunter. I just expect you to help me get my daughter out safely."

"Got it," Jack said, mock saluting. "Let's go."

* * *

John found the opening to the access tunnel and brushed away the foliage that had grown overtop the heavy doors. They looked like rusting storm cellar doors and sat low on the ground. It had been a long time since John had planned this out, and he was now finally going to do it. Today would be the day that Damien Amherst finally got the punishment he deserved, and Keira would finally be free.

It was unfortunate the she had been recaptured. John had very much wanted to keep her out of all of this. That's why he had sent her to Logan in the first place. He had not expected there to be a mole in the Gray Tower organization, which had foiled his initial plans. However, he still had the help of Gray Tower to pull this off, and Damien's resources were now spread incredibly thin.

The only thing that worried John was the possibility that Jason Savage decided to do something stupid. If that were the case, the man was dead.

"Help me get this thing open," John said.

Jack and another one of the team members grabbed the doors and lifted. The metal groaned a little, but after some tugging, the doors clanged back to reveal a pitch-black tunnel. The musty smell of stale air wafted up and hit his nostrils with full force.

"No lights I take it?" Hunter asked.

"No. The tunnel was supposed to be demolished," John told him. "Electricity was cut off a long time ago."

"And you're saying Amherst just took your word on it? He didn't check it himself?" Hunter asked.

"I was Damien's right-hand man. If I said something got done, there was no question otherwise."

Hunter nodded and shrugged.

"Okay, I just hope you're right. Let's do this."

The men moved forward, flashlights on their rifles turned on, dancing down the walls of the long tunnel.

"Hale, cover our back and make sure no one gets the jump on us from behind," Jack told one of his men as they proceeded forward.

"Yes, sir."

The access tunnel was about as clean as John could expect. There were cobwebs and rat shit all over the place, but it was otherwise unoccupied. John wished that he had brought a mask like Hunter's team just for the sake of keeping spider webs out of his mouth.

It seemed like forever as they walked toward Amherst Manor, though John knew it wasn't that far away. The tunnel itself started past the Amherst property line and went right under the security fencing. It had initially been built as an escape tunnel, but John had convinced Damien that it was more of a security hassle to monitor than an asset. Thus, the tunnel had been "imploded."

When they had finally gotten to end doors, John blew out a sigh of relief. It really looked as if Damien had taken John's word on the tunnel. However, he wouldn't know one hundred percent until they opened the doors. Damien had certainly become paranoid since John's departure.

John signaled to the door, which hopefully wasn't locked. It led out to a storage room that hadn't been used or cleaned in years, and he was hoping that no one had checked to see that it was unlocked. Otherwise, they'd have to use explosives, which would kill the surprise.

Hunter and one of his men pushed against the steel, and indeed, the door began to open but only partially.

"There's something stuck on the other side," Hunter said.

"It's a storage room. It's probably boxes."

"You'd better be right on this."

They continued pushing until there was enough space for each man to squeeze single file into the room, which was just as dark as the hallway.

John had been right that this was still one of the many "forgotten" rooms of the mansion. Boxes, old filing cabinets, and rotting desk chairs were stacked haphazardly. The room itself looked a lot spookier than it was with mounted lights on their weapons bouncing around in the dark.

There was light coming from under the door, however. That was the main hall of basement, which was a huge Biltmore-like area that included an old swimming pool that had been drained because of leaks.

Hunter tapped at the light on his rifle and everyone turned off their light source, leaving them in darkness except for the light coming underneath the doorway.

John had mapped out how the team would move, using schematics and floor plan that he had swiped long ago. They would move up through the main floor once the basement was secured. In the meantime, there was a much larger secondary group that would secure the grounds. Hopefully, they'd be able to take the manor by hitting Damien and his thugs from two angles.

Pointing to the door, one of his men slowly opened it, and they filed out, weapons at the ready.

Okay, John told himself. *Here we go...*

* * *

Keira clung to Logan as she saw the door opening.

No, not like this, she thought.

Logan was alive. Jason was dead. Everything was supposed to get better now.

However, she realized that they were still in Amherst Global's basement, and there were tons of guards everywhere. Now, they were about to be discovered, and her hope was about to disappear.

The man who appeared in the doorway was not a normal guard, though. He was dressed all in black and had what looked to be a compact rifle in his hands. She squinted as he walked closer to the light, and her hopes soared.

"John," she whispered when she recognized the man.

Relief washed over her. She couldn't believe that John was here. He had come for her. Again.

Logan coughed and groaned, saying, "You picked a hell of a time to show up, Stratton. I hope you have a plan to get us out of this."

Curse words flowed out of John's mouth as he surveyed the room.

Keira had to admit that it looked bad. Logan was covered in blood and still bleeding, and now she was covered in that same blood. And Jason was across the room, neck twisted grotesquely, face almost unrecognizable from what Logan had done to him.

"Are you hurt?" John demanded.

"No, but Logan is. He needs help."

"Don't worry about me," Logan said weakly. "She needs checked out. I think her cheekbone's bruised."

Keira reached up and touched her face where Jason had struck her and realized that it was puffy and tender. Sure, it had hurt when he had hit her, but after everything that had happened since then, she had temporarily forgotten her pain.

"Who hit her?" John growled.

Logan waved his hand toward Jason's body.

"It's taken care of."

If John was surprised that Jason was dead, he didn't show it. He just nodded.

"Uh, do you need medical attention for...other things?" Logan asked softly, looking at Keira.

The expression on his face made her heart break. She understood the question perfectly. He wanted to know if she had been raped.

Keira had thought that was going to be her fate as well. If Logan hadn't broken free when he did...

She shuddered at the idea.

"No, he didn't touch me," she reassured him. "Well, except for this shiner here."

She probed her cheek gingerly and winced when a streak of pain radiated across the side of her face.

Another figure appeared in the doorway, and Keira tensed. This one was also in all black but with a face mask covering the bottom half of his face, a larger rifle in hand. She tightened her hand around Logan's arm.

"Holy shit," said a familiar voice from underneath the mask. "Slade, you look like complete crap."

"Nice to see you too, Hunter," Logan replied wincing as he tried to sit up.

Hunter? Jack Hunter? The Gray Tower guy at the safe house who she couldn't stand? Well, she was certainly glad to see him now.

Jack turned to John and said, "Floor is clear. There were only two guys down here, and one of my guys took care of them with his knife real quiet-like. I'm about to signal the other team."

"Who else is here?" Logan asked as he attempted to stand.

Keira tried to help him as best as she could. He clutched his left side, where there was blood pooling against his palm.

"Cade, Hale, and Marshall, plus a group of twenty waiting to come in."

Jack pointed to his wound.

"You got yourself shot," he noted.

"Yeah, I thought it'd be a lot of fun," Logan growled as he limped forward, grimacing as he trudged toward them. "Please tell me you have a plan to extract us."

"Can we get them out through the tunnel?" John asked.

"Tunnel?" Keira asked, confused.

She had thought she knew every area of Amherst Manor. Apparently, she had been wrong.

"Your father hid quite a bit from you," John said solemnly. "But eventually, everything will all come out."

"We can get the Amherst girl, sure," Jack said. "But I doubt Slade is going to be able to walk that far."

"I'm sure I can do it," Logan said.

Jack shook his head.

"Not before you bleed all over the place and pass out," he commented. "No, I'll have to send her out with someone. Slade's going to have to come up out the front and hope we work quickly."

"No!" Kiera exclaimed and tightened her grip around Logan's arm. "I'm not leaving him. Not again."

The thought of being away from Logan again was agonizing, especially since he was hurt. She just couldn't handle being separated from him again. They'd have to drag her away from him at this point.

Jack shrugged his shoulders and said, "It's your call, Stratton. She's your responsibility now."

John shook his head and sighed.

"I doubt she's going to listen to me anyhow," he said. "You guys do your thing. I'll make sure they get to safety."

"At least give me your sidearm, Hunter," Logan said as he slowly walked toward him, Keira trying to steady him.

"I might be slow, but I'm not going to get caught without a weapon."

"Sure. Sure."

Jack pulled out a handgun and gave it to Logan. Keira watched as Logan looked relieved to have a weapon in his hands.

"Damn," Jack said, looking at Logan's swollen hands. "What the hell happened there?"

Logan jerked his head over to where Jason's lifeless body lay. Jack stared at it through his black tactical gear, processing the scene.

"I hope the dude had what was coming," he said.

"He did," Logan said, a look of grim satisfaction on his face.

Jack motioned to all of them and said, "Okay, then. Let's move out."

CHAPTER 27

L ogan was struggling as they walked up the steps to the main level of the house. He could already hear gunfire coming from the upstairs. The rest of the team—except for Stratton—had already moved ahead. They would work on securing the entire house.

More gunfire sounded from outside the mansion as well. That would be the secondary team moving in. Hopefully, Gray Tower could finally lay this mission to rest.

As they finally got to the main floor, there was more echoes of gunfire, but it seemed more distant now as if Jack and his team had moved to the second floor.

They passed a downed guard who was splayed by an open doorway. Luckily, with Jack leading, and with Marshall, Cade, and Hale as support, they'd make quick work of the building.

Keira gripped him tightly, apparently very serious about not leaving him. He felt a strange sense of pride that his woman—yes, *his* woman—wouldn't leave him, though the rational side of him was still annoyed. It was a stupid idea to allow her to stick around, but he was hurting too damned much to argue.

Logan tried to keep up as best as he could, but he knew this ordeal was catching up with him. He had no idea how much blood he had lost in the past twelve hours or so, but he was amazed that he was still alive and pushing through.

"Why are we going this way?" Logan heard Keira ask Stratton.

This sent warning bells off in Logan's head. Stratton had proven reliable—so far—but that didn't mean that Logan trusted him.

"Where the hell are you taking us?" He demanded.

"I need to make a little detour," Stratton said simply. "Don't be alarmed. It's to ensure that Keira stays safe forever."

Stratton gestured toward a heavy wooden door that had been flung open, most likely by Jack and his team.

"That's my father's office," Keira told him.

"And the Gray Tower team should have taken care of that room in their work to secure the building," Logan replied. "So, why are we here?"

"Please, Slade. You've trusted me this far, and I've never steered you wrong. Trust me now."

The rational part of Logan told him that this was a dumb move and could get them killed. However, Logan's instinct told him to follow Stratton. It was the same voice that had prevented him from shooting Stratton in the first place many months ago, and although that decision had put him through hell, he wouldn't have met Keira otherwise. Hell, she'd have still been locked up here, or worse, with Savage.

"Fine, but let's do this quickly. I have no idea how much longer I can run on my own steam."

As they entered, Logan looked around the room and couldn't help but roll his eyes. Everything about the room shouted over the top, old school money, though he knew that Damien Amherst was a self-made billionaire.

"I hate this room," Keira said quietly. "It's the first place that my father showed his true colors. This was the first place that he hit me."

Logan couldn't help but let the anger rise through him. Hopefully, Gray Tower would be able to nab Amherst here. If he escaped or hadn't even been here in the first place, then Keira would always be a target.

"Okay, Stratton," Logan said, irritation rising in his voice. "Why are we here?"

Stratton walked around the room slowly, his fingers tracing along the built-in wooden book shelves.

"Funny thing about being someone's trusted right-hand man," he began, a sneer forming across his face. "You're involved in everything. Every detail. The important things are left to you. Like, let's say the installation of a safe room."

The realization hit Logan like a ton of bricks.

"Are you telling me Amherst has a safe room here?" Logan demanded.

"Yes," Stratton replied. "Not only that, but he's in it right now."

He pulled out a large book to reveal a small keypad beneath. There was a small blinking light next to it.

"Well, I'll be damned," Logan said, shaking his head. "I suppose once we get the place secured, Gray Tower can try and blast him out of it."

"No need," Stratton said. "Damien got to pick his own passcode. Only he knows it. Not even me."

Logan was just about to give up on an immediate apprehension of Amherst when Stratton continued.

"Fortunately for us, I never told him about the override code that I know."

Stratton hit a few buttons and a bookshelf right next to the control panel opened, revealing a small, windowless room with a bed, toilet, supplies, and Damien Amherst, sitting there looking terrified.

Logan raised his gun and pointed it right at Keira's own flesh and blood, bitter emotions from the past week bubbling up to the surface again.

"You bastard," Logan growled.

"Oh, he's not armed," Stratton said, amusement now in his voice. "He never carried a gun. Thought it was beneath him. Always had others do his dirty work. Didn't you, Damien?"

"John, wait," Damien stammered, looking terrified. "We can work this out."

Then his attention turned toward Keira who was just standing there, staring at him.

"Keira, you've got to understand. This was all just business. I'll leave you alone. I'll leave you all alone."

"Do you know who I am?" Logan hissed.

Damien nodded, sweat visibly collecting on his brow.

"You're Slade, Logan Slade. Look, we have no issue. Let's just call this even and go our separate ways."

Logan laughed.

"Yeah, sure. As if you didn't leave me to get beaten to death by your little peon, Savage. He's dead, by the way."

Damien's eyes widened, and his hands began to shake.

"Just remember this when your rotting away in a jail cell," Logan said, limping right up to where Amherst sat, gun pointed straight at his face.

"*I'm* the guy who's going to marry your daughter. *I'm* the guy who's going to take care of her. *I'm* the guy who's going to make sure scum like you never cross her path again. Got it?

"Yeah...yeah," Amherst stammered.

With that, Logan pistol whipped his soon-to-be father-in-law across the face.

Blood spilled out of Amherst's nose, and Logan was pretty sure that a tooth came flying out too. Amherst took a knee to the floor, groaning and holding his face.

Satisfied, Logan limped back to where Keira and Stratton were standing, an odd expression on Keira's face.

"You...want to marry me?" She asked, a definite note of surprise in her voice.

"Yeah, sound good to you?" Logan asked, trying to sound casual, though now that the statement had come out of his mouth, he was as nervous as hell.

She blinked and then smiled.

"Yes," she said and threw her arms around him.

"Ow...ow," Logan groaned, and she immediately stopped.

"Sorry," she apologized, a grin spreading across her face. "You're hurting. Later."

It was then that Logan noticed John Stratton just standing there, staring at them. He had an odd expression on his face.

"What's the problem, Stratton?" Logan asked impatiently.

"When did...*this* happen?" Stratton asked.

"When did what happen?" Logan said, annoyed.

"You too, together. Falling in love. Deciding to get married. Hell, Slade, I told you to protect her, not *marry* her."

"Apparently, I took your advice a little too literally," Logan replied. "Besides, why the hell do you care? It's not like she's *your* daughter..."

He trailed off.

Then he looked at Stratton.

Then he looked at Keira.

And it all suddenly fell into place.

"She's your *daughter!*" He exclaimed.

* * *

The moment Logan's declaration left his lips, the happy moment of his proposal seemed to vanish, and Keira began to get light-headed. She grabbed at Logan as her vision temporarily went fuzzy. When it was clear, she was seated on a soft, leather chair near the safe room opening.

Keira looked up at John, her mind whirling.

No, this didn't make sense. He couldn't be her father, could he?

"So that's why you've been so keen to help her, right?" Logan continued. "I always wondered about that. Why would some guy like you care so much for his ex-buddy's daughter? In fact, why would he care so much to risk everything to save her life?"

She stared at John and asked pointedly, "Is this true?"

"Yes," John said without hesitation. "I'm sorry that I had to tell you this way. I had wished it to be under better circumstances."

"What do you mean she's *your* daughter?" Damien Amherst roared from behind them.

He was attempting to stand up, holding his nose that was gushing blood. His voice sounded odd with it injured in that way. If it hadn't been so garish, it would have been almost cartoonish.

"Stay down," Logan said, pointing his handgun at him.

For once, Damien Amherst took an order from someone. He sat but still looked ticked.

John began to laugh, something that started as a deep chuckle but then deepened into full-blown almost maniacal laughter. When he finally stopped, he smiled.

"This whole time you've been ranting and raving about your legacy and preserving your line," John said gleefully. "You've tumbled your organization in hopes of getting her back. You wanted grandkids so badly. And she's not even your kid!"

"No, no, no..." Damien trailed off. "Then that means that you and Lily..."

"She was the love of my life," John admitted, a hint of sadness in his voice. "She couldn't stand you, so she turned to me. Her and Keira were the only reason why I kept with you for so long."

"Are you sure she's not mine? There could be a chance..."

"I've got a DNA test that says otherwise."

This was too much for Keira. Too much to process. Too many emotions. She wanted to leave, escape with Logan and never have to deal with this again.

But then again, there was some relief in knowing that she was not related to one of the evilest men she had ever known. There was relief in knowing that she had a father who cared about her.

"I should have killed that bitch sooner!" Amherst shouted.

Keira blinked. Wait, what?

"What do you mean?" She asked, rising from her seat. "What did you just say?"

"It's the reason why we're here, Keira," John said quietly. "Justice. Tell her, Damien. Tell her what you did to her mother."

Amherst sneered, blood spitting out of his mouth as he defiantly said, "That's right. I killed her. She wanted a divorce. I wanted loyalty. In the end, I may have arranged a little accident with her car. Good riddance to her. Now I know why she was so desperate to leave. She was sleeping around with my best friend!"

John turned toward her and said, "Lily made the mistake of thinking that Damien would let her leave through the normal channels. She went against my wishes and asked for a straight up divorce to protect you. I wanted to quietly leave the country, but she was as stubborn as you are.

"Once I realized that had happened, it was too late. She was dead."

He looked back over at Amherst.

"And I've been planning for this moment ever since."

Keira expected anger and rage to pass her, but all she felt was numb. She felt absolutely nothing as if her body had just stopped processing emotions.

"It's over, Damien," John continued. "Gray Tower has all of Amherst Global's information. Everything. Every single dirty deal you've done. Every person you've killed. Everything. This whole organization that you've built? It'll be gone by the time the Feds move in. You're left with nothing. No legacy. No daughter. No business. Even your little buddy, Savage, is gone."

"No! No! No!" Amherst screamed. "You bastard! What have you done? What have you done?"

"Everything that you deserved, Damien," John said, his voice low. "Well, all except one thing."

John raised and aimed his rifle.

"Goodbye, Damien."

He fired.

"No!" Logan exclaimed, pointing his gun on John as Damien Amherst's body crumpled to the floor. "What the hell were you thinking? We were supposed to capture him alive if possible. This fucks up everything."

John shook his head.

"It would have never worked. Damien's got friends—or right now, mostly enemies—in some high places. They would have gotten to him first, even in your custody. You have no idea what can of worms your company is about to open up with this bust."

"Still," Logan continued, gun aimed steadily. "You're going to have to answer for all of this."

"I'm not going to fight you, Logan," John said softly. "I'll pay for my crimes, eventually. Take care of my daughter."

He turned to leave.

"Stratton, don't do it," Logan called out.

Keira wasn't sure if Logan would do anything or not, but she wasn't going to take any chances. She couldn't have him kill John.

"No!" She yelled and grabbed Logan's left arm. "Please don't shoot him. Please."

Logan lowered his gun and sighed heavily. John was out the door without another word, and they were alone.

Keira watched as Logan stumbled into a chair and sank down, resting his gun on a muscular thigh. She knew he was hurting but wasn't sure what she could do.

"I wasn't going to shoot him, you know," he told her. "I'm not that heartless."

"I know. I don't even know what I was thinking."

Logan tilted his head back in the chair and shut his eyes.

"Logan?" Keira said nervously.

He didn't respond.

"Logan?" She said again, louder this time.

She shook his arm, but he didn't move. Panic swept over her. Logan needed help. Now.

The universe must have known her desperation because it was only a few moments later that a man dressed in what she thought was Gray Tower gear entered the room.

"There you are," said the voice of Jack Hunter. "The grounds are secured. We're leaving before the Feds show up, though we didn't find Amherst."

He surveyed the room, confused.

"Why the hell are you guys in here? Where's Stratton? What's going on with Logan?"

Jack looked at where the safe room was located and noticed Damien Amherst's lifeless body.

"Fuck me. You guys found Amherst, apparently."

"Jack! Logan needs help!" Keira pleaded. "He's not responding."

"I can get a stretcher in here in less than a minute," he told her, picking up his radio and talking into it.

Keira sank down beside Logan's chair and held his hand. After everything that had happened, she couldn't lose him now. She just couldn't.

CHAPTER 28

Logan opened his eyes to see a bright light above him and an angel gazing down at him. Apparently, he hadn't made it after all and had succumbed to his injuries. That's what he got for planning a nice future. He could have really seen him and Keira together.

Keira...

Panic filled him. Where was she? What had happened to her?

"No! Keira!" He yelled and began thrashing around.

Pain spread across his body, especially down his left side where he had been shot. It was then that he realized that perhaps he wasn't dead after all.

Blinking, he tried to focus on his surroundings.

"I'm here," said his angel. "Try not to move too much. You don't want to pull your stitches again."

His eyes focused, and he saw Keira staring down at him, smiling. He could never quite get over how beautiful she really was.

"Oh, yeah," he said dumbly, figuring that someone somewhere must have been him pain medication.

Keira was sitting on the edge of a bed that Logan was lying on. The side of her face with turning purple and was swollen. He looked down to see his chest, stomach, and hands bandaged. An IV was attached to one arm.

Inspecting the rest of the area, he expected a hospital setting, but it looked to be more like a room on one of the sublevels of Gray Tower.

"Where are we?" He asked hoarsely, his throat dry.

Without being asked, she grabbed a cup with a straw and let him drink.

"At Gray Tower Headquarters," she told him as he took a few gulps. "I was told that they didn't want to take you to a hospital because gunshot wounds come with too many questions. Mr. Bryant was able to get a doctor and some equipment to make a little triage here. He was telling me that your medical wing wasn't ready yet."

Logan looked around at the concrete gray colored room. There were no decorations, just a light fixture and an IV line.

"Nothing's ready yet," he told her. "The whole place is one big construction zone."

"Yes, I noticed," she agreed. "This is an empty office on one of the bottom levels."

"Ah, that makes more sense now," Logan said, settling his head back down on a pillow.

"Oh! The bullet went straight through, and you don't need surgery!" She said brightly. "You do have several broken ribs, and you broke a couple of knuckles on both sides of your hands."

She grimaced as if remembering what had happened for him to get those broken knuckles.

"I'm sorry you ever had to see that," Logan apologized. "I acted like an animal."

"You saved my life," she corrected him. "And for that, I'm forever grateful."

She bent down and kissed him softly on the lips and for a moment, Logan didn't care about anything else but that fact that he and Keira were both alive and well. He deepened the kiss, feeling right for the first time in a long time.

The threat to Keira was gone. They were both alive. Those were the only things Logan cared about right now.

"Oh, my," said a female voice from behind them. "I'm very sorry to interrupt."

Keira's head popped up to reveal Alex Thorn grinning in the doorway.

"It's nice to see you awake, Logan," she said as she walked further into the room. "I was just coming in to check on Keira, but I'll tell Miles that you are awake. He *definitely* wants to talk with you."

"Ah, shit," Logan sigh. "How much trouble am I in?"

Then, reality seemed to come crashing back in. He knew that he'd eventually have to answer for all of the shit he pulled with his employer.

Alex cocked her head to the side, perplexed.

"None at all. Why do you ask?"

"Besides the huge fuck up of Keira and I getting captured? How about allowing John Stratton to shoot Amherst, so now our high value target is gone. And then I let Stratton just slip right through my fingers."

Alex shrugged.

"Stratton was always a wild card. Miles knew there was going to be some trouble there, regardless. However, it was you who pulled him out of the shadows. He gave us some of the best intel we've ever gotten as a company. Uncle Sam is *very* happy. You're the hero."

Logan grunted.

"Doesn't feel like it," he mumbled.

"It's true," Keira said. "Alex has been filling me in on what she could. It's amazing what John got on Amherst Global. Warrants are going out. Top level executives are dropping like flies. The company is going to file for bankruptcy."

"Good," Logan said. "Wait, you know Alex?"

"Yeah. She's been keeping me company while you've been out of it. Well, I should say her and her friend, Kat."

Logan tried to process the name "Kat" but couldn't think of anyone who worked at Gray Tower with that name.

"Who's Kat?" He asked.

"Oh! I should have told you," Alex continued. "She's going to be filling in for Brenden until we can get a replacement. Between you and me, Miles wants to hire her on full time."

"Wait, what happened to Brenden?" Logan asked, now really confused.

Alex's whole demeanor changed. She frowned and shook her head.

"He was the leak, Logan. When he was found out, he tried to take a hostage. Jack shot him dead."

Thoughts reeled through Logan's head. First, he was in shock. How could Brenden of all people be the leak? The kid was harmless—or so he had thought.

Then, he got pissed. That asshole put both him and Keira in peril. Logan could have been tortured and killed. And Keira could have ended up as Jason Savage's sex slave for the rest of her life.

He shook his head, trying to push the thought out of his mind. Right now, he just wanted to concentrate on the fact that he and Keira were safe. Playing the "what if" game never turned out well.

"Hey, look who finally decided to join us," Jack's voice came from the doorway. "Take a long enough nap, Slade?"

Logan shook his head, trying not to smile.

"Nice to see you too, Hunter," he said.

"You can thank me later for saving your ass," Jack said, flashing a smile.

Logan turned to Keira and said, "Watch, I'm never going to hear the end of it."

She smiled. Damn, it was good to see her happy for once.

"So, when's the wedding?" Alex asked, a glint in her eye.

"Alex!" Keira exclaimed, shooting her a glare. "I told you that in private."

"Sorry," Alex apologized. "I couldn't help myself."

"I mean, I don't even know if Logan wants to," Keira continued, a panicked expression on her face. "It was a tense situation. People say stuff. Things change. I don't know."

"I meant every word," Logan told her. "If you still want to, I'm down."

"Yes!" She said, bending down to kiss him again.

"I love you," he whispered.

"I love you," she told him.

"Oh, man!" Jack exclaimed. "What the fuck is this shit? Marriage? You've got to be kidding me, Slade. I told you to watch out for this girl. Now, you're going to marry her? What the hell were you two doing while you were out of contact?"

"Just shut up, Hunter," Logan said and kissed Keira again.

Then, it dawned on him.

"What happened with Mrs. Barber?" Logan asked. "Shit, her whole place was probably shot up."

"She's fine," said another man's voice from the doorway.

Miles Bryant strolled in the now crowded space. He had taken off his tie and now looked incredibly casual. It was one of the first times that Logan had seen the guy look so damned relaxed.

"She's one of the nicest people to work with," Miles continued. "Gray Tower is going to comp her for the damage. She was more concerned about you two, but she does know you are both safe now."

"Good," Logan said, nodding.

The last thing he had wanted was for Momma B to be in distress because of him.

"I wanted to stop by and see how you were doing," Bryant said. "But I also wanted to thank you personally."

"Like I was trying to tell Alex..." Logan started but was cut off by his boss.

"Just listen, Slade. The Feds are happy because—although Damien Amherst is gone—they now have enough information to prosecute a whole bunch of people in Amherst Global. They seized a ton of assets.

"Oh, and want to hear the best thing yet? Whoever was protecting the company has backed away. The whole organization is going down, and Gray Tower is getting a huge payday from it."

"Oh," Logan said, dumbfounded. "Well, good then."

"I'd also like to thank you for getting me in touch with our newest Gray Tower recruit," Bryant continued.

"Wait," Logan said, shaking his head, confused. "Who are you talking about?"

"Your fiancé is getting a job with us," Jack said, looking mildly annoyed.

Logan stared at Keira who was grinning from ear to ear. It was the happiest he'd ever seen her.

"You're going to work at Gray Tower?" Logan asked, stunned. "Are you guys serious? How long was I out?"

Keira shrugged and patted his thigh.

"Miles and I got to talking. He knew about my MBA, and though I've been out of work for a bit, he was impressed at what I had accomplished in my internships. I'm certainly motivated to help others in need as I was, and honestly, I need a job.

"I talked to a lawyer while you were out of it. Firstly, we looked at the legality of my marriage license to Jason. I don't even need an annulment, and I'm not a widower. It's already been thrown out."

Logan began to wonder how Savage had pulled that off, when she continued.

"Secondly, we had a quick look at my finances, and although I do have a trust that the Feds can't touch, a good deal of it is tied up in stakes at Amherst Global, which is now going bankrupt. Simply put: I'm broke."

"I'll be working closely with Miss Amherst in the hopes that she'll eventually be my second in command," Bryant continued. "It's going to be a lot to take on, but I have a feeling she'll be able to handle it."

"Well, damn, Keira," Logan said, shocked. "I guess congratulations is in order."

Jack laughed and said, "You do realize that your fiancé is going to be your boss, right?"

Logan grinned and said, "You do realize that she's going to be your boss too, right?"

"Touché!" Jack said and threw up his hands.

"One last thing," Miles continued. "I'd like to offer you a different position to you as well, Slade. With this new influx of cash and the new headquarters, we're going to be adding a ton of people, and I'd like to extend the number of employees who are in the field. I need someone to train these new hires and keep the current employees up to date on their skills. I want you to be that person."

Logan just sat there, stunned. It was the opportunity that he had always wanted. He'd be out of the field for the most part, working regular hours in a position that mattered. Hell, he'd be working in the same vicinity of Keira. They could have a real life, an actual honest-to-goodness happily ever after.

"This sounds too good to be true," he said. "Is this real, or are you guys just pulling my chain?"

"It's real," Miles confirmed. "Now, say you'll take it."

"Yes!" Logan said.

Keira smiled and kissed him again.

"Good," she whispered into his ear. "I was hoping that you'd stop your work out in the field and take something...a little less exciting for once."

"Okay!" Jack exclaimed. "Time to go and let these two lovebirds do mushy stuff or something."

Logan chuckled at his friend as the extra people filed out of the room. Then, he and Keira were alone again.

"This feels like a dream," he murmured to her.

"I know," she said. "I have to pinch myself sometimes to realize that this will be my life from now on. My father—I mean—Damien is gone. I'm free."

"How are you handling the news about John being your father? And what about the news of what actually happened with your mother? Are you okay?"

Keira shook her head and sighed.

"It was hard at first, but it all makes sense. I guess I feel a little bit better knowing I'm not related to that monster, though I'm still trying to process the news about my mother. I know Gray Tower wanted Damien alive, but I'm glad that he's dead. Now I don't have to worry about him ever again."

"That's understandable," he told her, bringing up a bandaged hand to touch her face. "Do you think you'll ever hear from your actual father again?"

"I don't know. I just want to concentrate what's right here and now."

"I can live with that," Logan said.

They kissed again, happily and deeply. And finally, the girl who didn't think she had a future, and the guy who was afraid to have one were about to begin one together.

EPILOGUE

Two Months Later

Keira squeezed Logan's hand, reassuringly. She knew he was tense. He should be as this was an important step for them both.

"Are you ready?" She asked him.

"Not really," he told her with a sigh. "But I'm going to do it anyway."

"That's the spirit," she said, laughing. "Let's do this."

They rang the doorbell.

Footsteps were heard from inside the house, and then the door opened to reveal an older man and woman. The man was tall and had graying black hair and a strong jawline. The woman was shorter than Keira and had a wide smile on her face.

The woman squealed and exclaimed, "You must be Keira! I'm Beverly Slade, and this is my husband Charles. We're *so* happy that you both could come."

Keira found herself being shoved into a hearty embrace from Beverly and then Logan's father.

Well, this is going well so far, Keira thought.

She and Logan were shuffled into a beautiful home that was smartly designed. It felt more like a "real" home than anything in Damien Amherst's overly elaborate mansion.

"Please, come into the family room," Beverly continued. "I've got refreshments for you. Oh look, dear! She's so beautiful. Isn't Logan's fiancé so beautiful?"

Charles Slade grunted in confirmation. Keira was starting to get the idea of what Logan had been talking about with his father. The man was intimidating.

Beverly continued chattering on as they moved through the home, though Keira was more concerned about Logan and his father. Charles had been oddly silent, almost sizing up Logan.

Keira was suddenly nervous that it had been wrong for her to push Logan into seeing his parents again. She had been talking with her new therapist about Logan's situation as part of her PTSD treatment and had gotten the idea. Keira had just thought that it seemed crazy that each side of the family wasn't talking, though she understood why. Logan had agreed to at least try and rebuild the relationship. However, she also knew that it would be up to his parents on how they reacted to the whole situation.

They all sat down on a set of couches. Keira pulled Logan close to her and eyed him nervously. He had gone from the sensitive man she had gotten to know to the stone-faced emotionless guy who had tied her up and threatened her with a knife.

"So, Keira," Beverly said. "Logan told me over the phone that you both work together. Isn't that lovely, Charles?"

Charles Slade nodded in agreement but said nothing else. Keira got more nervous for Logan. What if his father just decided not to talk to him at all?

"Is that how you two met?" Beverly continued. "Some type of workplace romance?"

Well, she supposed that it was for Logan. For her, it was a bit different.

"Actually, I guess I kind of stumbled into Logan's life, you could say."

Keira eyed Logan and smiled at him. Meanwhile, Beverly laughed nervously.

"That's nice, dear."

"So, what is it that you do now, Logan?" Charles Slade interrupted.

Keira had been warned that Logan's father had been very critical of him joining the Army instead of the family business. This must have been his father's way of sizing him up.

"I'm in charge of the training and skill development of all the field employees at Gray Tower."

The two men stared at each other for a moment before Charles grunted again, nodding his head, though Keira wasn't sure it was in approval or just an acknowledgement. The man was just as hard to read as Logan if not more so.

Then, Charles Slade said something unexpected.

"Well, I'm proud of what you've accomplished," Logan's father said. "That sounds like a damned nice job, and your fiancé is a delight."

If Logan was surprised, Keira couldn't tell. He kept his face expressionless.

"Not only that," Charles continued. "But your mom and I would like to apologize for how we've treated you in the past. I understand now that our frustration with Nathan was taken out on you, and that wasn't fair to you. I'd like to start anew, especially since you're starting your own family soon."

Logan nodded and said, "I'd like that."

Beverly clapped her hands together in excitement.

"Good! I'm so glad you two could work it out. Now, let me go get the refreshments. This is so exciting!"

Charles surprisingly began some small talk with the them while Logan's mom was away. Keira began to relax a little bit, knowing that the two men weren't going to get into an all-out brawl at least.

As for what Charles had said, she wasn't quite sure if she believed the older man. Damien Amherst had promised a lot of things too that never came to fruition. Only time would tell if Logan's parents wanted to seriously repair the relationship.

There was some banging around in the other room as Beverly rummaged around in the kitchen.

"Hey, sweetie," Logan's mom called from the other room. "Is this the mail on the counter?"

"Yes, dear," Charles replied. "I just brought it in not that long ago."

The small talk continued, and there was a few more moments later when Beverly called out again.

"Did you see there was a package here?"

"Yes, dear."

"Can I open it?"

"Do whatever you want, dear."

Keira had begun talking about what she was doing at Gray Tower when they heard a loud clatter in the kitchen. Everyone looked at each other before they all got up and ran to the noise.

Beverly Slade was in the kitchen, sobbing. There was an open box on the floor with its contents scattered about. Keira peered at the mess and frowned. There was jewelry spread around the floor as well as cash, rubber-banded into piles. It was an odd assortment to be sending in the mail.

"What the hell?" Logan said. "What is this?"

"Look...look!" Beverly stammered. "Look at the jewelry! It was mine!"

Keira peered down at some vintage pieces that looked expensive.

Charles frowned and said, "Yeah, it looks familiar."

"No! You don't understand!" Beverly continued. "It's the jewelry Nathan stole from me!"

She knelt on the floor and began rummaging through the contents, picking up each piece of jewelry and staring at it. More tears streamed down her face, and she shook her head in disbelief.

"It's all here. Every piece!" Beverly exclaimed.

Keira's eyes darted to Logan. His eyes grew wide, and he leaned down to inspect the fallen contents.

She knew that not having closure on his brother had been a huge issue for Logan. With this news, maybe he could finally figure out what had happened?

"There's a note here," Logan said, unfolding the paper and inspecting it. "It says, 'I'm sorry.' That's it. Shit. Are you guys thinking what I'm thinking?"

Beverly was now in hysterics, and Logan's dad was now trying to calm her down. Keira looked at Logan for some sense of the matter.

"It means my brother is alive," he said, voice hoarse. "My brother's...alive."

Keira breathed in deeply, kneeling next to Logan.

She hugged him and promised, "In that case, we'll go and find him."

* * *

Miles Bryant sat at his desk, trying to finish some work before calling it quits for the day. Gray Tower was finally getting to the vision that he had initially had of the company years ago. The headquarters was coming together. Keira Amherst was doing amazing at her job. They had more avenues of income now as they diversified their operations.

His only regret was the fact that he hadn't made any progress on those responsible for Jasmine's death. He had really thought that Amherst Global had been connected to the bomb that had killed her. Miles had received a tip a year ago that Amherst Global had been the ones responsible for shipping the required bomb-making items. Yet, he could find no information of that in anything Stratton had given him.

Now, Miles was at a dead end on that with no prospects coming down the pipe. It felt like the whole purpose for forming Gray Tower hadn't been quite fulfilled.

Miles shook his head as he continued to review more documents from the Stratton dump. The man had given them so much, and Miles had noted that there may be some new missions for Gray Tower when it came to Amherst's business associates. That was good news as Miles' company was growing.

However, the case on Amherst Global itself was closed. The company was now defunct. Damien was dead, and there were several high-profile court cases going on for some of the executives caught going along with Amherst's nefarious plans. This one was a win for Gray Tower.

Finishing the last document of the night, Miles flipped through his email one final time and noticed a new message from an unknown address with a title that made his stomach do a flip: Jasmine. Quickly opening it, Miles read the message that turned his world upside down:

Bryant:
This information is for your eyes only. It was not included in the initial information I gave you because I know it is something you will want to play close to the chest.
The organization that had your daughter killed is called the Conglomerate.

Just having their name can get you in a lot of trouble. They pull the strings of many of the infamous groups that your company tends to go after, including Amherst Global. You ticked them off in a business deal long ago, and Jasmine's death was your warning. Unfortunately, I was not able to get any other details.

I'm forever in your debt for what you have done for my daughter. If I ever come across more intel, I will pass it along to you immediately.
John Stratton

Miles leaned back in his seat and breathed out heavily.

"Well, I'll be damned."

ABOUT THE AUTHOR

J. M. Brister lives in sunny Northeastern Ohio with her husband, daughter, and three Siamese cats. When she's not writing romance novels, she enjoys hanging out with her family, editing for a gaming and geek culture web site, and spending way too much time playing video games. She is also very active on social media.

Check out her website at: http://jmbrister.blogspot.com

Printed in Great Britain
by Amazon